*"Please tell me I d... of the IRS. I'd ha... You're who?"*

"Raine. Raine Ashaway. You wrote me about the temple at Teotihuacan, and yes, the Feathered Serpent looks like a dinosaur."

*Bang!*

*"Oh!"* She lunged for McCord and hung on as the Land Rover swerved. "What was—?"

"That was my left headlight clipping the mountainside. So do you know of any place in the Copper Canyons where such a beast might have been found?"

She was no longer seeing triple. He had wonderful lips, though she knew that already. The man was a natural-born kisser. "What's *your* angle on this?"

"Aw, jeez—you're going to hold out on me, after I risked my neck to rescue you?"

"I never said that." But was she?

"So say it! 'McCord, I owe you my life. If I know where to find a dinosaur, it's yours with a bow on it.' Or would you rather I turn around and hang you back in the tree where I found you?"

Dear Reader,

Sometimes it's hard to say goodbye to a particularly vivid character. After *An Angel in Stone,* I meant to put professional bone hunter Raine Ashaway on the back burner, and move on to her younger sister Jaye. But then while prospecting for my next plot, I happened on a book on the Aztecs. I flipped to a page and there was a photo of the Temple of Quetzalcoatl, aka the Feathered Serpent. *Good Lord,* I thought, that carving looks like a dinosaur!

Next thing I knew, Raine had dashed off to the Copper Canyons of Mexico to check out the situation. A long, tall, wise-mouthed renegade Texan came wandering in from left field with his own agenda. I found a charming villain with a weakness for hummingbirds and…

Well, anyway, sometimes all an author can do is run at her heroine's heels, taking dictation as fast as the adventure happens. This was that kind of story. Hope you enjoy it!

Peggy Nicholson

# PEGGY NICHOLSON
# A SERPENT IN TURQUOISE

*Silhouette*®

# BOMBSHELL™

Published by Silhouette Books

**America's Publisher of Contemporary Romance**

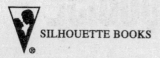

**SILHOUETTE BOOKS**

ISBN-13: 978-0-373-51429-8
ISBN-10:   0-373-51429-8

A SERPENT IN TURQUOISE

www.SilhouetteBombshell.com

**Printed in U.S.A.**

**Selected books by Peggy Nicholson**

Silhouette Bombshell

*An Angel in Stone* #48
*A Serpent in Turquoise* #115

Harlequin Superromance

*Soft Lies, Summer Light* #193
*Child's Play* #237
*The Light Fantastic* #290
*You Again* #698
*The Twenty-Third Man* #740
*The Scent of a Woman* #770
*Don't Mess with Texans* #834
*Her Bodyguard* #874
*The Baby Bargain* #929
*True Heart* #1025
*The Wildcatter* #1067
*Kelton's Rules* #1119
*More than a Cowboy* #1217

*The Bone Hunters

---

## PEGGY NICHOLSON

grew up in Texas with plans to be an astronaut, a jockey or a wild animal collector. Instead she majored in art at Brown University in Rhode Island (LARGE welded sculptures), then restored and lived aboard a 1920s wooden sailboat for ten years. She has worked as a high school art teacher, a chef to the country's crankiest nonagenarian millionaire, a waitress in an oyster bar and a full-time author. Her interests include antique rose gardening, Korat cats, ethnic cooking, offshore sailing and—but naturally!—reading romances. She says, "The best thing about writing is that, in the midst of life's worst pratfalls and disasters, I can always say, 'Wow, what a story this'll make!'" You can write to Peggy at P.O. Box 675, Newport, RI 02840.

To Ron duPrey, stars in his bow wave, attended by dolphins, reaching toward the dawn. Fair winds, my darling.

# Prologue

*Tenochtitlan, Valley of Mexico. Spring, 1520* A.D.

"This Cortés is a man, I say, and not a god! All this foolish talk in the marketplace that he is the Quetzalcoatl—*pah!*" The high priest spat into the brazier's flames. "You have only to look at his eyes, how they glow when he sees our gold! He burns for it like a boy in rut. He's no sort of a god. He's a soulless, hairy dog of an unbeliever, come to rob the Aztecs of all but their clouts!"

"If you say so, my lord." Like most traders, the *pochteca* was a practical man. He believed in a fair weight of cacao beans, and the sheen of parrot feathers. A leather pouch clicking with turquoise or coral. He'd leave the gods and their savage requirements to the bloody priests. One had to make a living in *this* world before he faced the gods in the next, he knew, though he'd never dare give voice to such an opinion.

"I do say it. But though this Cortés is a man, he brings our ruin. The city will fall."

The trader grunted in surprise. "I heard Cortés had fled, he and his men. After they murdered King Motecuhzoma. That they'd been driven from the city and were running for the east." The *pochteca* had returned only this morning from a profitable venture to the western ocean. He'd barely had time to bathe himself, then hurry his laughing young wife to bed, before the summons had come from the temple. From the high priest of Quetzalcoatl himself!

"Cortés will return, with more warriors than the fire ants. We have asked the one true Feathered Serpent, the *real* Quetzalcoatl, and so he says. Tenochtitlan will fall. Our men will be trampled like corn stalks beneath the hooves of their terrible beasts. Our women will be driven weeping into slavery. Our children will be meat for their sacrifice."

The *pochteca* swallowed a protesting laugh. One didn't laugh at a priest and live. "The god says this?" he asked weakly. Or his old women priests putting words into the Quetzalcoatl's mouth? Tenochtitlan was the finest, largest city in all the world, home to two hundred thousand of the bravest. Floating like a lily on its lake, the imperial capital could be approached only by guarded causeways or by canoe. To think that it could fall to a handful of rude, hairy, sweat-soaked foreigners? What nonsense.

"Already our end has begun. The strangers send a poison through the air before them. The people to the east of here breathe it and die—an illness of coughing and fever and spots on the face. The city will fall, says the Serpent. He says that if His children would survive this plague, they must return from whence they came. To Aztlan, the Place of the Herons."

"Aztlan," the trader repeated without inflection. Aztlan was no more than a tale to tell children. A fading dream of a homeland somewhere far to the north. Hundreds of rainy seasons ago the Aztecs had abandoned that city, but nobody remembered where it was located or why they'd fled. They'd marched south for year upon year till at last they came to an island in a lake, where they spied an eagle perched on a nopal cactus, devouring a serpent. There they'd stopped and founded Tenochtitlan, which became the navel of their empire.

But the *pochteca* had ventured north and west as far as a sensible man might walk in four moons of hard walking and he'd never heard a whisper of Aztlan. If such a place existed, he'd have learned of it. It would have markets same as any city, markets hungry for all the goods he traded and sold. A real city couldn't live on air. If ever the Place of the Herons had existed, it must have crumbled to dust. Its birds had flown.

"We return to Aztlan, those of us who have the vision and foresight to know what's coming. The courage to do what must be done. And you will lead the way."

The *pochteca* found spit enough to speak. "I, my lord? I—I don't deserve such an honor. I'm only a poor *pochteca*, a lowly merchant in obsidian and—"

"You will go before us, guiding an expedition that carries the temple treasure and the Feathered One himself. You will take your men and such priests and soldiers as I choose, to serve and guard the Quetzalcoatl as you travel."

His wife. Her feet were dainty as a deer's, softer than turkey down. And she was only beginning to swell with their first child. She'd never be strong enough to make a journey to nowhere, trudging north over mountain and desert for the gods knew how long—for years and dusty years?

Besides, the priests would never allow him to bring along a mere woman on a sacred journey. They valued only sacrifice, never human love. "Of course, my lord, if this is your wish. I'd be honored to do it. But first I'll need to go home, pack my gear, summon my men." If an entire people could flee, if a temple could pick up its gold and its gods and take to the road, then so could a single family. He'd take her west toward the ocean this very night. He knew a village on the coast; its people were openhanded and friendly, with gods that demanded fish and flowers, not beating hearts.

The priest smiled for the first time, a lipless turtle smile below eyes black as dried-up wells. "Ohhh, no need to go home! I'll send the slaves for whatever you require. We have much to discuss here tonight.

"This then will be your mission. You will find Aztlan. There you will raise a temple to house the Feathered One and his treasure. You'll prepare for the coming of His children.

"As soon as your expedition is safely on its way, I will call in the nobles and tell them my plan. Those who are wise enough to heed Quetzalcoatl's warning will gather their people, their slaves and their goods. We will follow no more than one moon on your heels, two at the most. And, Trader? Never fear. I'll keep your charming young wife safe, under my own hand."

"Very good, my lord." He felt the tears welling, warm as blood behind his lashes.

# Chapter 1

*State of Chihuahua, Mexico. July, present day*

Fourth in line for his bimonthly haircut and shave, Anson McCord lounged on the barber's porch, which overlooked the town of Creel, swinging hot spot of the Sierra Madres. Last approximation to civilization, north of the Copper Canyons.

Balanced on the back legs of his rickety chair, he thumbed through a year-old *National Geographic*. A couple of gringo mountain bikers whizzed past, nearly coming to grief as a mule and rider sauntered out of an alley and stopped halfway across the street to admire the view. McCord turned the page, glanced down at the next article. Blinked.

The photo had been taken in the midst of green jungle. A long-legged blonde sat on the skull of a dinosaur roughly the size of a Volkswagen Bug. She wore a broad-brim fedora tipped low against the tropic sun. Its shadow hid all but her knockout smile. Whoever she'd been smiling at must've landed on his butt.

"Hel*lo*!" McCord murmured under his breath. "Aren't *you* just something?" What he was feeling—hell, how could he be jealous of the fielder of that smile, when he'd never even met the woman?—call it wistfulness, or plain old-fashioned lust.

He dragged his eyes down to the caption. *Central Borneo. Raine Ashaway of the professional fossil-collecting firm Ashaway All poses with the only known specimen of an opalized T rex. Photo taken by her partner in the historic find: O.A. Kincade.*

"Good for you. Glad *somebody's* finding what she's looking for." McCord scratched his bristly jaw. Come to think of it, a dinosaur expert might even have some advice regarding his own quest. He brought his chair down with a thump and rose, to stride into the barbershop. "Felipe, *tienes papel?*" Might as well drop her a note, while he was waiting.

*New York City. October, present day*

"I couldn't find a kayak on the Somali coast, but I did meet a Frenchman who loaned me his windsurfer," Raine Ashaway told her younger sister, who'd picked her up at JFK airport. For the past half hour, they'd been stopped dead in traffic on the West Side Highway, not a mile from the apartment that served as the east coast base for Ashaway All, whenever any of the family hit New York City.

Time enough for Raine to tell about her scouting expedition to Ethiopia. She'd found a promising dig site in the gorge of the Blue Nile. A rich fossil stratum of the proper period, if not bones of *Paralititan* himself. But the war was heating up again. Bringing in a field crew was unthinkable, for the present.

Done with that topic, Jaye had insisted on hearing about

Raine's detour, after her Ethiopian venture. Now she pulled her sunglasses down her nose, the better to give her sister the fish eye. "You *windsurfed* out to an offshore oil rig in the Red Sea?"

"Just the last few miles. I hitched a ride on an Arab fishing dhow. Paid 'em to take me as near as they dared sail to Cade's rig. Asked 'em to wait for me." Raine unclipped her ripply, pale-blond hair and shook it out on her shoulders. She kicked off her sandals, then twisted her long jet-lagged body around, so she could prop her shoulders against the door of Jaye's ancient pickup.

"You're lucky they didn't blast you right out of the water! After Kincade's rig was blown up by terrorists, they've got to be taking a dim view of drop-ins."

"Actually, I was more afraid of the sharks. Red Sea sharks have this reputation…"

"Since you're here, I take it you didn't meet any. When did Kincade's guards spot you?"

With flat seas and a light breeze, they'd seen her coming about a mile out from the rig. Backlit by the fast-sinking sun, her rainbow-colored sail would be hard to miss, if anybody happened to glance down from the platform. Apparently somebody had. An amplified warning like the wrath of Allah himself had thundered out overhead—in Arabic, but the meaning was crystal-clear: "Back off or take the consequences."

But she'd come too far, loved him too well, waited too long to hear his voice to give up now.

She swerved the board to run parallel with the monstrous black tower, so that the sail wouldn't block their view of her. She'd worn a T-shirt over her bikini top, but it was soaked with salt spray and it clung to her body. "See? No dynamite, no *plastique,* no Uzi, guys, just a woman who wants a straight answer."

A wavering wolf howl floated down from above. She

grinned, leaned back against her harness to wave, then swerved back to her attack line. If Kincade was aboard this rig—and her sources said that he was—then she and he were going to talk.

"So did you?" Jaye eased the pickup forward and braked again.

"A Brit met me down at the boat landing platform, all muscles and pressed khaki and a semiautomatic in a shoulder holster—a bodyguard. He informed me, oh so regretfully, that I seemed to be trespassing." Raine tipped back her head to stare out the open window at a smoggy sky flecked with pigeons.

"What the heck is going on? That man was crazy for you."

"Wish I knew. Everything seemed fine between us when I left for Ethiopia. But then I tried to call Cade when I reached Cairo, got his voice mail. Tried again from Addis Ababa, and his phone number had been cancelled. That seemed weird, but I called the Okab Oil number here in Manhattan. Left a series of messages with his personal assistant that he assured me he'd pass on. After that, I couldn't call Cade, or anybody, for the three months while I was down in a mile-deep gorge."

"Maybe you two were just not connecting. His first rig was bombed about a week after you hit the backcountry. His partner in Okab Oil was critically injured. It makes sense that he'd return to Kurat, pick up the pieces, rally the troops. How could somebody like Cade be a silent partner at a time like this?"

"Of course he couldn't. But however busy he was, he had time enough to reach me on my sat phone."

"Oh, Raine, I'm sorry." Jaye inched the truck forward another few precious feet. "But what about Mr. British Muscles? Did he invite you up for tea?"

"No. He said that Cade was aboard, but that he was too busy to see me."

"Maybe he was lying? Maybe Cade was asleep, or—"

"Nobody could have slept through that warning. And most of his crew was hanging over the rails of the platform, whistling and cheering, by the time I sailed in at its base. Somebody was bound to tell Cade that a woman was sailing around out there." *And he'd have known it was me.* "No, Jaye, I finally got the message. That was a brush-off."

"So did you punch Muscles in the nose, and ask him to please pass *that* on?"

"Tempted, but no. He was doing his best to arrange my transportation to anywhere in the world I wished to go. I could have the use of the rig's chopper, with a transfer to the company jet. Or he'd take me ashore himself, in a crew boat. I could have anything I wanted." Except access to Cade.

"So, did you take him up on his offer?"

"Are you kidding? I stomped back to my surfboard and sailed back to the dhow." Cade's bodyguard had idled along behind her in a crashboat, till he'd seen her safely aboard. And if anything convinced her that he was acting under Kincade's direct orders, it was that final courtesy. Cade telling her by proxy that he cared for her.

But it was over. Now she blinked rapidly in the gathering dusk and swung to stare at the chains of red taillights, which miraculously had begun to move.

Home at last—or as near as Raine had to a home these days. The top floor of an old brownstone in the West Eighties, with fresh flowers in every room, and a bar of chocolate on her pillow. The welcoming touches came thanks to Eric Bradley, the freelance writer who lived on the floor below and traded office space in the seldom-used apartment for occasional concierge duties.

His fat orange tomcat came swarming up the fire escape as soon as he heard footsteps overhead. Strolling in from the balcony through the open French windows, Otto leaped to the desk and sat down on the heap of mail waiting there. Ignoring both women, he spit-washed his cheeks and nose, then he tongued his left shoulder.

"I met a lion in the Blue Mountains that had better manners than you," Raine told him, "and a better figure, too."

"Don't let's discuss figures, if we're ordering pizza." Jaye reached for the phone book. "I'll do that, if you want to shower. Barbecue chicken and pineapple, with onions?"

"Yum. And there were a few bottles of Chianti under the kitchen counter when I left. If nobody has guzzled it all…"

The apartment served as a pied-à-terre for any member of the footloose clan who might be passing through the city. Their father and his twin brother had bought the place some forty years ago, long before the neighborhood had become fashionable, while they'd been working at the nearby Museum of Natural History.

"Still here," Jaye called with her head in the cabinet. "Now go get that shower."

When Raine returned, combing her damp hair, she wore a blue Indonesian block-print sarong. Cade had bought it for her in Borneo. She'd hesitated now before choosing it, then she'd made a face and slipped it around her bare body. Just because a man had barged into her heart, then wandered out again, she was damned if she'd mourn. Life was too short for that. Carpe diem was the family motto. Seize the day, seize the opportunity, seize the dinosaur, cherish every pleasure. Paleontological fieldwork was one of the most dangerous careers in the world, right up there with test pilots and smoke jumpers. If you lived on the edge, then you learned to savor each moment as if it were your last. You couldn't do that looking wistfully over your shoulder at what might have been.

"Another twenty minutes till the pizza," Jaye reported, handing her a glass of wine. She returned to the desk where she'd been sorting the mail, to tug another piece out from under the cat. "Not much here beyond the usual junk. We missed an opening at the Smithsonian last month: fossilized ferns." She handed that over and drew out a long, smudged letter from beneath its furry paperweight. Jaye studied the return address printed on its backside. "Who do we know in Mexico?"

"Beats me. Maybe it's for Trey?" The expediter for Ashaway All was an ex-SEAL, probably also an ex-mercenary. In his dubious travels to unspecified places, he'd collected a raffish circle of friends and contacts. But mail for Trey usually went to Ashaway headquarters in Grand Junction, Colorado.

Jaye reversed the envelope. "Nope. It's for you, care of *National Geographic*."

"Oh?" Raine ripped it open, drew out a single sheet of rather grubby paper and read aloud. "'Dear Ms. Ashaway. Don't know if anyone's ever asked you this before, but if you'll glance at the enclosed photo of the temple of *Quetzalcoatl* at Teotihuacan—could the stone faces there with the snouts that stick out—be depictions of some kind of dinosaur?'"

She exchanged a glance with Jaye and they burst out laughing. "Another kid."

Since Raine's discovery of the world's only known specimen of a fire opal *Tyrannosaurus rex,* then its subsequent sale at Sotheby's auction house for fifty-seven million dollars, she'd been getting loads of letters from strangers. Most of her correspondents were male; most of them were under the age of twelve. Each was bursting to tell her his latest theory about the coloration or speed or near-human IQ of *T rex.* Or he was writing to volunteer, offering to drive her Land Rover and tote her rifle on her next bone-hunting expedition.

Or he wanted to send her what he was firmly convinced was a dinosaur fossil—no matter what his dad said about it being just a dirty old cow bone—if she'd promise to put it up for auction at Sotheby's, then send him a million dollars when it sold.

Raine could sympathize with dreamers, even when she couldn't oblige them in their schemes. She was a hunter and a dreamer and a schemer herself. So she lifted the photo in question and studied it with an indulgent sigh.

Gradually her brows drew together. She reached past Otto for a magnifying glass. She could see what the writer meant. He'd sent a close-up shot of a decorative frieze, carved along the top rim of what seemed to be a large rectangular temple. It showed a repeating motif of a grotesque stone face that seemed vaguely human, alternating with the sculpted head of an animal with a spiked neck-frill and a massive, beaky muzzle. If one stretched one's imagination, added in the missing nose horn and discounted a bit of artistic license on the part of the carver, the creature did look...

"He's not entirely nuts," she said, passing the photo to Jaye. "This does look like a cousin of *Triceratops*, maybe crossed with *Styracosaurus*." Not a known ceratopid, but some species yet to be discovered.

And, of course, that was what every Ashaway of Ashaway All, the world's foremost fossil supply house, lived to discover. New species of dinosaurs.

"So what's he proposing?" Jaye murmured whimsically. "That the Aztecs hung out with dinosaurs?" *Triceratops* had vanished from this earth at the end of the Cretaceous Period, some 65 million years before the Aztecs' forebears strolled across the Bering Strait land bridge, then drifted south in search of sunnier real estate.

"Don't know." Raine resumed reading. "'And if you do see a resemblance, then here's a second question for you. Is there any place in Mexico or the southwestern USA where the fossil bones of this sort of dinosaur might be common? Where an Aztec might have uncovered one?' Ah, so that's what he'd been getting at!" Dinosaurs were usually discovered when their bones were exposed by erosion of wind or water, a geologic process that would have been at work a thousand years ago, as well as today. "So he figures that some Aztec stumbled upon a dino skull, extrapolated what the live beast would look like, declared him a god—then carved his portrait all around the sides of this temple?"

"Aztec dinosaurs! Now I've heard everything." Jaye jumped as the downstairs buzzer announced the arrival of their pizza. "Back in a flash."

Raine studied the signature at the bottom of the page. A flourishing, angular, indubitably male signature. Too bold and quirky for a twelve-year-old. "Professor Anson McCord," she murmured as she deciphered it. Nobody she'd ever heard of, but she could picture him. He'd be one of her juvenile dino-lovers grown large. Dry and dusty from years of academic pondering and pontificating. Horn-rim glasses hiding blinky blue eyes, and freckles galore. He'd be gangly as Ichabod Crane, earnest in the extreme. Not a professor of paleontology, or he wouldn't need to ask her about his "dinosaur."

A history prof, she'd bet, afflicted with a lingering case of his boyhood bone-fever. Probably he'd taken a vacation to Mexico City, toured the temple at nearby Teotihuacan and been thunderstruck with the daring and originality of his own theory, which he now desperately needed to share with a kindred soul. She resumed reading, *If you have any useful thoughts on this, I'd sure like to hear 'em,* he'd written in closing. *I collect my mail at the address below, whenever I come to town.*

"Magdalena's Cantina in Mipopo?" The bar's address placed it in the northwest of mainland Mexico, somewhere in the state of Chihuahua. Raine chose an atlas from one of a dozen that were wedged into the nearest overcrowded bookshelf. It took her magnifying glass to find the dot that was Mipopo. A speck of a town along a rim of the—"*Barrancas del Cobre*," Raine murmured aloud, savoring the words like music on the tongue. So the professor was poking around the Copper Canyons, one of the last truly wild regions in North America.

Looking for *Triceratops*. Or possibly for Aztecs. Which, come to think of it, must be just about as extinct as dodos and dinosaurs. Raine laughed softly and closed the atlas. She'd always had a weakness for academic eccentrics.

They ate out on the narrow balcony that overlooked the backyard gardens and balconies of the adjoining block. While they talked idly of family and friends, a candle burned on the table between them. "So what now?" Jaye asked when there was nothing left but the wine.

"I'm not sure. With Ethiopia on hold, my calendar's empty." Not good. She and her siblings were close, but the way their father and uncle had structured Ashaway All, the top earner in any year got first claim on operational funds in the following year to finance his or her next expedition. The others had to trim their sails and their projects accordingly. It was a tough but fair system that kept them all hustling. Unfortunately Ethiopia had been all out-go, with no resulting income. Raine sighed.

"You could help me and my guys while you're figuring it out." Jaye was excavating for prehistoric amber in the Pine Barrens of southern New Jersey. Most of her field crew were interns from Princeton. "Fastest way to forget about Kincade is to surround yourself with a pack of flirtatious, adorable, Ivy League hotties. Beefcake *and* brains is a treat to behold."

Raine snorted. "You're not poaching in the playpen, are you?"

"No, just waving back at 'em through the bars. That's thrill enough. And I do have a couple of grad students old enough to grow beards. Plus their professors cruise through whenever they get the urge to take off their ties and muck in the dirt."

"Sounds like you've got plenty of company already." Raine yawned, stretched, stared up at the night sky. Not a star to be seen; the city lights had banished every one. She was restless already. And this was no time to sit and brood. Miles and motion were what she needed right now.

That and something exciting—something wonderful—to chase. If by any miracle Professor McCord wasn't entirely a crackpot... If he'd seen some old bones, or heard of some... "I appreciate the offer, Jaye. But I'm thinking maybe I'll fly down for a few days and check out the Copper Canyons."

# Chapter 2

Mipopo didn't qualify as a town, in Raine's estimation. It was a squalid little crossroads, set back a quarter mile from the canyon's awesome rim, as if its original founders had feared it might grow dizzy and tip over. Its main street had a general store with a battered gas pump out front, perhaps a dozen ancient adobes still standing. The only inhabitants in sight were several discouraged dogs and a flock of optimistic chickens pecking the rutted road.

And if there was a bar in town, they were hiding it pretty well. Maybe the professor had made it all up? "When in doubt, ask," she muttered, swerving in to stop alongside the gas pump.

The ancient proprietor limped out to fill the tank on her topless Jeep, then wash her bug-splattered windshield. But when it came to directions, he was a man of few words. Make that one. *"Que?"*

"*La Cantina de Magdalena,*" Raine repeated in careful Spanish. "Could you tell me where it is?"

"*Que?*" Raising his voice, he smiled wide enough to show her his steel eye-tooth.

"Magdalena's bar?" Raine tried in English. Or maybe 'what' was all the Spanish he spoke, since that was the secondary language in these parts.

The Copper Canyons were home to the Tarahumara Indians, second largest tribe of native Americans in the northern hemisphere. According to the guidebook Raine had bought this morning in Creel, it took a linguist about twelve years to learn their language—if he had an exceptional ear. "What about a place to stay for the night?" she tried without much hope, as she settled behind the wheel of her Jeep.

She folded her hands, prayer-fashion, pressed them to one ear and cocked her head. Closing her eyes, she sighed blissfully, as if snuggling down into a comfy pillow.

"*Oh, sí! El doctor.*"

"Clearly we don't have a meeting of minds here. But *muchas gracias, señor,* all the same."

As she eased the Jeep past a swaggering rooster and onto the road, Raine figured she had two hours before the sun dipped below the craggy peaks beyond the canyon to her west. If she couldn't find a place to bed down in Mipopo, she supposed she could return to the motel where she'd stayed in Creel last night. Some eighty miles of butt-bruising road to the north, the little logging and tourist town boasted the main stop on the railway that skirted the canyon rim. It was the last place even pretending to civilization for a hundred miles in any direction.

On the other hand, she could press on regardless, heading south into the hinterlands. According to her map, a dotted line swerved off the rim road about ten miles past Mipopo. This track appeared to switch back down the canyon wall, dropping from bench to bench. If she made it down to the river before dark, she'd surely find a place to pitch a camp.

"Darn," she muttered aloud. She'd pictured herself finding the professor tonight. Professor McCord had started out as the longest of longshots, barely more than an excuse for this escapade. But after her discovery yesterday in the Creel gift shop, her urge to consult him had grown more urgent. "So how do I find you?" she murmured, then glanced to her right at the building she was passing—and stepped on the brakes.

It was one of the few two-story buildings in Mipopo, and there were three battered cars and an overloaded lumber truck parked in the vacant lot beside it. *Farmacia,* proclaimed the rusty sign that swung above its torn screen door and sagging boardwalk, though the blinking red, chili pepper Christmas tree lights that framed each window were sort of festive for a drugstore. Plus they were either too early or way too late, this being only the first week in October. Still, if there was a pharmacist lurking within, surely he'd speak Spanish? The screen door banged shut behind her and Raine stood, half-blind in the dusky light.

*"Dame una tequila!"* demanded someone at her ear in a metallic monotone. She spun to find herself eyeball to beady black eyeball with a mynah bird, perched on a plastic coat hanger suspended from the ceiling.

A hand-lettered sign hung from the bird's trapeze. "Magdalena," Raine read aloud. "You're Magdalena? Then this must be—"

*"¡Una tequila o tu vida!"* A tequila or your life! Feathers brushed her ear as the bird swooped away.

Turning to follow its flight, Raine saw the bird flutter down behind a long marble counter, fronted by a row of red-topped stools. Back in some distant and glorious past, this must have been the town's ice cream parlor and drugstore. The round white wrought-iron tables remained, but nowadays they didn't accommodate miners' wives and children, sipping ice cream sodas and *limonada*. Half a dozen men slouched here and there, with their beers frozen halfway to their open mouths and their dark eyes drilling into Raine.

"*Buenas tardes,*" she said to the room in general.

Nobody smiled back or even twitched.

Wonderful. Raine walked between the tables and up to the bar.

Somewhere overhead, a woman burst into wild laughter. A bed creaked, then kept on creaking, settling into an age-old, familiar rhythm. "Great taste in post offices, Professor," Raine muttered under her breath. From upstairs she heard two distinctly different guttural groans of masculine bliss added to the woman's rolling giggles. So there was a trio up there.

"How d'you get a drink around here?" she asked the bird, now perched on a beer tap, as raptly attentive as the rest of Raine's audience. Choosing one of the tattered vinyl stools, she turned her back on the tables.

As a girl brushed through the beaded curtain that hung over the doorway behind the bar, Raine greeted her. "*¡Hola!*" The kid teetered on the low edge of her teens, with big black eyes and long black pigtails. "*Una cerveza, por favor.*"

The girl reached for a heavy glass stein. She whisked the mynah off its perch; with an indignant squawk, it hopped down to strut along the countertop.

"*Yo busco*—I'm looking for—*un norteamericano,*" Raine said as the amber liquid rose inside the glass. "*Se llama Professor McCord.*"

The girl paused in the act of serving Raine the drink. Her eyes narrowed to slits.

"You know him?" Clearly she'd heard of him.

The kid shrugged, rummaged under the counter, drew out

a second stein. This one had a smear of red lipstick along its rim. Deliberately she poured the beer from the clean glass into the dirty one, and then thumped it down before Raine.

"And welcome to Mipopo." Raine contemplated the spillage while somebody snickered behind her. The girl moved down the bar, to pick up a rag and scrub an invisible stain.

From her shoulder bag, Raine fished out her prize souvenir of the trip so far. Wrapped in a red bandanna to protect it, it was a mug made of low-fired local clay. She'd found it in Creel, in a gallery near the train station. After she'd spotted it, she'd realized that this trip might not be entirely a fool's errand. That she really ought to find Professor McCord and pump him for information.

Against a creamy background, the design was glazed in irregular squares of mottled greenish blue. Glaring out from the side of the mug, the critter's beaky face looked precisely like the professor's photo of the carvings on the temple of the Feathered Serpent at Teotihuacan—except for one added feature: The hornless *Triceratops* appeared to be covered with a turquoise mosaic.

Raine leaned across the bar to fill her blue dino-mug from the tap. With a toast to the outraged child, she took a long cool swallow. *"Delicioso!"* she assured the girl. Then she skated the dirty stein down the counter.

The kid caught it before it flew off the end. *"Una bebida para la pájara,"* Raine directed. A drink for the bird. "Or give her a tequila, if she prefers. *Con gusano.*" The premier tequila always came with a pickled worm in its bottle.

Behind her, one of the men gave a snorting guffaw and then instantly hushed. The screen door banged, as somebody walked into the cantina.

Just for a change, could it be someone sociable? Raine petitioned, staring straight before her as she drank.

Whoever the newcomer was, he smelled of peppermint and cigars. He was big enough to make the stool creak as he settled in, leaving only one seat between them. Not a local, judging from the well-cut shirt sleeve and crisp khaki trousers Raine could see from the corner of her eye. Neither was he an American professor, she concluded, stealing a glance while the stranger ordered a beer in halting Spanish. This guy was German or Swiss, if you added his sandy mustache and ruddy coloring to his syntax.

The kid gave him a come-hither smile, and he responded with courtly boredom, his gaze locked on the glass she held hostage.

Raine drew a notepad from her bag and penned a quick note:

Professor McCord,
Got your letter regarding the temple at Teotihuacan and your question's intriguing. I happen to be in the area for a week or two, so could I buy you a drink? I'll check back here at Magdalena's whenever I can these next few days. Set a date and a place at your convenience and I'll be happy to meet you.
Yours sincerely,
Raine Ashaway

She folded the page in thirds, then sealed the message with a strip of tape from her bag. She addressed it to the professor, then set it to one side with a five-dollar peace offering laid on top.

"A most handsome cup," observed the stranger, swinging on his stool to face her. "Might I please examine it?" His suntanned fingers were already extended.

Pushy, but she supposed he meant well, and for an ice-breaker, it beat the weather. Raine handed the cup over with a smile. "Like it? I understand the artist is local."

The German inspected it gravely. "It is really quite…
charming." His blue eyes lifted to include her in the compliment. "Might I introduce myself?"

He might. His name was Johann Grunwald, and he insisted
on standing Raine to a second beer while they moved casually
from names, to observations about Mexican pottery, to their
reasons for being there.

Not that Raine told the truth. You never knew when you
were going to bump into the competition these days. Even
if Grunwald had no interest in paleontology, he might talk,
and news spread fast where there was little to gossip about.
"I'm just a wandering travel writer. I've heard about the
Copper Canyons for years. Deeper than the Grand Canyon,
with almost three times its area. Thought they might be
worth an article."

That launched Grunwald into an oration on the most spectacular of the canyons; the trails offering the finest panoramas or the best swimming holes. He'd be *delighted* to show
her his favorite spots, since it was so very easy to get lost
down there. Beyond the point where the roads played out, the
canyon system branched like a gigantic labyrinth. The footpaths vanished or changed with each flash flood or rockslide.
The maps were imprecise, GPS reception was abysmal and
the natives were hardly helpful.

"But after six months of surveying the terrain, I assure you
I know my way around. My men and I study the geological
structures and the hydrographics in anticipation that my
company—" beaming with pride, he named one of the biggest
contractors in the world "—will soon build a dam hereabouts.
A most magnificent and enormous dam."

In that case, the kid could have him. Raine didn't believe
in drowning natural wonders for the convenience of mankind.
Even if she had, she'd noticed in her travels that building dams

might be a lucrative pastime for politicos and engineers, but it rarely improved the lot of the natives.

But why waste her breath arguing? Her companion wasn't the type to be shaken in his convictions. Raine dried her cup with the bandanna, preparing to tuck it away.

"That really is a most delightful cup," Grunwald observed. "I hope you will not be offended, but I have been seeking a gift for my, uh, sister, to send for her birthday. You would not, by any chance, consider selling to me this mug?"

He needed a gift for someone nearer and dearer than a sister, Raine suspected. He didn't wear a ring; still she'd lay money that he had a wife back in Hamburg. "Sorry, but I'm quite attached to it. And I'm afraid I bought the last one in Creel. The gallery owner said its maker was a new artist, a young Tarahumara she'd never dealt with before. She took only a few of his designs on trial. But perhaps you could buy something from the artist directly," Raine suggested at Grunwald's look of chagrin. "The shop owner said that he's built his kiln at a town called Lagarto."

Boot heels shuffled on the plank floors and Raine glanced behind to find one of the men from the tables standing at her shoulder with an empty mug. She turned back to the engineer. "In fact, do you know where Lagarto is?" After she located Professor McCord, she meant to track down the artist, ask him where he'd gotten his idea for the turquoise creature.

While the kid drew a refill for her thirsty customer, then exchanged a few rapid words with him in a language that sure wasn't Spanish, Grunwald explained that Lagarto was a *ranchito* some sixty miles south, on a branch of the Rio Verde. "It is not a town. Many of the names you will see on your map are *ranchitos*—just the little farm of some *Indio* family, no more than that. There will be no stores to buy food or drink, no one to rent you a bed. The Tarahumaras are shy and

standoffish, not fond of strangers. You must carry your own
supplies down in the canyons, and even so, without a knowledgeable and trustworthy guide…" He patted her fingers re-
assuringly where they rested on the cool marble.

"I see." Raine smiled and drew back her hand. She should
go. Grunwald was pleasant enough in small doses, but he was
starting to lean too close and lick his fleshy lips too often. "I
had one other question. Do you happen to know an American
hereabouts—a Professor McCord?"

"Anson McCord, the archaeologist? Yes, I've run into
him down in the canyons once or twice. We share an
interest in caves."

"Ah." So the professor wasn't a scholar of history, though
she'd not been too far off the mark—ancient man instead of
modern. "Do you know where I could—" But she paused at the
clatter of several sets of feet on an unseen stairway, then the
sound of a body slipping and crashing the rest of the way down.

A burst of drunken hilarity was followed by a man's bitter
cursing in Spanish. Two men staggered through the beaded
curtain. The skinny one held a bleeding elbow as he swore,
while his hulking companion laughed uproariously. Behind
them stalked a dark-haired woman with the seething impatience of a caged panther. With her bed-tossed hair and her
kiss-swollen lips, she was surely the giggler from upstairs, but
she was amused no longer.

The kid ran to her, stood on tiptoe to hiss in her ear. The
woman's eyes swerved like black lasers to focus on Raine.

"Ah, Magdalena," said Grunwald under his breath.
"*Cuidado!* She's in one of her moods."

"I thought—" Raine glanced at the mynah bird, who'd
discovered the rejected beer down the counter, and was
dipping its beak.

"That's Magdalenita, but this one is— How do you say it?

The real thing." Grunwald stood to make a gallant introduction, but Magdalena glared at Raine, ignoring the hand she'd offered across the bar.

*"Mucho gusto,"* Raine said pleasantly, though it wasn't. "I was asking Señor Grunwald if he could direct me to *el profesor* McCord. Or I understand that he collects his mail here. Perhaps you might tell me where to find him?"

"We know of no such man around here!" snapped Magdalena.

"Er, ah, well—" objected Grunwald.

The barkeeper raised her black brows at him. *"None* of us know such a man, *do* we?"

The German shut his mouth and sat down.

Wimp. Raine shouldered her bag, then handed Magdalena the note she'd prepared along with the fiver. *"Todo el mismo—* all the same—should you encounter this man McCord, I'd be grateful if you give him this. I would pay another twenty dollars gladly if by any chance he receives it." In all likelihood, Magdalena would toss her message, but what else could she do?

She turned to bid Grunwald an ironic farewell, but the German muttered something about using the facilities. He ducked around the bar, then through a door.

Raine dropped bills on the counter, headed for the exit. But threading between the tables, she stopped as a pair of long legs stretched out to block her path. The hulking thug from upstairs smirked up at her, then shaped her a wet kiss.

His skinny pal scooted his chair back to extend the blockade. At the next table, the young man she'd crossed gazes with at the counter was dreamily contemplating the rear wall. No help would be coming from him.

*"Perdóname,"* Raine said, deadpan. Dogs generally didn't bite till you showed fear.

*"Hoy es mi cumpleaños,"* confided Señor Double-wide, his smirk broadening to show teeth he ought to have hid.

"Happy birthday. You don't look a day over twelve."

His single ear-to-ear eyebrow bunched in confusion, then his smile turned mean. "So where's my present, *puta?* How 'bout you gimme that pretty mug?"

Ah, a crafts lover of impeccable taste. "I don't think so." If she tried a detour, he'd just block her new path. Raine stepped over his legs—then spun back fiercely as he grabbed her wrist. "Don't touch!" Her boot toe caught him square in his sweaty armpit.

As he squealed and doubled over, she chopped his elbow and jerked her wrist free. Kicked his chair out from under him. He crashed to the floor in a welter of clanging iron tables and smashing beer steins, and Raine walked out the door.

# Chapter 3

As Raine turned the corner of the building, cutting past the overloaded lumber truck toward her Jeep, a man stuck his head out a window. Grunwald.

"Pssst! Miss Ashaway! Raine! Over here!"

In spite of herself, she swerved to stand below him. "Gotta run, Johann. Thanks for the drink."

"I must apologize for my manners. But this is the only place to find a cold beer or a home-cooked meal in fifty miles. If I offend Magdalena…"

"I understand. But about the professor. Can you tell me where to find him?"

"I can only say where I last encountered the man, about a month ago. He was conducting one of his digs along the Rio San Ignácio, east of its junction with the Batopilas. You cannot miss his camp." He glanced nervously over his shoulder. "I think that perhaps I'd better—"

"Me, too," she agreed as he withdrew like a gopher down its hole.

Raine started her Jeep, glanced toward the front of the cantina. No sign of pursuit yet. She spread her map out on the seat beside her. Back to Creel or onward?

"I said I'd give you twenty *dólares Americano* for the mug—not to make a fool of yourself," Antonio said, squatting on his boot heels beside the fallen *mestizo*. The young man pulled the bill out of his pocket, waved it before the other's flushed face. "Do you still want it? Then go after *la rubia.*" The blonde.

"I go stomp that bitch for free, but first, for my troubles—!"

The big man ripped the bill from the other's fingers. Laughter clogged in his throat as the switchblade flicked into view.

"Ah, no," Antonio said gently, touching the point to the fool's lower eyelid. "You haven't earned it yet." He plucked his bill from slack fingers, tucked it away.

"I'll—I'll *kill* you for that," blustered the big man, blinking frantically as a bead of blood oozed along the bright steel.

"You may try at your pleasure, but meanwhile, *la rubia* drives away, laughing. She'll tell all her rich fancy lovers back in the city how she met a fool in Mipopo. 'So easy,' she'll say. 'One kick and I brought him to his knees. And he was a *cobarde*—a whimpering coward. He took my abuse and tucked his tail like a puppy!'"

"Oh, yeah?" bellowed the big man, as the knife snapped back into its handle and moved away. "If that's what she thinks!" He staggered to a swaying stand. "Once I've done her I'll be back with the mug—to break it over your lice-ridden head, you dirty *indio!*" He slammed out the screen door.

His skinny friend giggled and trotted after to watch the fun.

"Ah, Antonio, you were always a troublemaker," Magdalena said fondly from behind her bar. "Now pick up my damn tables."

Raine steered the Jeep across the bumpy lot toward the road. She stole a glance toward the cantina. Still no sign of trouble. Maybe Señor Double-wide had passed out from mortification? "Fine by me," she muttered, easing her foot off the clutch.

With a blast of its horn, a pickup loomed up on her blind side. Storming out of the north, it cleared the winch on her front bumper by a foot.

Raine stomped on the brake, staring after the dwindling truck, and the herd of black-and-white goats that filled its rusty bed.

Having stalled the Jeep, she coaxed it back to life, then sat in Neutral. Might as well give the cloud of dust that the pickup had raised a minute to settle—along with her heart. She glanced toward the cantina's screen door just as it banged open. The barroom brawler plus his skinny pal lurched out onto the boardwalk. "Uh-oh."

As he spotted her, the hulking man pointed her way, and the two broke into a purposeful trot.

Raine turned out onto the road and ran smoothly up through the gears. The Jeep reached the veil of dust that swirled in the pickup's wake. The last rays of the sinking sun struck it and Mipopo vanished beyond a wall of shimmering copper. Raine stomped the pedal to the metal.

Within minutes she caught up to the pickup with its four-legged cargo. "Pull over and let me by!" she fumed, beeping her horn.

But here in the land that invented machismo, the driver had his honor to defend. The pickup swung out to the crown of the road and trundled on at its top speed. The goats gazed back at her with demonic yellow eyes, their wispy white beards blowing in the breeze.

And behind her, she heard the first rumbles of pursuit. The dust cloud swirled as they rounded a bend, and Raine caught a glimpse behind. Here came the lumber truck, its pile of raw pine logs towering above the battered cab, the whole top-heavy load swaying monstrously on the curve.

Trey had trained her and all her siblings in hand-to-hand combat, but the foremost lesson the ex-SEAL had drilled into their heads was: "Run when you can. Fight only when you must."

Given an open road, she could outrun that truck. Then with a few miles lead, she could dive down the side trail she'd intended to take and vanish down into the canyon before they had a clue where she'd gone. The road widened suddenly and Raine pulled out to pass, but the pickup swerved to block her. "You son of a—" She got a grip and swung back to the right.

Behind her, Señor Skinny leaned halfway out the passenger window to jeer and hoot as he pumped his bony arm.

Okay, forget about passing. She supposed she could simply follow the pickup till her lunatic lumberjacks grew bored with the chase. "Hey!" she yelped as the truck made a roaring charge at her back bumper. She stepped on the gas and surged ahead, till the goats could have leaped out onto her hood.

"What is with you guys?" Harassing a lone foreign female seemed just their style, but instigating a three-way pileup was downright suicide.

If they knocked her off the road, she had to respond at maximum intensity. She hadn't brought a gun this trip; flying made it impossible. And her usual weapons, her blowpipe and her knife, she'd stowed with the rest of her gear beneath a tarp in the back, before she'd strolled into Magdalena's.

There'd be no time to put her pipe together, but maybe she could get to her knife in time. Meanwhile, she leaned toward the glove compartment, fished out a heavy flashlight and laid it in her lap as, up ahead, the road took a rising bend to the right. And there at last, beyond a screen of wind-tortured pines, the rim of the canyon yawned, a dark slash in the ground, falling away out of sight.

If she remembered correctly, the road snaked back to the east just beyond that promontory, while a side road cut away to her right and down. At this speed it lay maybe a minute ahead.

Just then the truck crunched her bumper, and Raine's teeth clicked together as her head slammed back against her headrest.

"So *be* that way!" She grabbed the flashlight, flipped it up and over her shoulder.

In her rearview mirror, she saw the truck's windshield glitter in a crazy spiderweb of cracks. Above the cab, the logs groaned against their chains. An outraged bellow sounded over the engine's roar.

Up ahead, the goat chauffeur was finally realizing he was traveling in bad company. The pickup belched smoke and squeezed out a few more miles per hour, but Raine didn't close the gap. She'd gut it out, ride the lumber truck's front bumper for another quarter mile, then hang a last-second hairpin right down the canyon trail. The truck's greater momentum should carry it well past the turn.

The engine behind her revved, roared. She gritted her teeth and eased ahead, hoping to soften the oncoming crash.

"Ooff!" Another blow like that and she'd be riding with the goats. She kept her eyes trained for her turn. Couldn't be more than a hundred yards to go…then fifty, then… "Where the hell is it?"

* * *

McCord was driving up the last switchback on the trail out of the canyon, when the coyote popped up on his right. "No *way!*" He braked the ancient Land Rover, raising a wave of sandy gravel, as the dusky form flashed past his front bumper then flowed over the drop-off to his left. *"Jorge?"* McCord cut the ignition and leaned out of his doorless vehicle to whistle, then call, "George-boy? C'mere, fella." He scanned the brush that edged the track, the top branches of a pine jutting up from below.

"No way that coulda been George." He'd left the mangy beggar back at camp, forty miles down the gorge. The coyote liked to tag his tracks, but he'd never have followed him this far. Besides, he couldn't have gotten ahead of him, if he *had* followed.

*"Jorgito?* If that's you, go home. Take it from one who knows, city life's not what it's cracked up to be." Magdalena kept a shotgun behind the bar, and the only varmints she tolerated walked on two legs. "Follow me there and she'll chop you up for chili."

No answer but a breeze, sighing through the pine needles.

McCord engaged the parking brake, then reached for the canteen on the seat beside him. He swung around to watch the sun flaming on a purple peak, far beyond the far rim of the canyon. He took a cool swallow while the light faded from copper to blue, sighing happily at the thought of the cold beers to follow, with a plate of *tamales* and *mole* on the side. Definitely a slice of real bread; he was sick of campfire biscuits and hush puppies. His stomach rumbled at the thought.

It had been complaining ever since he'd declined an invitation to supper when he'd stopped by the doc's place, an hour back down the trail. But McCord had his first-night rituals for whenever he straggled out of the canyons. It was best to ease back into civilization like a bather into a hot tub, and Magdalena's made a good halfway stop on the road to polite society. His first night out from camp, he didn't need stimulating conversation or a fight for his life on the doc's treacherous chessboard. He'd rather kick back, let a warm, curvaceous woman swaddle him in comfort and admiration.

Whilst he'd sat there anticipating, the sun had sunk itself, curving off toward the Gulf of California, and Baja beyond. "The Blue Hour," he mused aloud, then frowned at the noise coming from just above—a big roaring diesel rasping at the quiet, rumbling down the road from Mipopo. One of those damned lumber trucks, carting off pine trees that had struggled a thousand years or more to attain their rightful growth, cherishing every drop of rain, standing fast against landslides and winter gale—only to fall to some greedy little guy with a rusty chainsaw.

With a rueful grunt, McCord glanced back down the long sloping track that clung to the canyon wall. Too late for supper at the doc's? Maybe he wasn't in the right mood for the *cantina* tonight. It was no place to pick a fight. If that crowd ever suspected he was a closet tree hugger…

On the other hand, if he meant to change his mind, he'd have to drive the last little stretch up to the main road, then turn around there. Only a fool would attempt a K-turn on this one-lane ramp that was scarcely wide enough for two burros. And if he got as far as the main road, then he might as well—

He'd swung back around with this resolution and now McCord sat, transfixed. "What the—" A car plunged out of the twilight, heading straight at him, its left flank hugging the mountainside, scraping a shower of sparks as it came. "Shit! *Stop,* you—"

No time to start his engine, no place to swerve aside if he

did. He dove for the passenger door. Jump the other way and next stop was the canyon floor, about a half mile below.

The car clipped his left headlight. Head and shoulders out of the Rover, he clung to the doorframe as it spun counterclockwise.

Tree limbs crackled; the pine tree groaned like a wounded beast. Glass shattered, metal shrieked. His heart was going to burst right out of his chest and run for high ground!

Shaking and swearing, McCord lay, staring at the road only inches below his face. He listened for the sound of the other car striking the canyon floor.

It was a long way down, but still… He blew out a breath. Should have struck by now, and serve the jerk right. Driving at that speed, without his headlights? He struggled to a sitting position. "What the—" Almost afraid to look, he swung slowly around. "Sweet Jeez in the morning."

The other car—a topless Jeep—hung at his eye level, wedged in the branches of the pine tree that grew up the cliff face.

"Good God." McCord scrambled out onto the road till his knees gave out, and he landed on his butt, contemplating this miracle. "You're the luckiest damn fool in the—"

Something cracked. The Jeep settled gradually, rolling toward its left side as it sank. It paused, still cradled by the pine, suspended out there, maybe five feet beyond the edge of the cliff. "Oh, boy." McCord pulled himself up the Rover's fender to his feet. That wasn't a very big tree, and if—

Another branch cracked. The Jeep listed a few more degrees, allowing him to see the driver, who still gripped the wheel as if he meant to drive out of this mess—or straight on to Kingdom Come. "I, uh, think you better get outta there." McCord limped closer, swallowing hard.

"No kidding!" She reached out the gap where a door would be in a standard car to grope for a hold, only to touch thin air.

It was a woman, he realized, noticing her pale-colored braid now. And what was the matter with her, just sitting there so calm? Was she drunk or stoned?

Or maybe stunned. He swallowed and said casually, "Got your seat belt fastened?" If the Jeep tipped any farther and she didn't, she'd better have packed a parachute.

"Yeah." She swung her arm again. "What am I hung up on?"

Another snap of a branch and the Jeep rolled ten more degrees.

"I'm in a…tree?"

She'd hit her head, he decided. Was concussed. Maybe in shock. "That's about the size of it. Now listen, honey, I want you to just sit tight, while I…" Whatever damn-fool thing he did, it entailed going out there and getting the crazy bitch. Or maybe— "Hang on. Don't move. I'll be right back." He spun, heading for the rear of the Rover.

"What happens if I move?" she called behind him.

"You don't wanna know." Returning on the run with a rope, he built a bowline loop. "I'm going to throw you a rope now, okay?"

She grabbed in the wrong direction. It slipped past her fingers and fell away.

"I'll try again."

And damned if she didn't miss again. "Um, by any chance, do you wear glasses?" And she'd lost them in the wreck.

"I'm seeing triple, okay? Now throw me the fricking rope!" An edge of panic laced her husky voice.

"Sorry. Maybe if you— Oh, jeez!" he yelled as, in a crackle-storm of snapping branches, the Jeep rolled toward him—entirely upside-down. With its wheels turned up to the sky, it looked like a dying animal.

"Oh, shoot me," came her voice, from somewhere down below. "I'm off the edge, aren't I?"

"I'm afraid so." He tied the tail end of his rope to the roll bar on the Rover.

Down below the cliff face, she'd started laughing. "Lost the love of your life? Chased by rabid lumberjacks? No *problemo!* Come to the Copper Canyons and leave your troubles behind!"

"Least it puts 'em all in perspective," he agreed absently as he twisted the rope over his hip and shoulders in a body rappel. He was a firm believer in equality of the sexes; theoretically there was no reason he should risk his neck for a damned woman driver. Not that reason and women mixed very often, in his experience.

It was her husky laughter that was the clincher. She wasn't hysterical; she just had a fine black appreciation for life's little pratfalls, on top of what must be a whopping concussion. Still, if she showed that kind of guts in the face of disaster, what could he do but match her? "Just hang on now."

"Oh, believe me, I'm hanging."

Paying out rope, he walked down the cliff face, till he was looking up at the Jeep and the Dangling Beauty.

An ice cube slid down his spine. Only a couple of big limbs remained; the weight of the car had settled upon them. If they let go—*when* they let go, he amended, seeing the jagged crack in the crotch of the closer one—then down would come the Jeep like a Detroit-made guillotine, on his head. Two tons of dusty steel would ride him and the woman down to the ground.

"I'm gonna toss you the rope again," he said as he coiled up its dangling tail. "And this time, believe me, you want to catch it. Now let your arms hang." She'd never do it, he realized as he spoke. Though the belt ought to hold her weight, instinct would weld her hands to the steering wheel.

She drew an audible breath, then said in a rueful moan,

"Oh, man." She let go the steering wheel to hang, arms extended, swaying faintly in the breeze.

"Good girl. Here it comes." The loop slapped her wrists and she clawed for it frantically, finally capturing it.

"Now get the loop around your waist," McCord instructed.

Somehow she wriggled into it. "Beautiful!" Quickly he explained what she had to do. She had to release her seat belt, but hang on tightly to the steering wheel, and get herself aimed head-up, feet-down. "I'm wedged in right over here, and I'll take in your slack. When you're ready, all you do is let go, then I'll do the rest. I won't let you fall."

She'd swing into the cliff below him and bang herself good, but she ought to hit feet-first, not head-on. It might work. Except that nobody in his right mind would release that seat belt, no matter how much he wanted to live.

But she fooled him again. Her hand fumbled at the buckle.

"Oh, honey, we're gonna do this," he almost sang. She was one in a million.

Somewhere in the tree, something snapped.

"Um, I hate to say this, Tex, but the buckle seems to be jammed."

Another branch crackled—and the Jeep settled one foot closer to Kiss Your Ass Goodbye.

# Chapter 4

*Not a minute to lose,* McCord told himself when the Jeep stopped moving. He scrambled back up to road level, then realized what he had to do. Bending low, he called down through the gap between the car and the cliff. "Uh, honey? Guess we'll have to do it the hard way. You've gotta untie that loop and let it drop."

"Are you outta your tiny mind?"

"Trust me on this. Drop the rope." That loop around her waist must have felt like her last link to life, but if the Jeep fell when he added his weight to it, the line would saw her in half. A half-mile drop would be kinder.

She muttered something surly. The rope shivered, then slackened, and McCord was amazed all over again as he coiled it and slung it over one shoulder. "Okay, you're going to hear a thump, but don't worry. That's just me."

He leaped—and landed dead center on the Jeep's chassis,

flapping his arms for balance as the Jeep wobbled and wood crackled. His ankle touched hot metal and he swallowed a yelp. "Piece of cake."

"Yeah," she agreed bitterly. "Angel food."

She was hyperventilating, it sounded like, as he picked his way along the hot greasy metal till he could reach an upper branch of the pine. It was the only unbroken one in a position to help, and it *might* hold the two of them.

"What are you doing up there?" she snarled.

"Just making us a sky hook," he said soothingly as he tied the rope around the branch, then knotted in foot loops. Once he'd done that, he shinnied down the rope, to swing there level with her, toeing frantically for the last loop. He found it and settled his weight into it, then drawled cheerily, "Well, hey!"

Her upside-down face turned back and forth, then homed in when he whistled softly. "This is *not* the brightest idea you ever had in your life."

"You always this bitchy when you're scared?" He snagged the doorframe to pull himself closer. "Okay, here's the drill." He'd cut her loose, while she hung on to the steering wheel. Then she'd rotate, till they were no longer in sixty-nine position. "And then—"

"I get the picture. Just do it!"

"Right." Drawing his Buck Knife from its sheath, he sawed at the seat belt. "Okay, here it comes. It's all yours!"

Panting with terror and effort, she worked her legs out, her knees knocking him in the chest as she rotated upright. Then she dangled, treading air, her head stuck somewhere up in the Jeep's foot well. "N-now what?"

He grabbed the wheel, pulled himself closer. "Get your legs around my waist."

Easier said than done, but they managed. She had miles of

leg, and he'd swear she wrapped them twice around, squeezing him like an anaconda.

"Now all you have to do is let go of the wheel, and wrap your arms around my neck. Just let go, honey, and reach for me."

"I—I can't."

He opened his mouth to argue—and the Jeep shifted. With a screech, she let go and boarded him, hugging him in a stranglehold. The car slid farther and McCord kicked off its moving side. As they pendulumed outward, tons of steel sighed and slipped past and was gone.

"Yowsa!" he said reverently as their lips met. No telling who kissed whom, but still they brushed, and brushed again, then locked on tight.

Half a mile below, the Jeep pancaked on rock. The sparks singed him from here, or maybe that was the hot woman, almost welded to his belly. No sane man would feel a twinge of arousal, dangling over his own death on not much more than a healthy twig, but with the way she shuddered against him and the wild, wet taste of her…

*Wham…wham…wham…wham…* The echoes bounced off the far wall of the canyon and back again. McCord rubbed his lips across her cheek and up through her hair. She smelled like a surfer girl, whiff of coconut oil and sun-kissed sweat. He must be purely out of his mind. He glanced up at the bending branch. "There's just one thing more we have to do."

The first ten feet was the hardest part, but she had the slender arms of a rock climber and McCord gave her a boost. She swarmed up his body, then the rope.

By the time they heaved themselves over the cliff edge to collapse face-down and gasping on the road, it was just about pitch-dark. McCord rolled over and lay beaming gratefully up at the sky.

"God!" She groaned and flopped over beside him. Her

shoulder was pressed against his and it started to shake. He swung his head to look at her. So here came the girlish tears at last, and who could blame her? But no, this was laughter, bubbling and building from a silent chortle to wholehearted hoots of relief as he joined in. They struggled to a sitting position and clung to each other, yelping like a couple of moonstruck coyotes.

At last they wound down, till they sat, shaking with their last spasms, his arm around her shoulders, their foreheads resting comfortably against each other's. She pulled away to lean back on her hands in the dirt. "Th-thanks."

"Heck, I only climbed down there to get the name of your insurance company. Next thing I know, I'm hanging by my fingernails, wearing—" *You.* And she'd fit him better than his favorite wet suit. McCord turned to study her. Her pale, tousled hair and long, lithe form, backlit by the first stars were about all he could make out, but there was something about her growly, soft voice that curled his toes. *Down, boy,* he told himself absently, then stood. "Stay right there, honey."

"Name's Raine," she called as he walked to the Rover to find his flashlight.

And she didn't care to be patronized, he noted with a grin; not with her feet on solid ground. "Watch your eyes." He aimed the light down at the gravel and switched it on, wondering if the rest of her matched that come-to-bed voice. "Well," he said, and found himself grinning wider. He must look like George the coyote when McCord pulled a chunk of rabbit off the fire and prepared to toss him his share.

She must be used to that reaction. Her smile quirked wry and resigned as she met his eyes. Or tried to. Instead she focused somewhere left of his ear.

"Still seeing double?" he asked her.

*Actually, I figured you for the Twirling Triplets from Texas.*
"Guess I banged my head on the steering wheel."

"That's not good." He touched her forehead, making her jump. "Easy. Sorry. I just want to check you out." His gentle, work-roughened fingertips explored her temples with feathery strokes that set off ripples in her stomach. "Yeah, you've got a split here, right at your hairline. You'll need a few stitches and a good shampoo." His voice went brisk with decision. "I think the doc better have a look at you."

It took him nearly fifteen minutes of inching forward and back to turn his car from its slewed position till it pointed downhill. Finally he helped her into the passenger seat, then fastened her seat belt. "Not that you're going to need this. I'm the world's best driver, so just lean back and relax." He adjusted the seat till she was tipped almost horizontal.

The fear had left her drained and it would have felt good to lie back, if it hadn't made her feel less in control, being carried off into the dizzy dark. She fumbled for the lever as he walked around to his side, but she couldn't find it. "Really, I don't need a doctor," she tried again as he climbed in beside her and drove away.

"Probably not, but I can't leave you sitting in the road, and I don't think you'd care to be dropped off at Magdalena's Cantina. Might get more help than you need."

"God, no. That's where all my troubles started!" She told him about the lumberjacks. "I guess their truck was too wide for this track. That must be why they stopped chasing. But what I'm wondering is why they hassled me in the first place. Maybe Magdalena sicced them on me?"

He swore as the car bounced through a pothole, then landed with a sickening slither on the gravel. "Why would she do that?"

"I was trying to connect with a guy, a Professor McCord, who picks up his mail at the cantina. She seems to think she owns him."

"Huh." He drove in silence for a while, then muttered, "I suppose Magdalena figures she's got a lease on every man who walks through her door."

"She's welcome to 'em. I've no intention of jumping her claim. My interest is strictly professional."

"Hmmm. You're a...travel writer?"

"Nope." She winced as she realized she'd just blown her cover.

"Ah, a mountain climber. You're lookin' to hire a camp manager."

"Not me. But McCord does that?" She shifted to look at him, then winced as it hit her again; there were three overlapping images where there ought to be one.

"When he's trying to scrape some cash together, he's been known to do that. And worse things," he added under his breath as the car slid again and he shifted to low. "You with the ATF? The DEA?"

"McCord runs guns? Or dope?"

"Not if he wants to live. That's strictly a local franchise, no *gringos* welcome. But the damn feds—and the *federales*—are always shopping for snitches down here. No, McCord keeps his nose clean and he keeps to himself."

"Sounds like you know him pretty well."

"Too well."

"So maybe I could get an introduction?"

"'Fraid we're way past that. I'm McCord, and who the heck are you? Tell me please I didn't kiss an agent of the IRS, hell-bent on an audit. I'd have to shoot myself. You're Lorraine who?"

"Not Lorraine—Raine. As in Raine Ashaway. You wrote

me about the temple at Teotihuacan, and yes, the Feathered Serpent looks like a dinosaur."

Just then the car slid again, and this time what remained of his left headlight clipped the mountainside.

"So you thought so, too—that it looks like a dinosaur?" he asked after he regained control of the car.

"Given a bit of artistic license on the part of the carver, yes. Something like a *Styracosaurus,* with that spiked neck-frill."

"Bless you! But what about my other question—the biggie. Do you know of any place in the world—preferably around here—where such a beast might've been found?"

"It's not a known species, so I haven't a clue. Though, actually—" She remembered her mug, which by now must be bits of ceramic sand at the bottom of the canyon.

"What?"

At his tone, she turned toward him—and blinked. At the center of her vision, all his shuffling images had steadied to one silhouetted profile, led by a nose like the bow of a distant icebreaker.

"What?" He stopped the car in the middle of the road to poke her in the shoulder. "Come on, Ashaway, give! You thought of a clue? Where to look?"

"What's…" Enchanted by the miracle of sight—functional sight—Raine found it hard to heed mere words. He had wonderfully carved lips when she moved her focus, though she should know that already. The man was a natural-born kisser, if she'd ever met one. "What's *your* angle on this?"

"Aw, jeez, you're going to hold out on me, after I risked my neck to rescue you?"

"No. I never said that." But the reflex had been ingrained from childhood: *Guard your information.* Bone hunting was the Ashaways' livelihood; you shared your finds with the family and the firm, but never with strangers.

"So say it! 'McCord, I owe you my sorry life. If I know where to find a dino, it's yours with a bow on it.' Or would you rather I turn around and hang you back in the tree where I found you?"

She smiled in spite of herself at this show of temper; he didn't mean it. "I owe you my life and I swear I don't know where to find this dino—if it even exists. I was thinking about a ceramic mug I lost. It was in my luggage."

"Oh." He drove in silence for a minute, then growled, "I'll see about salvaging what's left of your gear in the morning. But as for a tacky tourist mug, it'll be busted to smithereens."

*And, but for you, I would have been down there with it.* She touched his arm and confessed, "The mug had a design on it. Exactly like the photo you sent me."

# Chapter 5

Raine drifted up from sleep to the fragrance of honeysuckle, the murmur of bees outside the open window beside her bed. She lay blinking at a rough plaster ceiling, tinged gold by the rich slant of light. Must be morning, she realized, stretching full-length. A soft tap on the door brought her up to one elbow. "Come in!" she called, assuming it would be McCord.

Last night he'd practically carried her into the *Casa de los Picaflores,* the House of the Hummingbirds, home and guesthouse of Dr. Sergio Luna. The aftereffects of adrenaline, followed by the car's vibrations on the long, rumbling descent into the canyon, had wiped her out. She dimly remembered McCord's arm around her waist as he helped her up the crude stone stairs of a winding path. Moonflowers and honeysuckle twining around the cedar pillars of a long porch. A flood of lamplight as a massive door opened.

Then the embrace of a big leather chair and a deeper-than-deep voice behind a moving candle flame, asking her to follow the light. A soft aside to McCord in Spanish noted that her pupils reacted to light, that he could see nothing to cause a man worry.

"At least, not that kind of worry," McCord drawled in the same language.

The doctor gave her a warm potion, bitter with herbs, laced with wild honey. It must have contained a painkiller, because when he stitched the gash at her hairline, it didn't hurt. After that she remembered McCord's arms again, easing her down a long hall. But beyond that? Some time later she'd stumbled into the adjoining bathroom, once by starlight, then once again by daylight, and now...Raine blinked. Was this morning, or—

The door creaked and a tiny, elderly woman nudged it open with the tray she held. With a timid smile she shuffled across the room to set it on a bedside table.

*"Buenas días,"* Raine said, adding a fervent *"gracias"* as the smell of coffee tickled her nose. There was bread with slices of papaya on a plate; it must be morning. *"Puede decirme, señora*—could you tell me—" She paused as the woman's brown, wrinkled face produced a smile of shy confusion.

The woman murmured soft apologetic sounds in a language that wasn't Spanish, ducked her scarfed head, then retreated and shut the door.

A Tarahumara, Raine guessed, as she hitched up against the headboard to pour herself a cup of coffee flavored with cinnamon and chocolate. Her questions would have to wait, which was fine by her stomach. It awoke with a lurch and practically leaped at her fingers as she tore off chunks of *pan dulce,* a bread of melting sweetness, to feed the ravening beast.

Once her first pangs had been quelled, Raine yawned, then rolled out to meet the day. Wrapping her naked body in a lighter blanket from the foot of the bed—and just who had undressed her?—she drifted over to sit on the wide sill. "Whoa!" she murmured aloud. Below the house, the hillside fell away in broad terraces till it vanished in purple, plunging shadows. A mile beyond the abyss rose sheer cliffs, crowned by a forest of toothpick-size trees.

So the House of the Hummingbirds wasn't at the bottom of the gorge, but perched on a bench carved by the river she'd yet to see. A rambling one-story adobe, it followed the contours of the hillside like a train of sugar cubes. Its walls were painted pink by the rising sun, which had just cleared the far side of the canyon.

"Wait a minute." Raine straightened with a frown. The track where she'd come to grief had descended from the eastern rim. Had McCord driven her clear across the canyon last night, and she was looking back the way they'd come? No, she'd dozed off through much of the journey, but still, surely she'd have noticed a river crossing. Which meant she must be looking west and the sun was setting! "I slept through a whole darn day?"

To her left, someone stepped out from behind a vine-covered pillar and started down the steps of the porch. A man, but not McCord. This one was short and almost portly. Supported by a cane, he moved with an awkward limping lurch. The doctor? She'd been too befuddled last night to note more than his voice and his suturing skills.

He paused where the first run of steps opened out onto a stone ledge, and swept off the Panama hat that had hidden his face. The gesture revealed ruddy, sun-weathered skin, a bold hawk's nose on a man of middle years. Plucking a crimson trumpet flower from the buttonhole of his white tropical suit, he called in a loud voice, *"Venga, bellezza!"* Come, beauty! He placed the stem of the flower between his teeth, spread his arms wide and tipped back his dark head.

He had to be the doctor, Raine told herself, with that voice deep as a canyon, but what on earth was he doing?

If she'd blinked at that moment she'd have missed it; a shimmering ruby-and-emerald colored hummingbird arrowed in to the prize. It hovered before the man's face, sipped—and flashed away. With a laugh, the doctor drew the plundered blossom from his lips, kissed it lightly and tossed it to the molten air. Donning his hat, he limped toward the next flight of stairs.

"The House of the Hummingbirds," Raine mused, smiling to herself.

He couldn't have heard her, yet, he turned, swept his hat off again with a flourish as their eyes met. "Señorita Ashaway, *buenas tardes!* I trust you slept well?"

"Wonderfully, thank you." And where was McCord? Still snoozing somewhere down the hall?

"As you can see, I'm off to visit my *clínica*. Evening rounds. But when I return, I hope you'll dine with me." He aimed his cane at a sliver of crescent moon, chasing the sun. "About the hour that she sets, shall we say?"

"With pleasure!" Then, as Raine ducked back into the room, she realized she had nothing but a blanket to wear. Or no, wait—there was her duffel bag and her pack, on the floor beyond the bureau. "Bless you!" she said to the absent McCord. She'd feared it would take a jaws of life to rescue her gear.

Best of all, he'd salvaged her parasol; it lay propped across her bag. Opening it, she sighted along the length of its lead-dipped, aluminum shaft, which didn't seem unusually thick, unless you really scrutinized it. "Not bent," she muttered gratefully. A blowgun didn't work worth a darn with a kink in it.

If anyone did look twice at her parasol—say, a customs agent—the design on its top served to divert his or her attention. An orange Chinese tiger painted in elegant brushstrokes on silk, the cat sat grinning through his whiskers against a sky-blue background. Raine twirled him and smiled. She'd been born in the Year of the Tiger, which meant, according to every place mat she'd ever read in a Chinese restaurant, that she should have been a race car driver. "Next life, maybe." Raine set it aside and dove into her bag. Since the doctor was a dude, she'd wear something dressy for supper. How about a midnight-blue tank top of heavy satin, plus her calf-length rainbow-hued skirt, with its broomstick pleats that defied every wrinkle? And her opals, of course.

Her hands paused as it hit her. Where was her leather shoulder bag, with her passport, her wallet…and the mug?

"Professor McCord isn't joining us tonight?" Raine asked, as soon as she decently could. Clearly he was not. There'd been only two places set at the long table before the crackling fire when she came in to supper. She'd made small talk with Dr. Luna while the same elderly servant poured apple cider into green crystal goblets, then brought them a first course of goat cheese with a delectable peasant bread. So far she'd learned about the doctor's free clinic down the hill. This was a service he provided gladly for the locals, the only medical care available for all this southern region of the canyons. He also ventured out to the surrounding *ranchitos,* when his patients were too sick to make the journey here.

To his own amiable prodding, Raine had replied simply that she was here on vacation, and that she was a fossil hunter back in the States. Too late to lie now, since she hadn't a clue what McCord might have told him. Besides which, there was something about this man's dark gaze that commanded confidences.

"Ah, no, I'm sorry to say. The professor has gone to Creel.

Had some arrangements to make, I believe, concerning his next group."

"His group? I'm afraid he and I didn't have much time to chat."

"So I would think! Professor McCord hosts digs for…how shall I say this? For rich amateurs; Americans who would play at archaeology. He teaches them the techniques of excavation, and they help him in his work for a week or two. With many a break for exploration and swimming, when the work grows hot and boring, I understand." He made an impish face. "But how can I condemn? The professor employs my nephew, Antonio, as his cook and assistant in this enterprise. And I also profit, when these same Americans stop here at my inn, coming and going."

"I see." Raine turned her glass in the dancing light cast by a silver candelabra. How could she say that, of course, she meant to pay for his hospitality, without offending the man?

He chuckled and shook his finger playfully as she opened her mouth to try. "Do not even think it, Raine! You are my honored guest, a delight at my table. The only payment I'll accept is that you listen to an old man's tales, and that, perhaps you join me later in a game of chess?"

Raine laughed. "Of course, if you like. My father's been trouncing me all my life at chess, so I've got lots of practice in losing."

"Somehow I doubt that. I smell a—how do you Americans call it? A setup."

Should she warn him that her father could have been a Grand Master, but he'd preferred to chase dinosaurs around the world?

They paused as the servant returned with bowls of dark, spicy stew—venison cooked with onions, peppers and *pozole,* the doctor explained. He said something to the woman, and she replied in her soft, oddly clicking speech, then departed.

"She's a Tarahumara?" Raine asked, once she'd gone.

"She's a Raramuri," Luna corrected, the warmth fading from his voice. "Tarahumara is the name the Conquistadores imposed on the tribe, in their arrogance and ignorance. They misheard the word, or they couldn't pronounce it, or they did not care. Raramuri means the People who run."

"They run?"

"They're renowned throughout the world for their endurance. Men and women both. We sent runners to your state of Colorado a while back, for a footrace of one hundred miles through the mountains, at a town called Leadville. The Raramuri raced in their sandals soled with worn-out truck tires, against young professional athletes wearing their fine running shoes. All the same, the Raramuri placed first, second and fifth. The winner was fifty-five years old."

Raine whistled her appreciation. "And you, sir? Are you one of the People who run?" He'd said "we," but should she dared to have asked? In some parts of class-conscious Mexico, the word *indio* was still a term of contempt, connoting poverty and backwardness. In spite of his urbane manners, clearly Luna wasn't Castilian Spanish, but if he cared to maintain that fiction? Bad move, she told herself as the silence stretched.

"One can only wonder," he said at last, with cool obscurity. "There were other people here, long before the coming of the Raramuri. The Raramuri retreated to the *Barrancas del Cobre* in the early 1600's, fleeing west before the Spanish soldiers and the Jesuits, who would tame them to their missions."

So you're not a Raramuri? With his beaked nose and his deep-set eyes below a broad craggy brow, Luna's features did seem harsher and more rugged than his servant's. But that might be simply individual variation. Whatever, she'd gotten too personal. "So…if Professor McCord left this morning for

Creel, he won't be back tonight?" And what made her think he'd return at all?

"He left yesterday, not this morning. But I suspect you have truth. He'll stay in Creel till his business is accomplished."

Her fork froze halfway to her rounding mouth. "He left yesterday? But that means—"

The doctor smiled. "It means you were very tired after your mishap."

Tired enough to lose a whole precious day and a half? She'd never done that before!

"What's wrong, Raine? The stew does not please you?"

"Oh, no. It's...delicious."

After supper, the doctor led her to his library. While Raine paced its book-lined walls, scanning medical tomes, histories of Mexico and Central America, firsthand accounts of the conquests, Machiavelli and Sun Tzu's military strategies, Luna brought out a chessboard from a side table. Its pieces were warriors carved of green onyx and white. "But you're in the midst of a game," she protested.

"Yes. The professor is beaten, though he won't yet admit it."

"And now he won't have to," she said, as the doctor returned the chessmen to their original ranks.

"Ah, but he will. I'll set the pieces as they were, once we're done."

Meaning he could remember the position of two dozen pieces? In that case, this might be a very short game. The doctor excused himself for a moment, and Raine returned to his books. One floor-to-ceiling case was devoted to birds, everything from Petersen's field guides to an Audubon facsimile. "Why hummingbirds?" she wondered aloud, when he limped up behind her.

"Well, herons won't stop here so far above water."

As good a non sequitur as any. She laughed and sat down to the board.

"That's how I met your friend McCord," the doctor recalled, waiting for white's first move. "He heard that I'm an authority, hereabouts, on birds. He stopped by for a visit, asked me if I knew anything about herons, if they nest around here."

"Herons?" She had the oddest feeling that he was holding his breath for her response. "Why herons?"

Luna shrugged, smiled; if she hadn't imagined the tension, it faded to self-deprecating charm. "I wrote a book about the migrations of wading birds, once, back when I was young and foolish enough to think I had time for hobbies."

But why would McCord want to know?

"Your move, *señorita*."

He was too sharp for her to throw him the game discreetly, Raine told herself a half hour later as she sat, her knight poised in midair, considering. Jump it there, and she'd checkmate him in four moves. Land it beside his bishop, and she could prolong the game, perhaps sparing his ego.

"That reminds me." The doctor stood abruptly, lurched across the room to open a cabinet and pulled out her shoulder bag.

"Why, there it is! I figured McCord couldn't find it—that it'd fallen out of my Jeep. Or he'd kept it." And since you had it all along, why wait till now to hand it over?

"And the professor left this note for you, along with a request that I show you this." The doctor limped over to another shelf, chose a small carving from among several. He handed her a blue lizard, shaped from wood, painted in patches that looked like stylized scales.

"It's charming." Puzzled, she turned it in her hands, then opened the folded note.

Hey, sleepyhead!

I stuck around as long as I could, then gave up and went on errands. Back tomorrow or the next, then my wheels are yours to command. Meantime, I looked for your mug and found a heap of shards in a bandanna. But here's a thought: check out the doc's carving of a *cielito* lizard. Five'll get you ten that's the critter on your mug. Till you see me, kick back and stay put, okay? The canyons are no place to snoop around without a guide.

Yours,

McCord.

PS. Don't play chess with the doc if you like to win.

Second man in two days—no, blast it, make that three— who wanted to be her guide. Raine turned the lizard till it faced her head-on, tipped her head and frowned. Could this be what the potter had been thinking of when he'd glazed her mug? "No neck-frill," she murmured.

"Your pardon?" The doctor had returned to the chessboard and sat, contemplating his fate.

"Oh, just thinking. It's a lovely lizard. Now, where were we?"

"Your move."

"Yes." Might as well put him out of his misery, so she could straggle off to bed. Raine lifted her knight again—and blinked. That pawn there, last time she'd looked, had been sitting on the f4 square.

Yet now it rested demurely on g5, blocking her attack. She glanced up through her lashes to find the doctor smiling benevolently into the distance, his hands crossed on his rounded vest.

Well, that changed everything.

# Chapter 6

Though the view from this overlook was no more spectacular than the previous ten they'd passed this morning, something about it grabbed the burro. Pausing on an outcrop above a sheer two-hundred foot drop to the green river, the jenny braced her stubby legs, lowered her grizzled neck and let loose with a truly astonishing, *"Haw, hee-hawng, hee-hawng."*

As the echoes bounced, then died, Raine took her fingers from her ears. "Well, if they didn't know we were coming before, they know it now." She set off, tugging on the burro's lead. "You wouldn't consider going any faster, would you?"

Apparently not. This was a beast that believed in *mañana*, if not next week. They'd covered perhaps twenty miles yesterday, Raine estimated, after leaving the *Casa de los Pica-flores* in the early afternoon. She'd waited for McCord to return, but finally she'd lost patience.

She'd asked the doctor for directions to the *ranchito* of Lagarto, home of the potter who'd made her mug. When he couldn't persuade her to wait another day, he'd insisted she take his spare burro, Poquita, to carry her backpack.

She'd have made much better time without her. But while the vegetation changed from temperate to near tropical as they switchbacked deeper and deeper into the canyons, the temperature climbed to the low eighties. And somewhere in the next twenty miles or so, the doctor had advised that she'd come to a point where nothing on four legs could handle the trail. Might as well spare her own back, while she could.

The doctor had assured her that she'd recognize this point when she came to it. Then Raine should remove Poquita's lead so she wouldn't trip on it, turn her around and shoo her on her way. "I'll send a boy to meet her and hurry her home, but in truth, it is not necessary. She knows where to find her oats."

Without stopping, Raine reached high up the wall of rock on her left, to pick a clump of dry grass. She offered the burro one blade to munch, tucked the rest of the bribe in the hip pocket of her khaki pants, where it wagged enticingly. That gained them maybe a tenth of a mile per hour. At this rate they hadn't a prayer of reaching Lagarto by nightfall, and the doctor had warned that she should not attempt the trails in the dark.

"Besides the danger of falling, there are rattlesnakes and..." He'd paused, then added in a regretful whisper, "worse things!"

"Bats, scorpions, what are we talking here?" she'd teased.

He'd shrugged good-naturedly. "That depends on who you ask. The Raramuri have legends of werewolves and ghosts and witches."

She'd met none of that crew last night, when she and

Poquita had camped in a lush little meadow. In fact, she'd felt more comfortable alone out under the stars than she had at the *Casa de los Picaflores.* The doctor was a sweetie, but still, there was something about him. She had an odd sense of un-plumbed depths... Something moving below that playful surface. Anyway, she was glad to be on her own again. At least, till she met up with McCord.

*If* they met up again.

"If McCord goes sniffing after *la rubia,* instead of search-ing for the treasure, this is no good! Time flows like water through our fingers. I say she should fall from a high place. It could be easily done."

"A man should trample flowers only when he finds no stones to run upon." The doctor chose an apple from the basket beside his chair on the veranda, then drew a handkerchief from his breast pocket. While he polished the fruit, he gazed dreamily across the canyon. "No, do nothing till I have considered this."

"But, my uncle—"

"*Ssszt!* You begin to argue like a *gringo.* And speak your own language, lest you forget it."

"If I do," Antonio growled in Raramuri, "it's because you sent me to live with a *gringo.* To wash his pots and pans! To carry his pickax and shovels like a pack mule!"

"To be my eyes and my ears, Antonio. To be the raven that perches in the pine and sees all."

"And does nothing!"

"When the time comes, then may you swoop." The doctor crunched through the apple's rosy skin. "While we speak of doing, what have you done since the night you came here to tell me of the mug you saw at Magdalena's—only to find I had its blond owner already in my hands?"

"I've done no more than you directed." The young man

dropped down on the steps beside his uncle's feet, to gaze glumly into the distance. "I went to Creel. Looked in all the tourist shops for more such mugs and found *nada.*"

"That is good news. If the design on this mug looked like the Quetzalcoatl as you say, then it could attract attention, draw interest, should a person of learning chance to see it. We need no more seekers after treasure here in the canyons. McCord is hard enough to control." The doctor took another bite, munched thoughtfully. "And so, you went to Creel. It must have taken you all of an afternoon to search the shops. But since then, my brother's son? What have you been doing? Perhaps you have a sweetheart in Creel. Young men like to keep such matters secret. And provided she's of the Blood, in this I see no harm."

"Maybe I do." Antonio twitched his wiry shoulders.

"Or perhaps there was a— How do you say this? An Internet café where you wasted your hard-earned money?"

Antonio jerked half around. "You—I—Who told you that?"

"A little bird." The doctor showed his teeth in a lazy smile. "They hum all sorts of news in my ear. Of good things and bad. Like Internet cafés, where young men worship new gods. War games to rot their brains and harden their souls. Photos of naked *gringas* to steal their hearts. By the Sun God, Antonio, if you're to be seduced, at least choose a warm, sighing woman, not a picture of one! You can't lie with a computer."

"I don't look at photos of women," Antonio protested. "I look at things. Places to travel. Like Hollywood. Or New York City."

"Canyons filled with honking cars and choking smog instead of singing birds and a running river? Now there's a bargain! A very fine trade.

"And do you know what those people in the city do? They look into their computers and dream of escape to a world of peace and beauty—a world such as this." The doctor had risen to sweep his cane around the sun-drenched vastness. Now he limped to the closest pillar and buried his nose in the honeysuckle. With a gusty sigh he plucked a scarlet blossom, stooped to tuck it behind his nephew's ear. "It's a wise man who knows his luck while it perches on his hand, Antonio. A wiser one who refuses to let it fly away."

"Yes, uncle."

"So." The doctor settled again into his chair and laced his fingers on his paunch. "I've had some news while you were gone. There's a man in Batopilas, a man of the People. He works in one of the silver mines. He sent word that he can liberate us a case of dynamite, possibly two."

"Excellent!" Antonio shot to his feet. "I'll go at once."

"Ah, but there's no hurry, nephew. I doubt we'll need it for a few weeks yet. Unless…" The doctor twiddled his fingers to some inner thought. "The big German…you said he, also, was at the cantina? Perhaps it is time to— Well, we'll speak more of this once you've completed your task."

"And what's that?"

"Antonio, Antonio, I keep telling you, you must learn to think ahead. To see not just the path before your running feet, but the next canyon, the next season. Why, if a wise man listens carefully, he can hear the rumble of the coming flood months before it sweeps the fool away."

"*Sí*, my uncle, I'm sure this is so. But what would you have me do?"

"*Bueno*. If an ignorant village potter makes a mug painted with the face of the Quetzalcoatl, then tell me: How did he know what the God looks like?"

They reached the river around noon. Poquita waded to her knees and drank deep of the chuckling current. "Think we should stop and have a swim?" Raine asked the burro.

Nothing but slurps and a belch in reply.

"Better not," Raine decided. Stop now, and in all conscience she'd have to unsaddle the jenny. By the time they got moving again, they'd have lost hours, and she was determined to reach Lagarto on the morrow. "Maybe this evening we'll find a swimming hole."

Preferably some spot more private than this. The paths through the canyons were the roads of the Raramuri, the doctor had told her. And this time of year the People were on the move.

Most Raramuri had two seasonal homes, he'd explained. A little cabin on the cool heights, safe from the torrid summer floods. Then another cabin—or frequently a cave—in the warm depths of the canyons, when the winter snows fell above. Some families were more nomadic—with a third shelter near good grazing for their animals, perhaps a fourth where they'd planted beans and corn.

So far Raine had been overtaken by three bands of Raramuri. First would come the men, striding on ahead; they carried massive loads on their backs, supported by the tumplines across their brown foreheads. Behind them trotted the boys, bearing burdens according to their size. The women brought up the rear. With babies tucked in their shawls, they herded the goats, a few cows if this was a prosperous family.

The black eyes of the men would slant sideways at Raine as they passed, then flick away. If they understood her greetings in Spanish they didn't deign to respond. The boys were gleefully fascinated; they elbowed each other and whispered. The women were shy, but not austere like their husbands. They'd steal glances, then cover their mouths and giggle, ducking their scarved heads as they hurried past.

Raine was used to being a source of amusement in foreign lands. If her pale-blond, ripply hair didn't strike the locals as bizarre enough, there was always her height. At five foot eight, she was taller than most Raramuri men, nearly a foot higher than their women. She must look like a big gawky white bird, blown down from the north. "As long as you leave 'em laughing, you're doing fine," her father had always advised. "It's the ones who can't take a joke you have to look out for."

An hour's walk brought them to the end of the floodplain. The canyon boxed in on both sides to rise a thousand feet straight up from the water, while the path climbed the left wall—and narrowed. "We meet any oncoming traffic here and somebody'll have to back up," Raine told the burro. Or dive into the river, which now tumbled over toothy rapids, some fifty feet below.

She must have sensed something subconsciously. A minute later, she could hear it clearly, the drumbeat of overtaking footfalls. Her pulse quickened to match their padding rhythm. In her experience, a runner sometimes brought bad news, even danger.

But in the world of the People who run, this must be a standard encounter. They'd come to a slightly wider stretch of trail and Raine swung her back to the cliff, then tugged Poquita inward—at least she tried to. The donkey swerved toward a clump of weed growing along the brink. "Poquita, dammit, not *now!*"

Intent on the prize, the jenny flattened her long ears, stretched out her neck. With the lead pulled tight between them, they'd trip the runner, if they didn't watch out! Raine swore and stepped out to stand alongside the rebel, with a hand on her halter. The runner would have to squeeze past on the inside. "Look out!" she called toward the oncoming sound.

He burst around a shoulder of the cliff, startled at the sight of them, then bounded on. A young man, lean and fit, stripped to the waist; for an instant Raine thought he must be an Anglo. The Raramuri were prim about showing skin. But no, even if he was breaking the dress code, this one had the face and coloring of an *indio*. His black eyes locked on hers and Raine blinked. Prolonged eye contact was unusual, and— *Where have I seen you before?*

He slapped the burro's rump as he passed, and not with a smile.

"*¡Hola!*" Raine said as he drew abreast. "*¿Sabe usted si*— Oh!*"

His flying foot hooked behind her knee and she spun backwards into space.

# Chapter 7

But a burro makes a good anchor—if her halter holds. Raine's left hand clutched Poquita's cheek strap. Dangling over the gorge with one arm flailing and her feet scrabbling at stone, she found no foothold.

Eyes rimmed with white, Poquita ducked her head and braced her short legs as she brayed her outrage at these *gringo* antics.

Half-deafened, Raine got her other hand on the halter. "You think this was *my* idea?"

Snorting and jerking her head, the burro hunched backwards along the path, doing her best to shake herself free.

"*Calmate,* you jackass!" Raine's boot toe found a protruding rock. She stomped upward just as the jenny tossed her head, and Raine's knee crested the ledge. She rolled inward to land on her back, panting in the dirt, clinging to the burro.

Noses only inches apart, they glared at each other, upside-down to right-way up. Poquita gave a snort that summed up *her* opinion.

"Are we having fun yet?" Raine found the lead, gave the beast some slack. She shifted to lean against the cliff. Arms clasping elbows to hold in her shudders, she gazed out over the drop-off. "*Whew*, that was a close one."

After a long, disgruntled pause, the burro noticed the same clump of weed that had started the trouble. While she swallowed it, grubby roots and all, Raine muttered, "But what d'you think, was it an accident?"

Whether that shove had been a silent "*gringa*, go home" or mere clumsiness, it was over, the runner long gone. So they went on their way—slowly at first, till Raine's knees stopped wobbling. Another hour's walk brought them again to the canyon floor. The river had twisted to flow due west, and the sun was setting straight down this slot in a bonfire that dazzled their eyes. "Next thing that looks like a swimming hole, we're stopping," she assured the jenny.

At the moment, the path cut through a field of chest-high green weeds. The river ran somewhere off to their right, but Raine preferred not to bushwhack. "With our luck, there're werewolves or witches out there, and I've had enough excitement for one— Hey!" She staggered backwards as Poquita crouched on her haunches, yanking the lead. "What the—?"

An eerie buzzing filled the hot air. The burro squealed and scuttled backwards, dragging Raine with her.

The fine hairs stood straight up on her arms as her slower instincts kicked in. Rattler! But where?

When it came to snakes, anywhere was too near. They retreated another five yards, then wheeled, peering wildly. Raine shielded her eyes with a palm against the glare—and there it was. A diamondback—a big sucker, easily as long as

Raine was tall. He lay coiled in the middle of their path, shaking like a meth-crazed marimba band.

"Good spotting!" Raine rubbed the burro's fuzzy ears, which for once, were standing straight up at attention. "That's two I owe you."

Poquita whuffled and jerked at her lead, trying to swing right around.

"No, no, we can't go home yet. Not for a silly snake. We just scared him is all." Raine leaned to scoop up a fistful of pebbles. "Snakes are all cowards at heart. Go on, shoo!" She tossed the gravel underhanded.

The snake struck at the missiles. He slithered a yard closer—and coiled again. The burro squeaked and retreated, hauling Raine with her.

"Great. We have to meet the tough guy." Raine scooped up more rocks to pelt him. "Go on, beat it! Don't make me break out my blowgun."

The snake struck and advanced—assumed the position and rattled his intentions.

This would be a whole lot less amusing once the sun went down. "Okay. If that's the way you want it." Raine chose a rock the size of a cantaloupe—and bowled it down the trail. "Scat!"

That broke the thug's nerve. He flinched at the oncoming menace, then whiplashed off into the bushes at a speed that made Raine gulp. But once he started moving, he'd keep on going. She patted her heart a few times; it refused to be comforted.

That went double for the burro. When Raine tugged on her lead, she flattened her ears and engaged the parking brake. "Hey, this is no time to play the diva. Get over it. He's gone. We get past this field and we'll call it a day. Find a nice waterhole, take off your saddle, settle in for a lovely night of grazing. How's that sound?" Raine rubbed the spot beneath the ear strap where the burro liked to be scratched. "Good girl, you ready now? Then why don't we—"

The burro braced her forelegs and practically sat.

A hearty smack of the leather lead on her fat gray fanny, and Raine knew she could stampede the jenny past the point of contention. But that seemed sort of ungrateful. "Take ten," she said, glancing at the sun. They could just spare it. Slackening the lead, she let the burro retreat to its length. Given Poquita's attention span, a ten-minute break should erase the problem. "Grab a bite, and then we hustle."

While the burro tugged uneasily at her lead, then dropped her head, Raine stood, keeping a sharp eye out for serpents. No sound but a mourning dove somewhere down by the river...then the sound of a bush being yanked and the soft munch of a snacking burro. Raine smiled to herself.

The cliffs to either side warmed from cream and ochre to glowing rust. Beyond the field, sparkles of fire paved the river. Two nights ago at dinner, the doctor had told her that the Copper Canyons were rich in silver, with perhaps a few veins of gold. But copper had never been mined here; the name came from the burning colors the stone took on as the sun went down. "Beautiful," Raine murmured to herself, then turned to the jenny. "So what d'you think? You ready to—"

Munching busily, Poquita faced her. A swath of leaves fluttered from her lips, jerking gradually inward with each grind of her long yellow teeth.

"Is that—?" But there was no mistaking those five-bladed, serrated leaves. Without moving her head, Raine skated her eyes left, then right.

All the plants in this field were of a height. Planted at the same time. She should have noticed. They were standing in the middle of somebody's million-dollar marijuana crop.

And nobody left a million dollars unattended. In the last five minutes, Poquita must have eaten twice her worth in weed.

There were rules to this situation, Raine recalled, walking calmly to the burro. People who broke them tended to end up dead.

Rule One: Never look like a drug agent when you stumble into somebody's dope patch. Unbuttoning her cotton work shirt, she stripped it off and stuffed it in a saddlebag. Then, lacing her fingers, she raised her arms lazily overhead as she rose on tiptoe, to stretch full-length. She ended the move with a sensuous shimmy that ought to give the invisible watcher an eyeful of her black sports bra. She pulled the rawhide thong off her braid and shook out her hair on her shoulders. "Now, do I look like a *federale?*"

Rule Two: Never let on that you have a clue you've stumbled into a pot field. 'Cause if you don't know what you're looking at, then you can't snitch to the cops, can you? "In other words," Raine muttered as she unstrapped her parasol from the saddle, "act like an innocent, a nitwit or a crazy." Even better, all three.

She opened her parasol with a snap. "See the pretty tiger?" she murmured to the watcher above. He'd be somewhere up on the cliffs this side of the river, where he could cover the whole field. He'd have something with a long range. A lot of the drug farmers favored AK-47s, she'd heard. Cheap, readily available, deadly. "But you don't need to waste bullets on *us*. Narcs don't carry silk parasols, and they sure don't chum around with donkeys."

Rule Three: Looking suitably befuddled, turn around and wander off the same way you wandered in. Do *not* proceed, because this might be the first field of many. But she was going to gamble on breaking that one, and keep heading for Lagarto.

Hemmed in by this gorge, there was no way she could make a detour. It was straight on through or forget it. And what bone hunter worth her salt could forgo a dino that might turn out to be the original Feathered Serpent?

"Even if McCord thinks there's nothing to it, we're going to make sure, aren't we, girl?" Gathering in the lead, Raine stepped to the burro's side. "So *vamonos,* shall we?" She vaulted up onto the pack saddle. And for idiot moves, that one was a doozy.

There came a thunderstruck, cogitating pause—then the jenny bounced for the sky. It came down with all hooves bunched.

"Dammit, now cut that out!" She'd expected a sit-down strike, not a rodeo! They jackhammered down the path—four crow hops, five, six…. Without stirrups, Raine clutched frantically with knees and one hand, while the other brandished her parasol. Riding a full-size bronc was one thing, but here the center of gravity was all wrong, and the jolts came twice as fast.

"*Calmate,* you moon-eyed bitch! It's me! I'm not a panther!"

She should never have tried this with a parasol. In a world of mountain lions, strange shapes from above were *not* negotiable. The burro bolted off the trail, tunneling through bushes that smacked Raine in the teeth. "Oh, shit! Remember the rattlers!" And the guard, watching them raze his money crop.

Raine hauled back on the lead, till Poquita's neck bowed left. Smashing their way in a bucketing circle, they burst onto the path again. The burro stopped short.

"Good, now can we just discuss— Ow!"

Snaking her grizzled head around, the diva chomped down on Raine's boot.

"Ouch!"

Somewhere high above, helpless hoots of masculine laughter peeled out.

"Dammit, let me go!" What if the jenny took off her toes—or yanked her under those sharp little hooves and started stomping? So much for mature conflict resolution. Raine leaned forward, grabbed a gray ear—and bit down. Hard.

Poquita squealed, let go and set off down the trail at a shattering trot that was worse than any gallop. The guard on the cliff was howling; if he didn't watch out, he'd fall on his head. To add to the merriment, he shot off a clip.

Glancing behind, Raine saw the train of puffs and sparks smoking down the path—bullets snapping at their heels! She slammed the parasol across Poquita's fat fanny. Bucking and braying, they rocketed away, pursued by whoops of blissful laughter.

For a man who hated heights, he'd sure seen his share these last few days. And all the fault of the blonde. McCord collapsed at the first level spot in the trail he'd come to, and wedged himself behind a boulder while he panted for breath. "Flippin' Ashaway!" If he had a lick of sense, he'd leave her to learn her own lessons the hard way.

Craning his head back till he went dizzy, he measured the distance he'd made from the rim—maybe two-thirds of the way down? But the last third was the worst, according to the herdsman who'd told him about this trail. Not suitable for goats, he'd said. "Yeah, well, anywhere a goat won't go is no place for this poor boy."

Yet, here he was. The cliffs on the far side of the gorge looked awash in blood, so he estimated half an hour till dark. He did *not* want to be hanging by his eyelashes come nightfall. "Friggin' Ashaway."

When he'd reached the *Casa de los Picaflores* this morning, he'd nearly stepped on his own jaw when Luna told him she'd set off alone. And after he'd warned her to stay put!

"How could you let her go off like that?" he'd demanded. Surely the doc had heard that the drug lords were moving their biz into this stretch of the canyons.

Luna had shrugged and smiled that sleepy Buddha smile of his. "But, Anson, my friend, she insisted on leaving. What was I to do—tie her down?"

"Well, yeah, that would've worked."

"Perhaps for a *Tejano,* but for a civilized man like myself?"

The doctor traveled under an implicit flag of truce that let him go wherever he pleased in the *barrancas.* But could he really believe that a *gringa* blonde flying the drop-dead sexy banner would be granted the same safe passage as a pudgy old medicine man? McCord hadn't stopped to debate the point. He'd shoved his weary bones back into the Rover, backtracked two hours to the rim road, then flogged it south over mesa and mountaintop, till he'd surely outpaced a woman traveling at burro speed. Then he'd waved down the goatherd, persuaded him to tell a humble, frantic Anglo the best shortcut to the canyon floor—and here he was, hanging between heaven and the sluiceway to hell with the sun going down.

"Too late to turn back now." Pot fields had sprouted lately along this stretch of the river, he'd heard. Hadn't passed this way himself since the first year he'd reached the canyons. But if the news was true, and Ashaway wandered into *that* scene… If the guard took her for a narc of some sort… Or simply took her… Pulling a coil of rope from his pack, he anchored it around the boulder, tested it, swallowed hard and rappelled on down. "Ashaway, you're gonna owe me big-time for this!"

Thoughts of how she could gratefully repay him served to keep his acrophobia at bay for the next hundred feet. He braked, breathing hard, standing out from his doubled rope with his feet braced flat on the cliff wall, wondering just what he'd do if he ran out of line before he found another climbable pitch.

The stone rumbled, echoes bouncing all around him—the ugly stuttering of a far-off machine gun! It hit him like a shock wave. Like a punch to the heart. "Oh, sweet jeez on a biscuit!" He'd come too late. But still... The rope smoked through his gloves as he slid through the dusk.

# Chapter 8

When his boots hit the ground McCord gave one end of the line a hard yank, then ran. By the time the rest of the coil slithered to earth, he was around the first bend, while he groped over his shoulder for his gun.

Half a mile on, the trail dipped toward the river. The shooting had stopped, but how many bullets did it take to kill a sassy blonde? He shrugged out of his pack, dropped it behind a boulder and pounded on. He crashed through a stand of bamboo, then there was the river, sparkling in the last rays of the sun and—thank you, Jesus!—there she stood, large as life and apparently unperforated.

Like a mermaid she stood, waist-deep in the current, with a rainbow-colored parasol held on high. She wore a black brassiere, that sporty kind.

"I really oughta have my head examined." Shoving the revolver in his belt, he staggered to the river's edge. Maybe he was hallucinating—a mix of vain hope and no oxygen? A burro stood chest-deep, nuzzling the water. Here he'd near killed himself, while *they* were having a swim.

With the last rays of the sun haloing her wet blond hair and her skin all over dewdrops, she was a heart-stopping sight. Any drug dudes she'd met, she'd probably knocked 'em dead with looks alone. Why had he thought she needed *his* help? "What the hell are you doin' out there?"

"We've been chewing on each other. Now we're taking a time-out, if that's all right with you?"

She sounded about as crabby as he felt. "Sure, fine, whatever." Meanwhile the water looked cool. And the distinct whiff of sweat he was smelling wasn't the donkey. McCord set the .38 on a boulder, then covered it with his shirt. "Thought I heard some shooting goin' on." He kicked off his boots, unzipped his jeans, figuring after all he'd been through on her behalf, she could put up with his raggedy ol' boxers.

Her eyebrows shot up and he glanced down. Whoops. No boxers. He'd done his monthly laundry while in Creel. His clean clothes were still in the pack. Well, tough.

"Hello," she said as he sauntered into the water, hoping he'd reach a deep hole and soon.

"Fancy meetin' you here. I could have sworn I told you to wait for me back at the doc's."

"Excuse me? I must have water in my ears."

"You heard me. I didn't risk my neck prying you out of that flying Jeep fiasco, just to see you get your fool head shot off next time I turn around. And listen up. The Raramuri don't approve of half-naked women. Least not in public, they don't."

"Thank you, Professor, for this illuminating lecture. You never told me, by the way—your chair is at precisely *which* university?"

A low blow; he had no good answer for that one. His temper kicked up a notch. "So what were all the fireworks about back there?" He'd waded out to her depth, and now they faced off, an arm's length apart. Annoyed as he was, still he could picture his own arm rising...his fingers hooking into her velvety cleavage to draw her close enough for a kiss—and not a gentle one, with his adrenaline still spiked off the chart.

She told him briefly about the pot field and its trigger-happy guard.

"Cripes, that's just down the road and you stop for a bath?"

"I'm lucky we stopped at all. I had to run Poquita into the river, to slow her down. She doesn't like parasols."

"Fashion positions aside, we've gotta make tracks! If your pal comes looking for you—" Toting an AK-47? No way would his .38 make much of an argument.

"I figured if he was going to hassle me, he'd have done it back there."

"Not necessarily. Once he goes off shift, and he's on his own time?" Out of sight was never out of mind when it came to a woman like this one. And down in the canyons, well, it was another world; no rules for the breaking. "If these guys respected the law, they'd be working at Wal-Mart, not growing dope."

"Who are they anyway, the Raramuri?"

"Hardly. The Raramuri are about as uncapitalistic a bunch as you'll ever find—and twice as moral, excepting their *tesguina*-guzzling parties. No, these are hard guys—*mestizos*—up from the city. They've been moving into the canyons these past few years. Plenty of isolation to grow and process their crop. Trading routes as old as time leading north through the Sierra Madres to the States, where their best clients live. No, they're nothing but bad news for the Raramuri 'cause when the army cracks down on the drug traffickers, the Raramuri get caught between." Damned if he wasn't lecturing. He ended gruffly, "Come on, we've gotta get moving while we can still see to walk."

"In a minute. Now that I'm wet..." She furled her parasol, then waded over to the burro, stowed it away and pulled out a tube of—

"Shampoo? Jeez, Ashaway, you'd risk our lives for clean hair?"

"Mine, yes, and who invited you?"

In lieu of strangling her, he took a turn around the pool, breaststroking so he could keep an eye out. But he found himself watching her, more than the track toward the pot field. The classical Greek sculptors had known their stuff. A shapely woman with her arms overhead could hold up a temple. Or bring a man to his knees.

As he cruised in alongside her, thinking sharkish thoughts, she finished her lathering. Crowned with a cap of foam, she gave him an enigmatic smile—and sank straight down out of sight. His blood quickened. If she attacked from below...

But no such luck. She rose, swishing her long hair back and forth, soap bubbles sailing away on the current. "Ah!"

Ah, indeed. He paddled behind her to shore, staying horizontal as long as he could. The water was cold and it occurred to him that he wouldn't be showing to best advantage, after a chill. And with his eyes locked on those slender hips rising out of the river, drenched khaki trousers clinging to every undulating curve, he was suddenly certain that, for the first time in a long, long while, Show and Tell was back on his agenda.

Insisting that he remembered a safe place to camp, McCord hustled her and Poquita off to the south. They stopped to collect his pack, then half a mile onward, they found his rope.

"That's the way we'll climb out of here in the morning," he said, nodding upward. "Same way I came down."

"You came down *that* without a parachute?"

"Well, maybe I missed the official route, the last fifty yards or so. It was getting hard to see. But come morning—"

"In the morning, *you* can climb out. I'll even give you a boost. But me, I'm bound for Lagarto."

"I told you, Ashaway, that design on your mug must've been a *cielito* lizard."

"I don't think so. Anyway, I intend to make sure." Tugging her donkey into motion, she left him flat-footed, mouth ajar.

With a growl, he caught up. "Help me out here. How did *my* quest become *your* quest?"

"If you didn't want me down here, you never should've written me that letter, asking about dinosaurs."

"Well, you got that right!" He grabbed a swatch of her hair. "Whoa. We hang a right here and cross the river."

They found the crack in the cliff he remembered, which opened out into a little side canyon. The creek still ran down its middle and there was plenty of graze for her burro. If the drug boys came hunting her tonight, with any luck they'd reckon she'd kept to the main trail, and look for her farther south.

All the same, McCord made sure the driftwood he chose for their fire was bone-dry; no use advertising their presence with smoke. And he strung his rope across the entrance to the canyon at knee height. Forewarned was half the battle.

By the time he returned from that task, she'd boiled a couple of bags of dehydrated stroganoff and noodles. He wolfed his portion with pleasure, pausing only to say, "Who'd have thought it, Ashaway. You've got a domestic streak."

Her teeth gleamed in the firelight. "I started going out on my father's digs when I was five. Any member of the field crew who didn't share camp chores was considered a worthless slacker."

"My apologies for the slur." He made a note to wash their forks and mess tins, once they were done. He supposed hiring Antonio to cook *had* sort of spoiled him.

"Think nothing of it." Seated cross-legged across the fire from him, she set her plate in her lap to stretch to the stars. "Whew! Long day."

And a longer night coming up. He meant to lurk in the boulders near the pass, keep watch till midnight. If they hadn't come by then, he could figure they weren't coming at all. Marijuana blunted the sex drive, or so his junior high teachers had always claimed. Probably the guards were back at their own camp, blowing smoke, telling each other fish stories about the *rubia* that got away.

"Tell me something," she said, breaking into his reverie. "How'd you come to write me in the first place?"

"Hmmph." He shifted against his backrest, embarrassed. "Purely by happenstance. Somebody left an old *National Geographic* in the barbershop at Creel. I thumbed through it, saw that photo of you with your fire opal *Tyrannosaurus*." And who'd have thought you'd be even hotter in person? "Anyway, the article made it sound like you knew your dinos. I was bored, so I dropped you a note. But I never expected you to come high-tailing it down here."

And much as he liked looking at her across the campfire, still a tiny alarm was clanging in the back of his brain. Last time a dynamite woman had helped him on a dig, she'd put the kibosh on his heart, his hopes, and—worst of all and least mendable—his career.

"Uh-oh!" Raine glanced toward the pass.

He dropped his plate in the dirt and grabbed his gun.

"She's definitely a diva." Raine rose and went to the burro, who stood, tangled in her stakeout rope and kicking petulantly. Alternately swearing and patting, she freed the beast, then returned.

"Hey, are you limping?" He transferred his frown from the remains of his dinner to her left boot. A bad foot out here was bad news.

"It's nothing much. She bit me is all, while I was riding."

"The hell you say. Let's have a look." He seated her on the driftwood log he'd been leaning against, then crouched before her.

"I can do that," she protested as he unlaced her boot.

But it pleased him to undress her, even if it was only from the ankle down. *Are you married?* he almost asked as he peeled off her sock. If she was, he'd pitch his bedroll on the far side of the creek. One brush with another man's wife had cured him of *that* particular fantasy forever.

Though sometimes ignorance was bliss. Resting her foot on his thigh, he examined her toes. "Does that hurt?" he asked, manipulating them gently.

"J-just a little."

"And that?" He stroked his thumb across the top of her foot.

She made a little sound deep in her throat, but it didn't sound like pain.

"Just bruised, and now your muscles are stiffening," he diagnosed, and let the AMA sue him for practicing without a license. "Let's see if I can loosen them up." Gripping her ankle with one hand, he rubbed his other thumb from her heel, along the high, soft instep to the ball of her foot, then slowly back again.

Her toes flexed, then curled; she made that sound again. He smiled to himself, and then did it again, nice and slow. He could feel the flutter of her pulse beneath his thumb.

She leaned closer, nearly close enough to kiss, and propped her forearms across her knees. "Are you…really an archaeologist?"

His thumb stopped. His pride stung. "Yup," he said after a minute.

"Then why would you care about a dinosaur? Are you switching fields?"

Couldn't make it in my own, you mean, so I'm poaching on yours? That came close enough to the truth to hurt. "Not exactly." He started stroking again, hoping to distract her.

"Then you're looking for the Feathered Serpent? But why in the north? Quetzalcoatl was an Aztec god, wasn't he? Or did the Raramuri worship him, too?"

"No, they're into gentler gods here in the canyons. A sun god and a moon god, all mish-mashed up with Catholicism, care of the Jesuits. Jesus isn't only the Son—he's the Sun. And the Virgin is the Moon. Plus they believe in the spirits within things—living in the river, or inside rocks, in certain trees, animals."

She nodded, her hair a silk curtain swaying in the firelight. "Animists, like in Borneo. So why'd you send me that photo of the Feathered Serpent?"

"'Cause I think maybe He and his friends passed this way, and possibly you could give me a clue as to where they were headed." Just picturing that caravan, he felt his heart quicken. "About four years back, I happened on an Aztec codex."

No happenstance about it; that was just modesty. He'd spent two long years scrounging through the basements and stacks of half the libraries in Europe, living on silverfish and cobwebs, before he crossed its trail. "Tracked it down, finally, to England, to the private library of an ancient, titled family. Back in the sixteenth century, they'd founded their fortune on privateering—piracy, licensed by the king."

His hand had paused in its stroking, and her foot did an odd little importunate wriggle that urged him to continue. Careful not to smile, he resumed his massage, saying, "Some ancestor sailed home from the Spanish Main with booty from a Mexican treasure ship. And when he swiped the Spaniards' gold, apparently he got their mailbag as well. Among the papers was this codex, along with a letter from a priest stationed in Mexico City in 1538. It had been intended for the priest's brother, back in Madrid.

"Anyway, I reckon Lord Swipe and Sink'em couldn't read Spanish. For sure, he wouldn't have been able to read a codex. And none of his descendants bothered to try. They just tucked the stuff away in a box on a top shelf."

"What's a codex?" she asked with a little hitch, as he transferred his attention to the top of her foot.

"The Aztecs had a written language, did you know that? Not a letter alphabet, but stylized pictures that a trained scribe could interpret. They used paper made from ficus tree bark, formed into scrolls, and a document painted on a scroll is called a codex. This particular codex showed what looked like a procession—priests carrying the Feathered Serpent and also heavy baskets, packs. They seemed to be marching toward mountains, then beyond the mountains stood some big gawky birds."

"Herons?"

His fingers stopped. "Why'd you say herons?"

"Oh, just a guess. Big standing birds might be long-legged waders. Like a great blue heron? Do they have those in Mexico?"

"You see 'em, once in a while. Anyway, at first I assumed the scroll showed a religious parade. A depiction of a feast day, or a day of sacrifice. Then I read the priest's letter that accompanied it."

He stopped, staring off into the dark, that same savage exultation roaring through his veins all over again. Here was salvation, vindication, fame and fortune all rolled in one! A way back to everything he'd lost. Lord, but he'd been young and naive, to think it'd be that easy!

She rubbed her bare foot up his thigh a few inches and he came back to the present with a jolt. "Why don't I tell you 'bout this some other time?" We've got more important things to attend to tonight.

The ends of her hair kissed his wrist as she shook her head. "No, now. Tell me."

And after? She was making no promises, but holding her gaze, he could feel the current sizzling between them. If words were what it took to keep her foot on his thigh, to coax her past this point, so be it. "The letter interpreted the codex and explained it. The priest wrote his brother saying he'd been given a slave, an Aztec woman, to do his housekeeping at the mission. From the way he described her, I reckon she warmed his bed, as well.

"Anyway, she'd spun the priest a tale about her husband, who'd been a *pochteca*. The *pochtecas* weren't members of the Aztec nobility, but they had their own kind of power. They were an elite class of traders who traveled far and wide, brought back luxury goods to Tenochtitlan, the Aztec capital on the lake, which is now Mexico City."

Little by little McCord told her, while her foot wandered up and down his thigh, that sensation melding with the pictures in his mind as he spoke: Of a priest, lying in his narrow bed, holding a dark, sorrowful woman—a Mexican moon to his Spanish sun. And had the slave seduced her master with her tale, or had he loved it out of her? Or had she just needed to tell somebody—anybody who cared enough to listen? Lying there in the steamy dark while she whispered of her cherished husband, who'd been stolen away by the high priest of Quetzalcoatl, to do his bidding.

To lead an expedition out of a city teetering on the brink of conquest and disaster. A caravan that carried the Feathered God himself, and all the treasures of his temple. A caravan in search of a safe haven—seeking a legendary, lost city somewhere far to the north: Aztlan, the Place of the Herons.

"But why didn't she follow? She and the rest of the temple priests and the people?" Raine's eyes glistened as she leaned over him, flames reflecting in brimming tears.

"Hey…" he said gently, and he tugged on her ankle. She slipped off the log to settle astride him where he knelt. He locked his hands behind her waist and trembled with the weight and feel of her.

He sighed and ran a fingertip below her wet lashes. "Because the plague came first. Smallpox, brought by the Europeans. Things fell apart. Chaos, invasion. The high priest who'd set it all in motion died."

"But she didn't? She survived?"

"She and the *pochteca's* son. Born after he'd headed north with the god."

"And she never saw him again?" The tears rolled down Raine's face—pearls in the firelight, beads of gold like Aztec treasure.

"I want to tell you yes." He wanted to say yes to all of her, all her shuddering warmth and fragrance, but… "Are you sure you're not married?" Or else what was this sorrow? Some betrayal of the heart.

She burst out laughing and shook her head, her hair stinging his face as it swung.

*Not married, but you wanted to be?* Whatever it was, she wasn't heart-free, not tonight. He'd been there before with a woman of two minds. An undecided woman could whipsaw a man in half before he knew if he was coming or going. "So kiss me and go to bed," he said gruffly.

She stilled, lips parting in surprise.

Think it's only girls that get to say no? He set his mouth to hers, intending nothing but a prim good-night peck—and then her lips opened beneath his. Self-righteousness sizzled, vanished in a starburst of heat. A curtain of silk wavered over a bonfire—rippled with running sparks, then greedy, spreading flames. Their kiss was a salty, smoky plunge toward blissful—

"Eeek!"

Not the response he'd expected. "Did I hurt you?"

"N-no, it's just that—" Her lashes brushed his cheek as her eyes widened. "—we've got company!"

His hand crept to the gun in his belt. But how could he roll into action with her straddling his legs? "Nice and easy," he murmured against her lips. "You need to get off me. Make it look convincing, like we're movin' to the next stage, gettin' horizontal. Then if bullets start flying, roll away from the fire."

"Not that kind of company. This one's on four legs. A...wild dog?"

"Not likely out here." Slowly he turned his head—and there sat the big gray bastard, fangs gleaming in the firelight as he yawned. "George? Jorgito?" And swear to God he was laughing!

Raine slipped off him to sit back down on the log. "You know this guy?"

"Can't be George. There's a coyote that hangs around my digs, cruises by every so often for scraps. But that's some sixty miles away, in another canyon. George, no way that's you. You got a doppelganger?"

The beast smiled, rose and faded off toward the pass.

"That was no coyote—too big. A Mexican wolf? Except I heard they were extinct." Raine stood, brushed herself off, went to her pack and pulled out a kit, then wandered down toward the creek.

Well, whoever he was, he was a spoiler. A spell breaker.
Whatever they'd had going was gone.

It didn't hit McCord till he was halfway through brushing
his own gritted teeth. He paused, toothbrush mid-stroke. What
about the donkey? Burros were famous for their alertness,
their nasty territoriality. Some herdsmen ran them with sheep,
for protection against predators.

Yet with their visitor tonight? Poquita hadn't even raised
her head from the grass, when the coyote strolled by.

## Chapter 9

"You sure she'll be all right?" Raine worried, looking after the jenny. Far below them, Poquita ambled back the way they'd come, stopping every ten yards to browse. "What if she meets up with a burro rustler?"

"The Raramuri aren't into stealing," McCord said shortly. He'd been grumpy on waking this morning, and his mood had only darkened when she'd refused to climb up to the rim with him, to abandon this trek to Lagarto, which he'd scorned as a silly goose chase—and *she* was the goose, wasting her time chasing tourist mugs tarted up with blue lizards!

When Raine had suggested that in that case, he should stop wasting *his* precious time, go about his own business and leave her to hers, he'd snarled and led the way south. But when the road to Lagarto left the river trail to climb a hundred-foot cliff in the western wall, it was time to send the burro on her way.

"If the Raramuri won't bother her, what about the guards at the pot field?"

"Even if they stop her, you said the doc's boy is coming to meet her. He'll set them straight. Nobody messes with the doc in these parts. He swings a lot of weight."

"Even with the drug crowd?"

"When they need curing of a snakebite, or a bullet dug out, who else are they gonna run to? Besides, the drug dudes know how the Raramuri handled Pancho Villa's troops, back in the Mexican Revolution. Anybody dissin' the doc, would answer to the locals."

"How *did* they handle Villa's men?"

"They discovered the wonders of gasoline. How to drain it out of an army truck. What happens when you splash it on a bivouac tent in the middle of the night, then toss a burning branch on top. Villa and company learned it was best not to mess with 'em. They're only peaceful long as they're left in peace, which t'my mind, is how it should be." With a shrug he set off again. The path led up a crumbling ridge to the western rim, where they could look out over endless miles of ragged buttes topped with pine forest. The land between the high points was fractured by dark, winding cracks—the myriad, branching canyons fading to blue-hazed distance.

They traveled on the cool windy skyline for most of the morning, then descended into another canyon. The temperature rose along with a dull thunder of falling water. Like ants on a staircase, they crawled down one eroded bench after another, till these sloped away to a sheer gorge, with a path meandering down its face. Far below rushed a ribbon of white water. "Not too much farther," McCord said, watching her stop and lift her left foot to massage it. "Not getting blisters, I hope?"

"No. It's just stiff." Their eyes connected for a moment. Her rueful smile kindled an answering glimmer, then he turned away and led on. "So the codex," she called. "Who made it? One of the priests left behind at the temple?"

"Nope. It was painted by the housekeeper's son—hers and the *pochteca*'s. Seems he became a translator for the Spanish, and a scribe. The Aztec written language limped on for a generation or two after the Conquest. There were scholars and priests who came over to the New World, as well as the soldiers. They salvaged as much of the culture and its records as they could."

"So the son based the codex on her tale? Illustrated it?"

"That's right." McCord stopped so suddenly she bumped into him. "Let's take a break."

When he sat and slouched back against the cliff face, she could see the path ahead. The trail tapered to a ledge not a foot in width. "A rockslide?"

"Hardly. This is still suitable for goats and local grannies. Me, I want my lunch first, so I can die happy."

They shared cheese, dried apples and crackers with their heels dangling over the abyss, their backs propped against the rocks. McCord passed his canteen and Raine took a long, grateful swallow. A trickle of water escaped her lips to run down her chin, her throat.

He reached to brush his knuckle beneath her bottom lip, then on down, tracing the cool track of the water. Her neck arched instinctively with the caress, then she checked the motion and looked aside. His finger paused at the V of her shirt, lifted away to accept the canteen she held up between them. "Tell me something? Why'd you cry last night?"

"It was a touching tale," she said, refusing to meet his eyes. "Sometimes, when I'm tired, I get overemotional."

"Right," he said wryly, and drank.

Changing the subject, she said, "But speaking of that...if the codex was written by the *pochteca*'s son, who never met his own father, then it couldn't have given you directions on how to find the lost city."

"That's right. All the codex said was that they'd set out in the spring of the year of the Conquest, heading north. All the folk tales of Aztlan say it lies to the north, but none say where. Only that there should be a lake—the Place of the Herons. And then some of the legends claim there're seven caves at Aztlan, one for each of the seven tribes of the Aztecs."

"Come to think of it, not only do you *not* know where the city was located—you don't know if the *pochteca* and his caravan ever found it."

"Only too true." McCord capped the canteen and set it between them.

"I mean, when you think of all that could have happened along the road… Bandits, disease, the deserts and mountains they'd have had to cross. The country must have been in an uproar, with rumors of Cortés's coming. A swell time to snatch a treasure and run for your life. Even the *pochteca* himself, if he didn't stay loyal…"

"You've gotta remember, he left a hostage behind. And the codex shows him guiding a whole band of priests. If his fingers grew sticky, they were along to chop 'em off. Nasty customers, those guys. Aztec priests give *me* the willies at a five-hundred-year remove. I make it a point not to think of Aztec priests and their hijinks after sundown, for fear it'll carry over into dreams."

He wasn't quite kidding, she realized, meeting his eyes. They were nice eyes, crinkled at the corners from squinting into too many Mexican suns, from being amused all too often. But then all of him was nice, in a lean, big-boned, battered sort of way. He was the first man she'd noticed since she'd met Kincade. She ought to be celebrating that there were at least two men on Earth who rang her chimes. Ought to be…

"Now with a ledge this narrow, you'll need to face the cliff," McCord said briskly, while they put the food away. "But you may have noticed that there's not much in the way of handholds, so it all comes down to balance. And doing the Copper Canyon two-step with forty pounds of pack trying to drag you backwards off the brink can get kinda…stimulating. Or maybe you'd like to reconsider visiting Lagarto?"

"McCord? Give it a rest." But she took his advice and chose not to wear her pack. She led the way, nudging and lifting her pack on before her, a few inches at a time, while the Texan followed, dragging his pack behind. Her palms tingling with suppressed terror, she sidestepped along the ledge, her nose almost brushing the stone. The abyss at her back seemed to suck at her body. She paused, knees trembling.

"You okay?" McCord drawled. He was following at a sensible two-arm's length.

"Marvelous." She had to applaud that he stayed out of grabbing range. There was no way one of them could save the other once a fall started. "How much farther till it widens out again?"

"Beats me."

"Oh. I thought—" From the way he'd bad-mouthed the *ranchito,* she'd assumed he'd been there. "You've never been to Lagarto before?"

"Not me. I tried to make it my first year, but I tried in the wet season. Half a cliff fell away, a few miles back, and nobody went in or out for months. Reckon this is the detour."

Another thirty feet and she started to develop sewing machine leg—lactic acid was building up in the tensed calf muscles, causing spasms that would only get worse.

"Hey," McCord called. "Come on back here." He'd found a crack overhead, six inches beyond her reach. He'd insinuated his fingers into the crevice, then made a fist jam, and now he stood at full stretch, his forehead resting against his arm. "It's a good hold. C'mere and take a load off."

She edged back, caught his belt. "Th-thanks."

"That won't do you much good. Get your leg in front of me, but nice and easy. Don't kick me off the cliff."

She snaked her left boot between McCord's shin and the rock, slithered to her left till his heat and bulk half overlapped her. A living wall between her and the chasm.

"That's good," he drawled soothingly in her ear. "Now, just rest all your weight on one leg for a while, while you loosen up the other."

She tried, but it was hard to relax with her butt nestled against his taut thigh. Impossible to ignore the changes in contour and temperature going on back there. Or his muffled groan as he dropped his face to her hair. "I've never understood how guys can think about sex at a time like this," she growled, trying not to shiver.

"Who's thinking? And my associate there, he's got his own credo in cases of flood, famine, war and unspeakable heights. Goes something like: Breed fast or die."

"You can tell him it's breed fast *and* die if he doesn't quit nudging me!"

"'Fraid he's not much for taking orders. How 'bout you distract him?"

"I'm all out of knock-knock jokes today. Why don't you tell us all a story? Like, how'd you end up in the Copper Canyons looking for lost Aztecs?"

So McCord told her, with his breath warming her ear and his heart thumping her shoulder blade. How, after he'd found the codex, he'd hired Mexico City roadworkers—tough *indios* in good condition and presumably of a similar size and stride—to help him calculate the weight the Aztecs could carry and their speed. "The god traveled on a gilded platform built on two long poles, carried by eight men to each side, if the codex was accurate. You know the Aztecs didn't have wheels, right? And no pack or riding animals; horses and mules and oxen arrived with the Spanish."

Figuring that they'd spell the bearers every few hours to maintain the same pace, he'd estimated they'd travel thirty miles per day. Once he had his daily mileage, McCord had caught a taxi to the *Templo Mayor* in downtown Mexico City. He'd slung on his backpack, strapped a pedometer to his ankle and started walking northwest.

Raine turned her head, saw nothing but a blurry glimpse of a brown unshaven jaw. "Why northwest instead of north?"

"Due north is too hot and dry; no dependable water. Plus the linguists tell us that the roots of Nahuatl, the Aztec language, lie in the southwestern U.S. It's related to Hopi and Ute. The best guess is that the Aztecs originally migrated down the western margin of the Rockies. Then the mountain chain continues on down the west coast of Mexico under a different name—the Sierra Madre Occidental, in the basement of which we're standing right now."

"But still, that's got to be thousands of square miles to search. And if you're a professor, didn't you have classes to teach?"

His body stiffened against her. "Let's say I was…on sabbatical. And, yeah, it was a crazy notion from the word go, but…" He'd decided to cut through a pass south of present-day Guadalajara, then walk up the western side of the Sierra Madres. There are more rivers on that side of the range, running down to the Pacific—reliable water. "Also, in the priest's letter, he mentioned a necklace his housekeeper wore, a carved seashell—a gift her husband had brought her from his last trading trip to the west."

"Meaning he'd traded as far as the Pacific?"

That was one more guess among many. But if the *pochteca* knew the coast, then McCord suspected he'd prefer the familiar. That he'd cling to known routes as long as he could, till the caravan marched right off his map and vanished into the north.

Raine shifted her weight to her rested leg, and McCord stifled a groan. She smiled to herself. "So you started walking in thirty-mile marches, but even so, their tracks would be long gone."

"Their footprints, sure. But the intangible traces, well, you'd be amazed. Folk tales, language, those kinds of clues can linger for centuries. For instance, look at Tule Lake, California. *Tula* or *Tule* is a word from the Toltec language. The Toltecs being the kissing cousins to the Aztecs; they preceded them into Mexico by several centuries. A tula is a species of bulrush, the kind of reed they'd have gathered to make baskets. So that name survived the coming of the Spanish, then the independence of Mexico, then the invasion of the Anglos. By now there's probably a mall on top of the marsh where the Toltecs once harvested their reeds, and nobody who shops there has a clue what the name means—and yet, there it stuck, for maybe a thousand years."

"Fossilized words," Raine mused to herself.

"More like ancient echoes than old bones, but yeah, language endures. And stories survive. Suppose you'd lived in a village where nothing much had happened for the past hundred years. Then one day, a *god* comes to town, carried by a parade of strange-talking, weird-looking foreigners. And maybe they stop long enough to trade for some food. And they build an altar in the main square.

"They buy or grab the prettiest virgin in the *pueblo*—and cut her heart out while her parents and her sweetheart and the whole town stand aghast. You think that event might not be remembered a good long while in local story or song?"

For a year McCord had walked north along the coast. At each village he came to he'd seek out its elders. Ask them to sing him their songs, tell him their stories, give him poetry, myths or even rumors. "But finally I hit on the best way to track my caravan. I asked the mothers how they scared their children into behaving." Here and there he'd find a town where the local bogeyman sounded just like an Aztec priest— with a sweet tooth for bad little boys and girls.

A creature who could terrify children across five hundred years? Raine shuddered.

McCord swore softly—and pressed his lips to the soft skin below her ear.

Suddenly she was drenched in heat. Fear and arousal twisted in her stomach. She *ached* to move against him, but one wriggle and she'd bump them off the cliff.

"You know," he drawled, smiling against her skin, "much as I'd like to stand here like this all day, my hand's going numb, so maybe…"

"Right." She drew in a steadying breath, and then inched out from beneath him.

## Chapter 10

They smelled Lagarto before they reached it. An odor of smoke and burned cooking fat drifted along their path, which followed a shallow river, rumbling over red cobblestones. When they came to a side trail Raine wrinkled her nose. "This way, I'd say."

The path bounded upward, alongside a ribbon of wind-blown waterfall. They arrived at its top, damp and breathless, to find themselves standing at the lip of a hanging canyon. A half-dozen tiny cabins made of wood and stone dotted the floor of the narrow valley.

A hundred yards in, men trudged back and forth from a slope of scree at the base of a cliff to a spot near the center of the *ranchito*—a patch of blackened ground and smoking embers, with a mound of rocks rising at its middle. An elderly white-haired man heaved a stone onto the pile. He straightened with a hand braced on his back, then froze, staring as they approached. His fellows wheeled to stare.

McCord stopped at a boulder beside the creek. "This is as far as we'd better go." He unslung his pack, turned his back on the villagers and sat. Pulling out his canteen, he offered her a swallow. "Crash course in local etiquette. You never stroll up to a Raramuri's holdings uninvited. That'd equivalent to standing on an American's toes while you introduce yourself. A Raramuri's land *is* his body and his soul. So now we wait while they look us over and decide if they want to chat."

"We came all this way and they might refuse to see us?"

"Their world, their rules, Ashaway. But don't worry. Sooner or later, somebody's bound to get curious."

Rocks crashed onto rocks behind them at painful intervals. The light changed from late-afternoon orange to blue as the sun sank toward the unseen horizon. A woman's voice rose in a bitter harangue, accompanied by the sound of smaller stones pelting the pile. McCord took out a bag of gorp, poured some into Raine's cupped hands, then took a mouthful.

"They're covering a bonfire back there?"

"You've got me. The Raramuri love a good fire. But if they'd had a *tesquinada* last night, we'd have heard the drums. And nobody'd be standing today, much less shifting rocks."

"A *tesquinada*'s a party?"

"*Tesguina* is fermented corn liquor and not for the fainthearted. A *tesquinada* is a three or four-day drinkathon around a bonfire, with elements of spouse-swapping, magic, religion, politics, sport and Lord knows what all thrown in. Gringos are generally not wel— Looks like we've got a nibble."

The elderly man they'd first noticed stood beside their boulder. Black, unwinking eyes inspected them each in turn. McCord rose to string together a series of clicking, glottalstopped syllables that, along with his posture, somehow conveyed respect.

The Raramuri jerked his chin in surprise, then offered a withered hand.

The two men stroked each other's fingers from first knuckle to fingertip, then their hands fell away. The old man broke into a rattling speech that sounded like a typewriter with hiccups.

McCord offered a rueful disclaimer. Abruptly the language shifted to Spanish, though it was an accent that Raine could hardly follow. After a moment, the Texan glanced at Raine. "Not to be macho about this, but I'll get more out of him alone. He's given us permission to pitch our camp in that little draw over there, so if you'll excuse us?"

"Fine by me."

The dark had socked in by the time McCord rejoined her, guided by the glow of the fire she'd started. "Just in time for supper," she said as he sat with a weary grunt.

While she dished out two servings of freeze-dried curry, he turned to his pack and rummaged. "So what's the score?" A mess plate in each hand, she dropped down beside him. "Did you meet my potter?"

"Don't happen to carry a gun, do you?" He loaded six bullets into a battered revolver, then snapped the cylinder back in place. He dropped extra cartridges in his shirt pocket.

"No." She glanced at her pack, which contained her throwing knife, as well as the parasol. But she made it a rule not to disclose her assets unless she had to. "Who'd I need to shoot if I had one?"

"Good question." He accepted his plate, then gave her the story between famished mouthfuls. "Seems that what's left of your potter is under that cairn they're building."

Lagarto was home to three interrelated families, he'd learned, most of whom were still on the way from their summer cabins on the rim. The potter, a young man named

Mateo, stayed here year-round, because of the valley's proximity to his source of clay. His widowed mother and a younger brother lived with him. But a few days ago, those two had walked to a distant *ranchito* to help in the delivery of a cousin's baby. "Mateo was halfway through firing a load of pots, so he stayed behind."

His mother had returned this morning, along with some other residents of Lagarto, whom she'd met on the journey, to find the remains of her cabin a heap of glowing charcoal. Only the stone half walls and a door clad in salvaged sheet metal had withstood the flames.

"And Mateo burned with it? Are they sure?"

"They found a skull and some bones. Since nobody else was at home in Lagarto, it seems a reasonable conclusion."

Raine set her plate aside. "An accident, I suppose. Maybe he smoked in bed?"

"Might have. But if the guy was alone, then who propped the rock against his door to wedge it shut?"

"Oh, boy." Raine twisted around to unzip the pack she'd been leaning against. She found her knife. "They have any idea who might have done it?"

"No. But they're pondering hard on that topic, and sooner or later, it's bound to hit them. Seems that the only strangers seen around Lagarto for the past six months are you and me."

The engineering textbook on dynamite was assuredly useful, but very dry. The doctor rose to limp restlessly about his bedroom. Books were all very well, but they spoke; they never listened. "Perhaps I should take a wife," he grumbled to his own reflection in the big Spanish looking glass. "But for which man would I seek a spouse?"

Taking the Panama hat from a peg on the wall beside his bureau, he adjusted it to a rakish tilt in the mirror. "For *el doctor, autor* and man of letters, a physician educated in the finest *universidad* in all Mexico? To appreciate *him*, I would need to find a cultured woman, a woman of poetry, taste and style. A woman who knows her way around a chessboard, yet can lose with grace and good humor. In short, a *criolla* from Mexico City, or perhaps an *Europea*.

"But such a paragon of femininity, would she consent to live in a canyon? And if I wished to discuss the shaping of charges to blow out a road or a bridge?" With a grimace, he rehung the hat. "No, she'd be shocked and—far worse— she'd be bored!

"For a proper partner to discuss explosions, sabotage, our fight for independence, I'd do better to seek a mate in Palestine or Iraq, no? But then she'd be all business, forever cleaning her guns and glowering. She'd probably use my *picaflores* for target practice, and that would never do.

"So…" From another peg he plucked the cloth cap of a traditional Raramuri male and snugged it down so its pointed end jutted over his forehead. "So I should be consistent in my convictions. At the next *tesquinada*, I'll stand before the fire and announce that I need a wife. Before the ladle goes once around the circle, the mamas will bury me in their plump, giggling daughters. And truly, if all I needed was a pair of doe eyes and a warm armful in bed, I could do no better. She would love the canyons as I do. She'd sing while she watered my flowers. My *tortillas* would be fresh every morning. But when I desired witty conversation?" He sighed and put the hat away.

"And as for the man who stands at my core, peering out through my eyes…the son of my unknown, uncaring father…" His hands caressed the knobs of the bureau, hesitated—then pulled open the top drawer. He drew out a box of polished madrone wood from its depths, and pressed a series of invisible slides. A seam parted to reveal a shallow hideaway. He lifted forth something that gleamed in the lantern light. "Who would I find to love he who wears *this?*"

Carefully, he fixed the gold clips in his nostrils. The pendant dangled from his nose, gold hammered smooth and sheer, forming the shape of a bold mustache—a butterfly with wings outspread. The ornament of an Aztec nobleman, it masked his cheeks and his smiling mouth as he turned his head to admire each profile. Truly, he'd been born to this!

Something stirred in the glass and he lurched around. His servant, Maria stood in the doorway, mouth agape, her old hands clutching a tray with a steaming carafe and a sugar pastry. Foolish woman, he'd told her to take the evening off! "Ah, Maria," he said heavily, advancing upon her, "I wish you had not seen this."

Just this side of the smoldering fire, they'd arranged their bedrolls into a couple of body-shaped bundles to serve for decoys if anyone came stalking. Raine and McCord had moved deeper into the draw. Sheltered by a fallen rock, they sat, shoulder pressed to shoulder. Raine faced inward to scan the walls of the arroyo in case of climbers, while McCord faced outward, peering around the edge of the boulder. "If you really think we're in danger, I say we move out," Raine whispered in his ear. They'd travel slowly in the dark, but still, they could be miles away by morning.

McCord huffed a soundless little laugh. "You know how the Raramuri hunt deer? There's usually an ancient rifle or two in every *ranchito*, but bullets are precious. They save the ammo for special occasions and they run the deer down. Takes about three days to run one to exhaustion, so they can stroll up and cut its throat. I don't know about you, but I'm out of practice for the marathon.

"Besides, right now they may be wondering, but if we

split, they'll *know* we're guilty. Better to brazen it out, I—" As Raine startled, he swung half around. "Trouble?"

She let out her breath. "Just an owl." Not a good omen.

"Ah." He turned back to his own lookout. "Then there's another thing to consider. If we go running from the Lagarto clan, who's to say we don't bolt straight into the arms of the murderer?"

She shrugged, savoring the warm friction of her arm against his. "Think he really exists? Imagination can be pretty vivid, places where it hasn't been blunted by TV. Maybe a stone rolled off the foundation during the fire. Fell against the door? No more than that."

"Could be. But even so, we'll still have to deal with their notions."

"Yeah." Raine smothered a yawn with her fist. "Tell me, what was going on with that woman, the one who was haranguing and stoning the cairn?"

"That was Mateo's mother. She was scolding him for leaving her. Calling him a faithless, no-good, lazy son."

"Seems sort of harsh. The poor guy didn't ask to be burnt."

"Ah, but that's not how the Raramuri see it. They believe that a person chooses how and when he'll die. Mateo wasn't murdered—he *consented* to be murdered. His mom thinks he could have shown more consideration with his timing." It was McCord's turn to muffle a yawn. "Not as heartless as it seems. Anger's a good way to drive out sadness."

"Give me your gun and get some sleep," Raine told him. "I'll take first watch." She had much to ponder. Like, if someone had killed Mateo—by Mateo's choice or quite the reverse—was she to blame? And if her interest in a simple mug had brought death down on an innocent man, then McCord was right. Sometimes anger was more useful than sorrow.

* * *

"Cut this much all over," the doctor instructed, measuring a corn kernel's breadth between his thumb and forefinger. Settling back on his stool, he clasped his hands under the sheet that protected his shoulders, and closed his eyes as Maria lifted the scissors and took the first timid snip.

With more snips, a feeling of warm contentment prickled his shoulders. Mercy was gratifying to the giver, as well as she who received. He was glad he'd reconsidered. Not acted in haste. After all, he'd concluded, Maria had no idea what she'd seen, and even if she had, she had limited means to describe it. She was an inarticulate woman in her native tongue of Raramuri, and she had no other. "And who would believe you, old woman?" he asked softly in Spanish. And who would cook his *pozole* to perfection if he threw her off a cliff?

No, the worst that could come of this was that a few more rumors would float around the canyons, whispers that the doctor was more than he seemed. That late at night, he wore gold like a prince. Well, he could live with such rumors. "And so can you, old woman."

But his price for mercy tonight was a haircut. Not that he really needed one, but he had need of conversation and of a woman's touch, even if it was only the touch of gnarled hands such as these. He sighed as her fingers brushed his ear. "Now that you've seen it, shall I tell you how I came to inherit such a bauble?" he asked in Spanish, raising the silver hand mirror to observe his barber.

Her black eyes peeped warily over the top of his reflected head. She recognized his tone as a question, if not his words' meaning, and nodded. Snipped again.

"This tale was told to me by my older brother, who was perhaps five at the time. It was the winter after a summer when the corn and beans failed from too much rain, and the goats died with rotted hooves. In order to feed his family, my mother's husband went off to work in the mines of Batopilas, leaving my brother and mother alone at our *ranchito*. This was in a valley so remote even you would not know it. All the men of that *ranchito* left to find work.

"And then, one night, a night of the full moon, when my brother could not sleep for his growling stomach, came a shirtless man with long ragged locks and bones in his ears. Gold gleamed at his nose and chest. He looked like nothing my brother had ever seen, spoke harsh words with no meaning." He'd pictured it so many times. The tall stranger stalking into their hut as if he owned it.

He'd bowled the boy out the door and barred it from the inside. "My brother beat on the door, but to no purpose, so he crouched there, listening to my mother's cries turn to whimpers, then sighs, and finally, just as the moon set, she made a sound like singing."

The boy must have fallen asleep soon after that, because the next thing he remembered was a tall shape looming over him—hands lifting him, tossing him over a hard, sweaty shoulder. Long strides carried him off through the night.

"Then, out of the dark flew my mother, screaming like the eagle as she dives! The tall stranger grunted, there was blood everywhere—on my brother, on the man's slippery shoulder. My mother flew in again, with a blade on high. But he caught her wrist and twisted her to her knees, tossed her knife off into the rocks.

"And then, Maria, holding her so, he looked down at himself, and he laughed. He wiped a hand across his own chest and chanting words in his unknown tongue, he flicked the drops on the earth—so and so and *just* so. He wiped his wound again, then he stroked my mother's cheek with his hot blood...and then he set her son on the ground. He walked away and he never looked back."

Maria pressed down on his head. Obediently, the doctor looked at his lap while she trimmed his nape. "The next morning, when my brother would speak of the night and the stranger, my mother told him he'd dreamed. And that he must never talk of nightmares, lest they come true."

"But my brother was a stubborn child, as am I. He searched the path out of our valley, and at last he found a few dark spots spattering the dust. Nearby he found the gold nose pendant that you saw tonight."

Maria lifted the sheet from around her master, then whisked it off his shoulders and stepped back with watchful eyes.

"On the ninth full moon after the moon of my brother's nightmare, I came into this world." The doctor lifted the mirror, inspected his haircut from every angle—then smiled. "Thank you, Maria," he said in Raramuri. "Now you may go."

# Chapter 11

Lying on her stomach with her cheek pillowed on her forearms, Raine woke to the sound of stealthy footsteps on gravel. Then silence as a foot paused. Somebody was sneaking up on her. McCord had taken the dawn watch. Had he fallen asleep on the job?

Her pulse surged. She took a slow, deliberate breath. She could feel the heat of a body bending over her. *Picture your move first and then strike.* She rolled, her knife slashing a bright circle, then she froze, with the blade nearly impaling the small blue lizard that hovered before her face.

"Jeez, Ashaway!" McCord flinched back on his heels, whisking the lizard out of reach. "You almost cut him! See if I buy *you* a present again."

"Reptiles before breakfast are *not* my way to start the day." She sheathed her knife, brushed the hair from her eyes. "Or is that breakfast?"

"It's a *cielito* lizard. I paid Oso my last quarter to catch him. Thought you might like to see the critter that inspired this whole goose chase."

Raine caught McCord's wrist, brought the chameleon-like creature almost to her nose. "He's cute, gorgeous color, but he's not the model for my mug. And who's Oso?"

"Mateo's kid brother, peeking round the rock there. Vastly disappointed that you failed to behave like a proper *gringa*." He turned to give the kid a palms-up shrug. "No screams, no faints, no hysterics, what can I say? Want your lizard back?"

"He probably would eat him. Give him to me." She escorted the *cielito* to the safety of some brush at the base of the cliff, returned grumpily. When McCord poured her a cup of cowboy coffee from the pan simmering on a nearby fire, she cheered up. "I take it they've decided we're not killers," she said, watching the kid scuff his casual way around their campsite in a steadily contracting spiral.

"Yep. Oso tells me that after much consideration they've identified the perp. An invisible pest known roundabouts Lagarto as the Heart Snatcher."

Raine choked mid-swallow.

"Usually this guy snatches the heart and throws the rest of the body off a high cliff. This time, they figure he held a barbecue for the remains."

"Is there any evidence that somebody really did take Mateo's heart?"

"I doubt it. Apparently he was too burned to tell much of anything. But consider, Ashaway: Here's another permutation of my bogeyman story. Clearest example I've heard yet in the canyons. You realize that when the priests of Quetzalcoatl made a sacrifice—took a living heart on the altar at the top of their temple pyramid—they flung the body down all those flights of stairs? The Conquistadores wrote that the steps were stained with blood from top to bottom."

"On second thought, who needs breakfast?"

Growing boys and joker Texans needed to break their fast, if she didn't. Once they'd put away an alarming amount of jerky, string cheese and reconstituted dried eggs, Raine sat down with the sketchpad she always carried and a pen. "This is what the mug looked like," she said when she'd finished.

McCord dropped his stack of cleaned mess tins in the dirt. "You're sure?"

"You've seen this motif before?"

"Not this one, no." He handed the sketchpad to the boy, who stared at it, then whispered something. "He says this is his brother's new design to paint on his mugs."

"New? Then ask him where he got the idea for—" But McCord was already speaking. Oso responded in that soft-voiced dialect of which Raine could recognize barely a word or two as Spanish. "What? Did Mateo see something, or—"

"Hang on." McCord fished in his back pocket and pulled out a folded US ten-dollar bill. He smoothed it out and handed it to the round-eyed kid with a few warm words. He patted him on his scrawny shoulder, then stood watching as the boy darted off toward the *ranchito*.

"Well?" Raine nudged him in the ribs.

He turned with a preoccupied frown. "That design you drew—the mug looked precisely like that?"

"That's what I've been trying to tell you! Just like one of the heads carved on the temple at Teotihuacan, shown front-on. But with blue-green patches or scales all over its surface."

McCord rubbed his jaw. "Now that I'm not thinking lizards, there's a couple of examples of Aztec art in the *Museo Nacional de Antropologiá* at Mexico City that put me in mind of that. One's a mask of a man's face, carved from obsidian. The other's an actual human skull. In each case, the artist decorated his work by inlaying chips and tiles of turquoise and coral and jade over all. Absolutely spectacular."

"You know, I've been meaning to ask you what the god *was* that the expedition carried. A temple statue?" That was what she'd been picturing. A carved stone idol, possibly replicating the skull of a dinosaur that some early Aztec had unearthed. Though not a fossil, such a find would still be a staggering coup for Ashaway All. As long as the carving was reasonably, recognizably accurate, it would extend the lore of dinosauria. Predict a new species that someday might be discovered.

But if the Feathered Serpent turned out to be an actual fossilized dino skull—the skull of a *new* species of dinosaur? Paleontological purists would fume at its lines being obscured by a mosaic of semi-precious stones, but the bones could still be mapped and studied by CAT scan. And such an artifact, with its visual glamour and its outrageous history would be adored by the public! Any major museum in the world would gladly give half its endowment to obtain such a find.

She'd give her first-born to be its finder. "What did Oso tell you? Where'd Mateo get his new idea?"

McCord had crouched to stow his mess tin in his pack. He rolled up his bedroll, then tied it to the frame. "Mateo came back from his last trip to dig clay, and the first pot he made, he painted that design on it. He told his brother he'd seen something amazing, and that someday, if Oso was very, very good, he'd show it to him." McCord stood, shrugged into his backpack.

"Does Oso know where his brother dug clay?"

"He does. I've just hired him to guide me there."

Raine paused, her pack dangling from her fingers. "Guide *you* there."

"Yep. And he says there's a friend of Mateo's, somebody trustworthy, who can take you back to the *Casa de los Pica-flores.*"

Men. Generosity with their bodies was one thing, but when it came to the important stuff… "Not into sharing the glory, McCord?"

"Not into sharing the danger. I don't believe that Mateo's killer is a Heart Snatcher. I'm starting to think he might be real. If Mateo knew a secret that points the way to treasure— and somebody learned that he had it—it could have cost him his life. It's hard enough watching my own back out here in the canyons, I can't watch you, too. I'll rest easier knowing you're safe." He turned to go.

"Hey!" Raine caught his sleeve. "You're not going to rest at *all,* if you try to leave me behind! Maybe I can't outrun a Raramuri, but I can run down a Texas weasel."

"Now, listen, honey—"

"No, *you* listen. I've earned a share in this hunt. You'd never have known there was a clue in Lagarto, if I hadn't told you about my mug."

"That's right." He pulled free and moved on. "And while you were blabbing, who else did you tell?"

*Nobody but you!* She swallowed the words as they leaped to her lips. Her eyes narrowed. No… *Not* possible. McCord was maddening, and apparently he could be selfish when it came to finds. But could she see him as a murderer?

No way. Except that nothing was ever quite what it seemed. How often had she learned that in her travels? And at what cost? "Not possible," she insisted aloud, as he strode off without a glance behind.

And even if there was the teeniest, tiniest, terrible chance that she'd entirely misjudged the man? A serpent in turquoise, just waiting to be discovered… Raine shouldered her pack and hurried after. She'd chase the Devil himself to bring back such a find.

"You disturb my breakfast to tell me that for all your efforts you learned *nothing?*" The doctor stirred sugar into his coffee, then mounded a teaspoonful onto the patio table at his elbow.

His nephew shifted from sandal to sandal on the sunlit flagstones, but he didn't dare sit without an invitation. "I did what I could to make him talk, but the potter was stubborn. Very stubborn. So I thought to scare him. I trapped him in his hut, set it on fire. Told him I'd let him out, if only he'd tell where he'd seen the Quetzalcoatl."

The doctor sighed wearily, reached for the cream for his coffee—paused as a small yellow bird fluttered down to the table.

"He didn't tell me. Never called out once. When I looked…"

The bananaquit cocked his head this way and that, inspecting his benefactor with black beady eyes. He hopped across the table to dip his bill in the sugar.

"Smoke inhalation after a beating? It wouldn't take long, Antonio. This was clumsy. Even worse, it was wasteful. After all our years of searching. If he knew something of value, something that could have helped us…" His eyes tracked the bird's flight, as it shot off into the *flamboyan* tree that shaded the back of the house.

"If the potter knew something, then his family will know it, too," Antonio said sullenly. "He told me while we were still friendly that he has—had—a mother and a little brother. One of them will know where he went, what he saw. After what happened I didn't think it was wise to wait for them to return."

"On that we agree!"

"But in a week or so, when all is quiet again, I can go back. I'll find the boy while he's out with his goats, and this time I'll—" He paused as his uncle held up a quelling hand.

"And what of Señorita Ashaway? By this time McCord must surely have found her. If she persuades him to travel on to Lagarto…"

Antonio smirked up at a passing cloud. "Oh, I doubt she'll do that."

"Never underestimate a woman's power to get her own way. If she still wishes to go to Lagarto, McCord will take her. Once there, if there's a secret to be learned, the professor will obtain it. You could study his methods, my nephew. Like me, he understands the uses of sugar." The bananaquit had returned, bringing his drab little mate to share in his good fortune.

"If McCord learns where to search, then I'll follow him to the treasure, as we planned from the start. Nothing has changed."

"You forget the blonde. A lucky blonde, to find what we've all been most desperately and diligently seeking, and in Creel of all places."

"*Sí,* my uncle, but luck can change. Something tells me she's had her share, and now it is my turn."

"*Bueno,* we'll hope you are right." He nodded at the chair opposite. "Sit, sit, and rest your swift feet. You must take a siesta after breakfast, and then…"

"You have another task for me?" Antonio took a roll from the basket.

"Off to Batopilas to fetch that dynamite before it goes astray."

"And after that, the big German? As I told you before, he'll soon make his final report on where to build the dam. If we don't stop him—"

"It will take money as well as violence to stop a dam such as this one, Antonio. Enormous sums of money to bribe the *políticos* in Mexico City who dream up such projects. With enough gold, I could persuade them to inflict their concrete obscenities on some other hapless people, in some other part of the country.

"No, our best hope of success is that McCord finds his treasure and soon! After you fetch the dynamite, you must go see what our friend has learned."

"But the German—"

"Enough. His time will come."

Fifty yards ahead on the trail, McCord paused at a rift in the canyon wall. He glanced down at something at his feet, then stepped into the shadows. They hadn't spoken to each other all morning. McCord was angry that she'd tagged along, and Raine preferred to keep her distance till she'd sorted out her suspicions. So they'd maintained this strung-out marching order, with Oso darting anxiously back and forth between them when he hadn't disappeared entirely, running somewhere on ahead.

The kid's energy was boundless. Raine suspected that he'd already covered the distance to his brother's clay pit three times over. She reached the cleft in the rock and glanced down to see two lines of pebbles laid parallel, pointing inward. Oso's trail mark, showing them where to follow. She glanced up and grimaced—the walls of the rift were barely ten feet apart. The crack of blue sky she could see overhead must be a thousand feet up. "What a place for a flash flood!" she muttered to herself.

Or an ambush. The rift didn't run straight into the rock, but meandered in sinuous, water-polished curves, beyond any of which somebody could be lurking. Her nerves had been jumping all day. *Could* McCord be Mateo's killer? She put the facts together. She'd described her mug to him, and though he'd insisted it depicted nothing but a *cielito* lizard, next day he'd vanished. He hadn't reappeared till they'd met at the river four days later. Plenty of time to reach Lagarto if he'd hustled. Then, when they'd met, he'd claimed to be coming from the *Casa de los Picaflores* by way of a hair-raising descent of the south rim.

But she had only his word for that. He might as easily have been returning from Lagarto. Which would certainly explain his reluctance to take her there. And then there were all his attempts to discourage her, as well as his seeming familiarity with the trail along the way.

So he'd had the means to murder and, Lord knew, he had the motive. By his own account he'd been obsessed for years with his near-mythic treasure. If Mateo had stood in his way of gaining it, refused to surrender his secret, could McCord have killed him?

Of course, when you added it all up, her case was entirely circumstantial, hardly enough to convict a man, especially a man that she liked. A man who'd saved her life.

Not that the courage he'd shown, plucking her from her doomed Jeep, was proof of innocence, Raine reminded herself as she rounded a twist in the trail. She'd known some dreadful villains who were brave as— She stopped short.

McCord stood with a palm upraised like a traffic cop. Beyond him, a wall of shattered stone blocked their way. A rockslide had created a steep slope of scree some four stories high by ten feet wide, with no possible detour.

"That'll be fun," she observed.

"Just a blast. And there's a rattler up there. I came back to tell you."

"Where?" She saw nothing but jumbled rocks and the shadowy gaps between them.

"Well, if I knew that I would have shot him, wouldn't I?"

"And shot yourself with a ricochet, while you were at it." Raine glanced around for a stick, but the gorge was scoured clear of driftwood. She shrugged and reached over her shoulder, pulled her parasol free of its pack scabbard.

"You're gonna dazzle him with your Paris umbrella?"

"It's Chinese, and no, not exactly." She unscrewed the silk head, pulled out the handle's telescoping inner pipe and locked the two three-foot shafts of her blow gun end to end.

"Neat. Instant snake prod."

"Just a hiking stick." There was no reason he'd guess that it was more than that, and she sure wasn't telling.

"Let's have it." McCord reached for the pole, and scowled as she swung it behind her. "Come on, Ashaway. I'm leading, so I'm the one who needs it."

"Sorry, but it's sort of a personal charm. If you'll let me go first…" She moved to step past him and bumped into his raised arm.

They stood toe to toe. Glaring. Bathed in each other's body heat. His eyes drifted down over her leisurely, rose back to her face. "You're awfully cute…for snake-bait."

"And you've been down a canyon too long. *Cute* isn't a compliment back in the real world."

"No? Well, whatever you care to call what you've got, I'd suck on your snakebite any ol' day, if you're foolish enough to get yourself bit."

"I'll keep that offer in mind." Raine ducked under his arm and started up.

He swore and caught her free hand. "No way I let a woman break rattlesnake trail for me!"

So they climbed the slope hand in hand, with Raine tapping the rocks ahead as they advanced. A third of the way up, the whirring started. An eerie, hair-raising challenge, the sound echoed off the stone walls.

"Sounds like a big one," McCord muttered between his teeth.

Raine's eyes scanned back and forth, trying to cover every twitch of movement. A snakebite out here, half a week from anywhere…

"Hold on." McCord let go her hand, caught her waist, drawing her to a halt.

"What? Where?"

"Right here." He ducked under the brim of her hat, laid a kiss on her jaw.

"Dammit, McCord, quit kidding!" She swung to frown at him, and he kissed her full-on, leaning into her, bending her back over his muscular arm, their sweat-soaked bodies fusing together. The snake buzzed; goose bumps stampeded across her arms, her breasts. She shuddered and kissed him back, then dragged her mouth away. "Crazy bastard! You'll get us both killed."

"Figured I owed myself one of those, if we're gonna die any—oh, shit, there he is!" Coming down to meet them in a rippling rush.

# Chapter 12

MCCord jerked her behind him and reached for his gun. Spun off balance, Raine smacked into the near wall, and the rocks slithered away. As she staggered and fell, McCord crashed down in a cascade of stones. He landed in a belly flop—and froze.

The rattler lay coiled not a foot from his face. Its ugly triangular head rose off the ground to hover, ready to strike. Its tail was a blur of buzzing motion. "Don't move!" Raine whispered.

She still held her rod, but she'd have to get to her knees to reach over McCord. There was no way to land a killing blow from here. Raine yanked off her hat, hung it on the end of the rod and fed it quickly out to one side of the Texan's right shoulder.

The viper's head tracked the new menace. Raine twitched the hat closer and the snake whiplashed into motion, fangs extending.

"Shit!" McCord rolled to his left, hit the wall and bounced back. The diamondback dropped the hat and swayed toward his movement.

"Don't do that." Raine nudged the discarded hat with her pole. The snake feinted at it, paused as if in thought, then swerved. Cutting a wide berth around their bodies, it slithered on and down—flowed away like water between dry rocks.

McCord scrambled up, then met her eyes with a shaken grin. "Okay, so go ahead and say it."

"What?"

"Something snide about who's watching whose back out here in the canyons."

"Oh, that." By her count, they weren't even yet. She shrugged, smiled, scooped up her snake-bit fedora. "Well, darn!" She rolled it poison-side in and shoved it in her pack. "Think I'll boil this before I wear it again."

McCord patted the rocks, scrambled to his feet to turn a slow, perplexed circle. "Where's my gun?"

They spent a broiling half hour lifting rocks, peering into cracks. They found several scorpions, but no revolver. "It slipped down some hole where we'll never find it," Raine concluded, wiping sweat off her brow.

"Dammit, I've had that Colt longer than I've had chest hair!"

"You keep hunting, I'm outta here." She left him swearing and slinging stones. A few miles' hike brought her to the end of the crevice, where she walked out of oven-baked shadows into the blaze of high noon. Sunlight seared the walls of the main canyon—well, another major canyon. Green and slow, a river looped around the towering buttress to her left and disappeared.

Oso's double line of pebbles led to her right down the

gorge. But a hundred yards on, the kid's sandal tracks crossed a bar of sand fine as sugar. The beach sloped from water's edge up into an alcove of inky shadows, where the river in flood had undercarved the cliff in lush, lazy curves. "Break time." Raine dumped her pack in the shade, changed quickly to her red camping bikini, found soap and shampoo and marched straight into the water.

By the time McCord arrived, she was clean and cool. Floating on her back, she drifted lazily downstream, with barn swallows swooping and chittering above, and a bottle-green dragonfly perched on her toes. McCord groaned in envy, doffed his pack, then his boots and clothes, and staggered into the river.

"Find it?"

"No."

She smiled and drifted on, leaving him to swim out his temper. In a few minutes she joined him where he sat brooding in knee-deep water. "Suppose we ought to catch up with the kid."

"He'll find us when he gets hungry. What's this?" McCord's fingers grazed her skin as he lifted the leather thong off her collarbone. "Opals?"

"Yes. One of my sidelines. Years ago, Dad told us to each specialize in a gem of our choice. You come across 'em now and then, prospecting for fossils."

"You do this for money?"

She smiled. "Sit in a river whenever I please? I'd *pay* to do this—we all feel that way—but to finance our fun, we've got to bring back something to sell."

"How many 'we's' make up Ashaway All?" Her opals were only an excuse to lean closer; it was her scent that entranced him—whiffs of coconut shampoo and sun-warmed skin. Didn't help his peace of mind, sitting buck-naked beside her. Or that her bikini top barely covered her breasts. One sign from her and he'd have jumped her then and there.

"Well, in my generation there's my brother Ash, who's getting his PhD in paleontology at Stanford. I'm next in line, then comes Dana. She's digging prehistoric whales in Ecuador; haven't seen her in almost two years. She deals in jade and emeralds on the side. Then there's Jaye; she's our amber expert, and Gina, our cousin-in-law, a latecomer with no expertise at all. She's back at headquarters, learning to clean and mount the fossils we find."

"I seem to remember the article mentioning that your company's been around for a couple of generations?"

"Longer than that. But Dad and his twin brother, my uncle Joe, kicked it up a notch and took us international."

"And do they still hunt bones?"

Her smile faded. "There was an accident three years back. They were excavating an *Allosaurus* out of a cliff face, under-cutting it, and…something collapsed. Joe and his son—my cousin Jack—were way deep inside. Dad was closer to the cliff edge. He survived, sort of. They didn't." She stood abruptly and launched herself out into deep water and stroked away.

"Dang families anyway," he muttered, watching her go. He washed out his clothes, hung them on a bush to dry, pulled on his other pair of khaki shorts and still she kept her distance. So he switched hats from would-be lover to archaeologist and set to quartering the site, eyes on the ground.

Raine found him half an hour later, on a ledge about a hundred feet above water level. Half the bench was sheltered by another overhang, but he sat at its open end, cross-legged, sketching in his fieldbook. "Take a look at this." He patted the bowl-shaped depression in the rock beside him. "A *metatl*."

"In Manhattan they call that a pothole."

McCord snorted. "It's where a woman grounds her maize

to make *tortillas,* back in the good ol' days when you all knew your proper place."

"Barefoot, knocked-up and in the kitchen?" Raine glanced around at the stark ledge as she sat. "But how could she complain with the latest in time-saving appliances *and* granite counter-tops." She accepted the rounded rock he handed her, made a half-hearted swipe at grinding it along the walls of the *metatl.*

"You always find them in situations like this. Since it took her six hours a day to do this chore, she'd have started her work early in the morning while the air was chilly. So she'd want to sit in the sun, which rises that way." He nodded down canyon. "And naturally she'd have kids to tend, and they'd be out looking for trouble as kids do, so she'd want a place where she could keep an eye on 'em while she worked." He waved a hand over the view and Raine saw that it commanded a quarter mile of riverbank.

She laughed softly. "Someone really did sit here once upon a time, didn't she?"

"That's the main trick of my trade. I just keep reminding myself that they were people, and people haven't changed at all. Not for fifty thousand years, probably not for a million. They loved, they hated, they needed, they wanted, they dreamed. I just close my eyes and think about what I'd need or want for any given location, then I can just about go straight to where they placed their fire, or built their shelter, or planted their crops."

"As easy as that?"

"Used to be," he said, something going brittle in his voice.

She glanced at his profile, the knot of muscle bunching in his jaw beneath the reddish bristles that were so much lighter than his dark-brown hair. She looked away, out over the river. "So who was she, who sat here? One of your wandering Aztecs?"

"Lord, no. On a mission for Quetzalcoatl, they'd have been

bachelors only. The *pochteca* and his men would have been the scouts and hunters. The priests went along to handle the rituals, with soldiers to defend the god and his treasure. The slaves as usual got the grunt work; they carried the burdens."

McCord ran a fingertip idly around the rim of the depression. "Consider the depth of this. It wasn't worn down this deep in a year, or even a lifetime, so nobody in transit shaped this. Her people may have come to this ledge a thousand years before my caravan passed by—if it ever passed by this particular spot."

"And she wouldn't have been Raramuri, I suppose. The doctor told me they migrated from the east, eighty years after Cortés conquered the Aztecs?"

"Fleeing the Spanish, right. But these canyons were peopled thousands of years before that. Just little families of hunter-gatherers here and there, enjoying good water and ample shelter, plenty of game and a temperate climate. You've got to reckon that the woman who looked up one day and saw a caravan trudging around that bend, well, she might have been the twentieth generation to use this *metatl*."

"And did she stand up and wave?" Raine mused.

"Hope she called her kids and ran like—" McCord's head snapped around to look the other way, upriver. "Shoot." He whipped his hat off, dropped it on Raine's head. "Tuck your hair under that, quick! Anybody who takes you for a guy needs his eyes examined, but if you don't stand up..."

A hundred yards off, on the opposite shore, a mule and rider picked their way along a trail. A couple of heavily laden pack mules straggled into view, followed by another, then another—by a whole train of fifteen burdened mules—with a second rider bringing up the rear. "You're sure they've spotted us?"

The lead rider yanked a rifle out of a scabbard, aimed—

"Look out!" As he dropped backwards, McCord swept his arm across her stomach, taking her with him.

*Crack!* A rock splintered on the cliff behind them.

"Shit, shit, *shit!*" McCord swore as he glanced around. They were pinned, Raine saw, looking also. Out of sight for the moment, but they'd be in plain view if they tried to climb the cliff at their back. And she'd left her blowpipe below.

"I lose my gun and what happens?" the Texan was muttering. "Every friggin' psycho in Mexico drops in for tea."

*Crack! Crack!*

"Cut it out!" McCord yelled in Spanish. "What do you want?"

*"Hablar contigo! Ahorita!"*

"You want to talk to us?" McCord yelled. "So who's stopping you?"

*"Venga aquí!"*

Raine rolled over and flattened her hands on his bare chest. "Don't you dare go down there!"

"I don't think I've got a lot of options here. This ledge was very defensible back in the Stone Age, when you could dump a rock on anybody who tried to climb up. But since the invention of gunpowder—"

*Crack!*

"Okay, okay, if you're going to start lecturing—" Raine jumped to her feet.

"Not you!" McCord snatched for her ankle, but she stepped aside. "He meant me! Now we're in trouble."

"Don't shoot!" Raine called, raising her hands. She pulled the hat off, shook her hair out with a big, sheepish smile. "I'll be happy to talk." Till she could reach her blowgun, she would. If she could duck into the alcove below, its shadows should hide her while she gummed her darts. By the time they forded the river to smoke her out, she could be ready.

*"Traiga el feo contigo, mujer!"*

"Insults, yeah, they're in a mood all right." Hands raised, McCord rose into view. "Now for chrissake, Ashaway, let me do the talking."

"When I make a break for the alcove, get down, all right?"

"Not all right!" McCord locked his fingers around her wrist. "That's a dead end. If they start shooting at me, you run like a rabbit for the crack in the cliff. Make it past the scree and they'll probably give up, since no mule would climb it."

They argued fiercely in whispers all the way down to the beach, then McCord dropped her hand. "Get ready to run for it."

"Fine." She would, but toward her weapon, not his bolt hole.

"So what do you want?" McCord called to the mule riders as he stepped into the river.

"We want to talk to you both!"

"Sorry, but she's shy, and she's too stupid for conversation. You can talk to me." Wading up to his knees, arms raised, McCord kept advancing with a smile.

The gunman glanced at Raine. "If you don't get your ass over here, I'll shoot your man's head like I'd shoot a watermelon."

And that settled that. Raine followed McCord across the river.

# Chapter 13

"I've never been so happy to be caught with a babe in all my life," McCord muttered a half hour later, as they stood, arms around each other's waist, watching the mule train plod away. "Whatever they're thinking, we didn't fit the profile."

The muleteers had been seeking the leader's younger brother. Only thirteen, he'd vanished two nights ago, from their camp up the river. "And we can thank our lucky stars that Oso didn't pop up in the middle of this," McCord continued. "If they'd seen us with one kid, they might have concluded we're in the market for more."

Which was why Raine had snuggled up to him, halfway through the inquisition. Better to look like a couple of honeymooners, too enamored of each other to want anyone else, much less a kid, underfoot. "I still don't understand," she said, frowning after them. "They were obviously upset. So why don't they hang around? Keep hunting for him?"

"What do you think was in all those packs, Ashaway?"

"Supplies for some *ranchito?*"

"Those were *mestizos*—mixed bloods—not Raramuri. They're packing marijuana out from some field. That's not a freelancer's profession around here. It's organized. There's always a *jefe,* who answers to some boss back in the city, and he's always a merciless son of a bitch. Those guys are delivering a million-dollar payload, and the *jefe*'d get nervous if they didn't show up when and where expected. If he starts wondering if maybe they stopped somewhere to skim the loads, hide some weed till they could come back later and collect it, well, they're dead. And he's not going to buy any sentimental excuse about a lost kid brother."

"I see." Still moving as one, they drifted down the bank toward the river. "But they said they searched all yesterday."

"Took guts to steal the time to do so."

"And what happened to the kid?"

McCord shook his shaggy head. "Fell down a crevice, got bit by a snake, drowned in the river? It's a wild, woolly world out here. With any luck Oso'll find him lost and hungry somewhere and bring him along."

But he didn't.

An hour later the boy appeared in his usual fashion—from out of nowhere. One moment Raine and McCord walked the trail, the next, Oso fell in between them.

"Your shadow's back."

"Oh?" McCord turned to grin at the solemn child. "Must be lunchtime."

While they ate, Raine tried to ask Oso if he'd seen the lost boy. If she spoke Spanish slowly and kept it simple, he seemed to understand. But she hadn't a clue what his shy whispers signified. "What's he saying?"

"He says he's seen nobody but the big man."

"That's you?" The two muleteers had been short and wiry.

"I suppose; he's not much for explaining. Though he's got to be ranging a good ten miles out ahead of us. Who knows who else is out here?"

"Well, then, ask him when we'll get to his brother's clay pit."

"I'd be wasting my breath asking a Raramuri."

"Still, it can't be much further. Clay is heavy, even if Mateo dried it out."

"Don't count on that. I've seen men toting half their own weight for days on end along these trails. Now if you want to worry about something, worry about when Junior's going to eat us out of house and home. If I had my gun, I could add some game to the pot, but seeing as I don't..."

They had a week of provisions left, Raine had already calculated. "Aren't there fish in the river?" That would be her chore tonight, she decided, shouldering her pack.

She led the way till Oso's macho little heart couldn't stand it anymore, then he hustled past her, while McCord lazed along in the rear. The kid was still with them an hour later, when Raine stopped to peer across the river. "A cave," she noted, as the Texan joined her. On the opposite side and set some fifty feet above the water, it wasn't a river-eroded alcove, but a ragged, man-size hole tunneling into darkness.

"Yeah. Looks like there's maybe a spring inside. See how green the vegetation is, following a seep line down from its mouth? Prime real estate." McCord rested a hand on Oso's shoulder and asked in Spanish, "Who lives there?"

The boy muttered something and darted off down the trail.

"He says it's haunted." McCord shrugged and walked on.

"Haunted by whom?" Raine called as she followed. "Or by what?"

"He wouldn't say. But caves are valuable shelter here in

the canyons. If no Raramuri have claimed it for a home, then it's got some seriously nasty vibes."

"Caused by what? Rabid bats? Killer cockroaches? Heart snatchers?"

"How 'bout all three? But just as likely it's something harmless—like a blowhole in the roof that makes a howling-ghost sound when the wind whistles through it. Though it could be something factual," McCord admitted. "Say a family died there of plague or cholera a hundred years back. The legend would linger long after the details were forgotten."

"Okay, but what about the missing little brother? Kids get into all kinds of jams, exploring. I think we should check it out."

"They were riding that side of the river, Ashaway. I'm sure they searched it."

"I suppose you're right. Then what about Mateo? He said he saw something amazing on his trip to the clay pit. Why are we assuming he saw it at journey's end? Could as easily have been something he found along the way."

"True, and I'm keeping my eyes open. But Raramuri take their superstitions seriously. If the cave is haunted, he'd have never gone near it."

She stood frowning while the Texan walked on. What he said made sense, and yet... Mateo hadn't been a typical Raramuri. He'd broken his tribe's customary isolation, found a way to bring his work to the tourist market in Creel. Adapted a design foreign to his own culture. What else might he have dared? If they didn't hit the jackpot at the clay pit, she promised herself, she'd definitely explore that cave on her way back.

Not half an hour later, McCord called a halt. They'd forded the waist-deep river at a slowly spinning pool, above which the canyon narrowed. Gigantic boulders jumbled the course of the descending waterway, breaking it into a series of foaming cascades. "A good place to stop for the night."

"This early? We could make a few more miles before dark."

"Yeah, but consider those clouds." McCord nodded north-west at a series of thunderheads. "This isn't flash flood season, but you can't bank on anything out here. If the water level jumps twenty feet, it'll be Blender City up ahead."

After they'd gathered enough driftwood for their campfire, Raine washed out her hat. True to their elusive gender, the guys vanished at the first whiff of domesticity. She shrugged, found some crumbled hardtack in her pack and set to catching supper.

When McCord rejoined her, she was lying on her stomach on the bank, up to her elbows in the river. "Lose something?"

"Hey, watch it! You're spooking the fish."

"You're joking, right?"

"Nope." Eyes fixed on the submerged, upturned fedora that she held, and the crumbs of cracker that floated within it, she waited, motionless as a hunting cat. A perch cruised past the brim of the hat and vanished with a flick of its tail.

"No way! Not even fish are *that* stupid."

"Really? See the sack in the water to my right?"

He looked. "You're using my Grateful Dead T-shirt as a fish pound?"

"Sautéed perch for supper," she sang seductively. "All you have to do is clean 'em."

"I knew you were dangerous, first time I laid eyes on you."

*"Ha!"* She tipped the brim up—hoisted the hat out of the water, with a frantic perch tearing around its perimeter. She drained the river out, then tucked her catch in the improvised bag and settled to the game again.

"I really have to clean 'em?"

"Only fair, since I'm doing the catching."

While another perch hovered near the trap, they chatted idly. "Meant to ask you," Raine murmured. "Is that some sort of artifact you wear?" She'd noticed the carved seashell hanging from a cord on his chest, while he was admiring her opals that afternoon.

"This?" He pulled the pendant up from the V of his shirt. In the manner of an Italian cameo, a cream-colored layer of shell had been carved intricately, delicately, down to its rosy background. A tiny woman knelt with her arms outstretched to a large, wolfish canine. Somehow the figures captured an aura of wistfulness, of yearning toward completion. Any moment, Raine imagined, the beast would wave his tail, step close enough to be hugged.

"It's lovely." She glanced again at the shell as McCord tucked it away. "Is that Aztec work?"

"It's…well, you can't call it a copy, since I never saw the original. Just a guess what it might have looked like."

"*You* carved it? Really?"

"Sure. Replicating technology is the best way for an archaeologist to understand it. I graduated from chipping Folsom spear points out of flint ages ago. You'll remember I told you that in his letter to his brother, the Spanish priest mentioned a shell necklace his slave—the *pochteca*'s wife—always wore?"

"The gift her husband brought back from his travels?"

"Yeah. It showed a woman kneeling to a coyote, a scene which the priest described as idolatrous, heathenish, but my hunch is he also found it titillating."

"Wow. I assumed this was a genuine artifact. That you must have dug it up around here."

"And kept it for myself?" His voice had gone chilly as the river.

"Well, I— Yes. I suppose that's exactly what I figured."

His laugh was harsh and unamused. "*Pothunter*'s a dirty word in some circles. Not much better than *graverobber*."

"But is that the circle you travel in?" He called himself a professor, yet, where were the trappings and perks of academia? The grad students, the excavation site, the university where he hung up his degrees and taught?

"It used to be, all right? And it will be again. All I need is one big find. But in the meantime, since you ask, no, I don't believe in pillaging history for profit—ripping up sites and selling off the sexiest pieces to the highest bidder. I'd have figured that was more *your* family's style, Ms. Bone Hunter."

Raine dumped out her hat and sat up to face him. "Then you figured dead wrong. When Ashaway All digs a dinosaur, we collect the skeleton—and its entire complex of facts: death-pose, maps, photos, vegetation, geology—all the background materials that surrounded it, same as any degreed paleontologists would harvest on-site. And we do a better job than a team of college kids and their academic babysitters would do. In terms of experience *they're* the amateurs; we're the professionals. And we bring back the goods—an undamaged fossil plus its whole matrix of knowledge. Every major museum in the world has dinosaurs supplied by Ashaway All."

"And I bet every major private collector has some, too."

"Well, of course. There're more bones out there than there are museums to house them, or academics to describe them. And they're fragile. Leave 'em *in situ* and they'll weather back to dust within a few years. Is that any kind of solution?"

"Hey, dig 'em all up and see if I care. Me, I'm gonna go clean some fish." McCord dragged his wriggling T-shirt out of the water and stalked off downstream.

Raine sighed, stretched out and rebaited her hat. "So much for dancing," she muttered. "Choose your partner, seek out his sorest toe—then stomp on it."

When she'd caught enough perch for supper, she sent her

remaining catch to the Texan via Oso, since they still weren't speaking. She'd have to find some way to make peace. Meanwhile, there was just enough light left for a dip and scrub.

He shouldn't have flown off the handle like that, McCord told himself, watching her swim. She'd hit a raw nerve, true enough, but she'd done so without malice. In any event, how long could a man stay mad with a blonde in a scarlet bikini?

It was the suspense that was setting him on edge. He wanted her. He'd dreamt about her again last night. And in spite of her wariness and waffling, he got the feeling that the feeling was mutual. Whenever they touched, it was flint to steel, sparks swarming like fireflies. Given the tiniest bit of tinder, then a chance to stoke the resulting flames...

But he'd made a mistake hiring Oso to be their guide. With the kid popping up over their horizon every half hour, there was no opportunity for wooing or dalliance. "Soon as we get to the clay pit, I pay him off," McCord promised himself. Later on he could send for the boy, offer him a job as camp gofer and general pest underfoot. Oso was eager and smart and, given the loss of his older brother, he surely deserved a break. "But so do I," McCord said aloud, collecting the fish he'd cleaned and rising. He glanced again toward Raine—and stiffened. "What the—"

She stood in the shallows on the opposite shore, flirting with a big bronzed-and-brawny type. Looking foolish in shorty hiking shorts and fuzzy legs, the intruder seemed to be contemplating a swan dive down the bosom of Raine's red bikini.

"Grunwald!" McCord shook his head in disgust. So here was the big man that Oso had forecast, but what the hell was the German doing out in the back of beyond?

"Look who dropped in for supper," Raine called cheerfully.

# Chapter 14

"A magnificent feast," Grunwald pronounced, as he scraped his plate. "My compliments to our charming chef. It takes the feminine touch, so I think, to work such magic in the center of a roaring wilderness."

"Yeah, she's a regular Suzie Homemaker," McCord agreed, sending Raine a private smirk. "We're *so* lucky to have her."

He was going to have a tin plate for a hat, if he kept on this way, Raine decided. She'd preferred him silent and surly, as he'd been for the first half of the meal. But McCord had picked up on the feelings she was working hard to hide. The more irritated and bored she became with their dinner guest, the cheerier he grew.

"Now, if you will permit me to provide the dessert?" Grunwald reached into the pack he'd been lounging against. "Yes?" He held a bottle triumphantly aloft and the campfire flames turned the Scotch to gold.

"Now you're talking!" McCord dumped the water out of his mug.

Freed of Grunwald's elephantine attentions while he poured out the treat, Raine studied the engineer. Feminine touches or no, this was a darned big roaring wilderness. The odds of their bumping into each other by chance were somewhere between lousy and nil. All her instincts had bristled when he hove into view. She'd invited him to supper with the intention of asking some questions, the first being *Where were you the night Mateo was murdered?*

Because the minute she'd seen him, it had hit her: He was another one who'd known about the blue-dino mug. He'd tried to buy it off her back at the cantina. She'd even told him where he could find its maker—in Lagarto.

Could Grunwald have realized that the mug might be a clue leading to treasure? Been willing to kill in pursuit of that prize? Have beaten them to Lagarto by only a day? Grunwald claimed that he'd arrived on the scene this morning, via an arroyo that cut in from the east, a few miles up the big-boulder canyon. A company helicopter had dropped him there, he said, and would return to collect him in a few days.

She'd stolen a glance at McCord when Grunwald mentioned the chopper, and seen her skepticism mirrored in his face. The canyon's acoustics were amazing. Wouldn't they have heard the machine's thumping echoes? Or maybe the tight angles of the rift would have baffled its sound.

As for why he'd come, the engineer claimed he was taking a week off for hiking, before he sat down to write his final report on the dam's placement. "My survey team and I passed this way months before," he'd explained. "There is a cave that I happened upon, only a few miles down this river. I had no chance to explore it, but it looked promising."

McCord's gaze had flicked across hers, then he'd drawled, "The Raramuri say that's a haunted cave."

"Do they? So much the better!" The German had laughed his boisterous laugh. "The *indios* are quite wonderfully superstitious. Isn't that so, *chico?*" He'd winked at Oso, whom McCord had drawn into their fire circle. Silent and shy, the boy had sat at the Texan's elbow all night.

"You mean to tell me that you have not explored it yourself?" the German continued, handing round the mugs. "This one has a passion for spelunking as do I," he confided to Raine. "You really should not miss the opportunity, my friend. In a few years it will be gone forever."

"That a fact?"

"Yes, truly." Grunwald patted the ground. "Here where we sit will also be under water. If my company accepts my recommendations—and they will—our dam will be sited seventy miles northeast of here. Once the river backs up, this will make the largest man-made lake in all of Mexico. It will be a magnet for tourism to rival Cancun. And now for our toast: To man's ingenuity, which will make a blooming paradise of this worthless desert!"

Raine couldn't drink to that. The canyons had their own stark and fragile beauty that was paradise enough. And when the engineers and the bureaucrats drowned it, how many irreplaceable fossils would vanish forever? Where would Oso's people go when the developers crowded up to the trough to build their lakeside condos?

"Oh, yes, let us drink to progress!" A man stepped out of the shadows to loom over them where they sat gaping. A slender young man strung tight as a bow. "There will be so many jobs for my people when you bury the canyons! There will be a need for waiters in the restaurants that will surely be built. A need for maids to make the beds of the rich tourists who come to the hotels along the lake shores. And for the golf courses, there must be caddies, is it not so?"

"Antonio, what the blue blazes are you doing out here?" McCord stood to offer his hand. The two men stroked each other's fingers from knuckle to fingertip, then McCord gave him his cup. "Sit down and drink to whatever you damn well please."

The third time the Scotch went round the circle, Raine passed. Killing a bottle was one way to smooth the rough edges of a mismatched dinner party, but for herself, she'd rather imitate Oso. Sit back in the shadows and observe the interactions among her companions. Look up at the stupendous stars and ponder.

Antonio. He was as complex as Grunwald seemed to be simple. An interesting development in himself and also for the light he'd thrown on McCord. The Raramuri worked as the Texan's cook, guide, dig-site foreman whenever McCord held one of his two-week seminars for paying volunteers. In much the way that a dude ranch imitates the real thing, the Texan sold the archaeology experience. "Archaeology Lite," he'd labeled it, with a breezy smile that didn't hide his embarrassment. "For those earnest types who want a smattering of education on their vacation. We camp out at one of the caves I've found along the Rio San Ignácio, always a site near a good waterhole. I lecture about the Copper Canyons' prehistory and history, show 'em how to set up a grid, collect potsherds. Antonio leads nature hikes and feeds 'em authentic Raramuri cuisine." He shrugged. "It pays the bills, keeps my hand in while…"

His voice had trailed away, but his eyes had sought Raine's with an urgent plea: *Don't talk about the Aztec caravan!* That quest must be private, she realized, in the way men so often hide their wildest dreams. Something he'd shared with her—and probably now regretted sharing.

She wondered if Antonio knew what McCord was really looking for, eyeing the young man across the fire. His lean face wavered in the flickering light, looking alternately fierce and too friendly, yet always familiar. *I've seen you before, haven't I?* But where? In Creel at the start of this venture, or more recently than that? Or was it merely that the Raramuri bred true to type? He easily might have been Oso's brother or cousin, or the son of the doctor's aging cook.

The flames leaped as his deep-set eyes moved her way—and stilled. In one pupil a red spark gleamed like a lamp in a distant cavern—some reflection off the guttering embers. *No, I've seen you before. Coming right at me, and with the same kind of malice I'm sensing now. You don't like me, do you, Antonio?* He hadn't addressed her directly all evening. And whenever she and McCord spoke to each other, he looked away, yet she could tell he was listening greedily.

Was he jealous of his boss's attentions? McCord treated him with the respectful affection that a professor bestows on a promising grad student, a whiff of mentor and protégé. Did Antonio imagine that she might intrude on that relationship?

Or maybe this was simply paranoia on her part. A product of too much Scotch on top of too many dangers for one day. *And with a cave full of haunts downriver, just waiting for us to nod off,* she mocked herself. Whatever, brooding about Antonio would do her no good. She stretched, rose to wander off and ready herself for bed.

When she returned, the conversation had changed subject and tone. "This was in one of the professor's books that I borrowed, about the gods of the Aztecs and their priests," Antonio was insisting.

McCord shifted restlessly. "They don't want to hear about that stuff, this time of night."

"Not so," protested Grunwald. "A scary tale around the

bonfire? It reminds me of summer camp. Please do tell us, and then I will tell one even better."

It wasn't a story, Raine realized as she listened—more a selection of nasty facts, recounted with a veiled pleasure and that same sudden, lancing gaze to measure their reactions. Hers in particular. Antonio described the racks of skulls of the sacrificed displayed at the base of the temple in Tenochtitlan—136,000 skulls, the Conquistadores had estimated.

He spoke of the priests of Quetzalcoatl, who practiced self-sacrifice when they lacked prisoners of war, or other victims. "There must be blood. Without an offering, the sun will not rise. So they pierced their own ears with maguey thorns— thorns as big as your finger—then they let the blood drip down through their long hair, and let it dry in their locks." Antonio turned to Oso with a kindly smile and switched to Raramuri.

"He doesn't need a translation!" McCord said sharply.

"But I only thought to include him."

"Well, don't. He's just lost his big brother in a fire. Last thing he needs is more material for nightmares."

"Ah?" Antonio swung to study the boy—then smiled, his teeth flashing in the firelight. "I am very sorry."

Expressed in English, the apology was worthless. McCord shrugged and stood, beckoned to Oso. "Reckon we'll go check out the river level."

Raine rose also, to arrange her bedroll and foam pad a little way from the fire. Presumably Antonio would soon desist, with his audience fading away.

But no, with Grunwald's encouragement he'd started on another. This tale was about a misunderstanding between the ancient Aztecs, newly arrived from Aztlan in the north, and the powerful tribe of the Culhua. "The Aztecs begged the Culhua for one of their princesses, so that they might worship her as a goddess. The king of the Culhua sent them a young beauty—his favorite daughter. Then soon after this, the Aztecs invited the king and his lords to a ceremony in honor of their new deity. But to the king's surprise, when they called forth the goddess, an Aztec priest stepped out to dance in the streets for all to see. And the costume he wore was…the flayed skin of the princess!"

Grunwald chortled in horrified delight. "Oh ho, now *that's* a scary story!"

And quite enough. Raine snatched up her bedroll and moved out of earshot. She lay a long time watching the moon rise above the canyon walls, remembering what McCord had told her the other night: that the Aztecs believed there was a rabbit in the moon. Tonight, there must be dust in the air, as a rusty stain marred the bunny. "Can't be a good omen," she murmured to herself, and slept.

Raine dreamed of dinosaurs, as she often did. This time it was a migration of *Hadrosaurs*. More numerous than the buffalo, they darkened the plains. Behind them tramped a species she'd never seen before. Like *Triceratops,* but without horns, they were turquoise in color, with parrot feathers edging their neck-frills and ringing their hefty ankles. She laughed in delight and stepped forward to meet them.

And they panicked. *Something dreadful coming.* The ground shook as they thundered past her, the whole herd stampeding for the river. She turned and ran, too, trying to head them off. In the swift current they'd drown, make lovely fossils for her to find millions of years in the future, but not if she could save them right now!

But the beasts splashed into the river and were swept away. *Something dreadful was coming.* And somebody was calling her, voice cracking in desperation. Water rising, mud sucking…

She bolted upright with a cry. It was a nightmare. With a hand on her hammering heart, she blew out a breath. Only a dream, thank God, but had she woken anyone? She looked around—and jumped violently.

Not ten feet away sat a dog—a wolf—something canine and too damn large! It was staring at her. "G-george?" she whispered. McCord's vanishing coyote. *"Jorge?"*

Were his intentions friendly? Or not? When had he eaten last? Slowly Raine pulled her legs up. She gripped the hilt of her knife, which she'd strapped to her ankle at bedtime.

The beast yawned luxuriously, rose and strolled off into the dark. She was still dreaming, she assured herself. She glanced over her shoulder.

No dream. The setting moon touched his rippling fur with silver. He sauntered up a rise, paused to look back at her from his crest—then vanished downstream.

Raine struggled into her pants, her boots. She grabbed a flashlight from her pack and hurried after. Whoever or whatever he was, he'd sent her an invitation.

Stepping lightly, she passed a bundle of blankets—then saw that they didn't cover a body. Somebody else was up and wandering, too? But the others had bedded down after she had; she didn't know who was on the prowl.

As for where her guide and she were bound, her conviction grew as she caught another glimpse of him, fifty yards ahead, moving steadily. Her sense of urgency was growing along with the certainty. *Something dreadful... Someone in need...* The blood strode relentlessly in her ears. For fear of snakes she had to use her flashlight, but that made her a target for anything lurking in the dark beyond her golden, bobbing circle. Still she gritted her teeth and hurried on.

When at last she reached the cave, the coyote waited for her at its mouth. Their eyes met for an instant, then he turned and vanished into the black. "McCord!" she whispered as she broke into a run. The abandoned bedroll must have been his!

He and the coyote were linked in some way. Could the shell around his neck somehow call the beast?

*Something dreadful was coming.* She scrambled up the slope, teetered on the lip of the cave. The Texan had told her it was haunted, but by what? "McCord?"

"Help! Oh, God, quick, help!" A man's voice—frantic with fear, hoarse from screaming, distorted by distance and echoes.

Raine gulped, drew her knife and walked in, sweeping her light. Spiderwebs iced the damp stone. Weedy bushes followed a trickle of moisture inward, growing pale and sickly as she moved beyond the reach of sunlight. "Hello?"

"Help, please help me!"

"I'm coming!" Into a trap? But if not, if the need was as urgent as the panic in the voice implied…. No time to run for reinforcements, she told herself. Not till she'd seen what she could do, here and now.

The trail twisted around a massive boulder. The tunnel widened into a cavern as she rounded it, her shaft of light swallowed by its immensity. "Where are you?" And where was the coyote?

"Here. Down here. D-d-don't come too close!"

The path sloped inward and gently down to where it widened into a smooth, flat floor, gleaming in her light. A skim of water lay over its gritty surface. And in its midst, casting a long shadow, was a small boulder.

The rock writhed grotesquely, revealing a half profile, a white-ringed eye, a gaping mouth. *Oh, God, where was the rest of him?* "Johann!" Not McCord. Even in her horror, Raine felt the relief.

"Oh, God, thank—" Grunwald babbled something in German, then shrieked as she started toward him. "No, no, stop, you idiot! It's quicksand!"

# Chapter 15

He was sunk to his neck. "Oh, Johann! Okay, okay, be calm, I'm here." Raine dropped to her knees, crawled closer, feeling the path before her. Her beam probed back and forth and found no edge to the pool; the saturated sand was the same color as the rock on which it floated. She reached the horizontal smoothness, put a finger into chilly muck and flinched. "How long have you been here?" The tawny mud grazed his uptilted chin.

"A year, a lifetime, I don't know. *Get me out!*"

"I will, I promise. But how fast are you going down?" Her eyes lit on his pack, tossed up onto the far bank. If she could break its aluminum tube frame, make a snorkel, that would buy him a little time.

"I'm not. It has stopped. I stand...upon something."

"Then, could you try to wade toward me, Johann?" He was four feet beyond her longest reach.

"No, no, I cannot! I tried that. I…" He paused, panting. "I believe that I stand upon…a boulder. It drops off in each direction. If I move…" He burst into tears.

"No, of course not! You stay right there. But, Johann, this is excellent news. You can stand there and be safe till I get you out, okay?" she said soothingly. As long as he didn't hyperventilate himself into a faint. "Your pack over there, is there any rope in it?"

"There is climbing line, but, woman, I weigh nearly twice what you do."

True, and combining his dead weight with the suction of the mud… Raine sat up, staring around. The margins of the pool—what she guessed were the margins—were without feature. No large rocks or stalagmites around which she could build a primitive purchase. "I'm going to need help to get you out, Johann."

*"Don't leave me!"* His voice teetered on the ragged edge of hysteria.

She didn't argue. "Do you have a flashlight in your pack?" She could run the trail back to camp in twenty minutes, but only if she didn't break her neck. Yet to leave him here in the dark…

"No, I dropped it when I stumbled and—" He gulped audibly. "It sank."

"No problem." She edged around the pool. The quicksand must form a level surface, so she could guess where its edges lay. But the damp stone banks sloped steeply toward the trap, must have funneled moisture and fine, windblown sand into the hole for centuries. Wouldn't help Grunwald if she tripped and joined him. "You've got matches in your pack, right? Maybe a candle lantern?"

"I…yes…somewhere… Oh, no! I left it by my bedroll!"

"Not a problem." She searched quickly through his pack,

found the matches, then in a side pocket— "Why, look, you've got a lighter."

"Ah, yes!" He laughed through his tears. "So I do."

She picked her way back to the path leading to the cave's entrance and knelt again. A few minutes more to calm him, then run like the devil. "So...how'd you happen to come here?" Had the coyote lured him, also? She played her light around the space but saw no sign of the creature. But twenty feet beyond the pool, the cavern narrowed to a doorway-size tunnel and burrowed on into the rock.

"I could not sleep. I decided, what the hell. In a cave it is always nighttime. Why wait till morning to explore? So I..." He managed a ghastly smile. "So here am I."

"It's going to make a terrific campfire story. You'll be dining out on this one for years." She gave him her warmest smile. "You didn't happen to see anybody or any animals on your way, did you?"

"A possum. A snake. No more than that, why?"

"Just wondered." She found a level spot on the slope at her side, drew his lighter out of her pocket. "Johann..."

"Yes, I know. You must go for help." He gulped again.

"I wish I could leave you my flashlight, but that would slow me down."

"Sooner is b-better." He blew out a breath. "I am better now, for talking to you. For knowing that someone— Yes, please to go quickly."

"Quick as ever I can." Raine flicked his lighter. Its flame was pitifully small to hold back the crouching dark. She balanced it on the rock. "I think this will burn for quite some time."

"Burning or not, I will wait for you here."

They smiled, sharing the feeble joke. "Be brave!" she whispered, then turned and walked up the slope, out of the cave. Reaching its mouth, she paused and glanced back toward a muffled sound. Had he called her?

No, that was a groan dredged up from his heart, she decided, and almost threw herself down the slope to the path along the river. She sucked in a breath and ran.

Small red eyes flickered in the bounding beam of her flashlight. A snake? Packrat? She slowed, and something dark scurried out of her path. She rushed onward, huffing and puffing, a stitch in her side. She was moving too fast, but all she could think was how terrified he must be!

Terror for him, terror dogging her heels… She couldn't shake the feeling that something dreadful lurked out there in the dark and she was an easy target—blinded by her own light, making noise to attract predators, unable to hear approaching danger above the tramp of her boots upon stone. The path rose as the trail climbed away from the river, mounting the canyon wall. She put her head down and slogged on, reached the crest with a grateful gasp—and slammed straight into a hard, hot body.

Hands grabbed her arms as she yelped. "Be quiet!" Antonio commanded, steadying her while she swayed. "Why do you run?"

"McCord, where is he?"

"Back at camp, asleep. I saw you'd gone walking and thought that was not wise."

"I'm fine, but Johann—" Quickly she told him of the German's plight. "If you'll run ahead of me back to camp, tell McCord."

"No, you go. I'll run on to the cave. I'm stronger. If he needs help…" The Raramuri whirled away and loped off into the night.

*Can he see in the dark?* she wondered, panting. And was

that a pack he'd been wearing? To walk out and find her? Odd. The thought brushed her mind, then retreated as she whirled, jogged on.

When he saw the German, Antonio burst into laughter. Reduced to his arrogant head, he was not so confident now!

The head stared upward with sheepish, pleading eyes. "Thank God! Where are the others?"

"Coming." He squatted on his heels by the pool. "So. Perhaps there is a little justice in this world. You would wreck our homeland for your profit, but the canyon bites back. It sucks on your toes!"

"Go ahead and laugh, *Indio!* But when I get out…"

"Ah, but what makes you think you'll crawl out of this?"

"Wh-what do you mean? Of course, I'll— Raine knows I'm here. She'll help me, even if you won't."

"But will there be anything to help, by the time she returns?" Antonio pulled off his pack and unzipped it. "Tell me, engineer. What will happen if you do not write that report? Perhaps your company of earth-wreckers will give up? Build their dam somewhere else?"

"It w-would make no difference! They'd send somebody else, check my notes, put the dam just where I recommended! This is madness, to think that by hurting me—" He stopped, gulped, softened his tone. "Please. *Please* do stop joking."

"So I must find your notes, back at your main camp. Destroy these, smash any computers I find. Yes, that can be done." Antonio nodded to himself. "Any delay that I can buy us… Any examples I can make, to show the others that resistance is possible… Ah, when I tell this one at the next *tesguinada*— how your eyes bugged like a bullfrog in a pond—everyone will laugh, I promise you! And so…" He drew a cylinder out of his pack. "You're the engineer. Do you recognize this?"

"Dynamite! You're crazy! *Loco!* Where did you get it?"

"From a friend of our cause. A brother who slaves in the mines. I have much to learn, before I know how to blow up a bridge or a railway. And I've been wanting to practice." He drew out a length of fuse. "I'm told that there is slow fuse and there is fast. Which do I have here?"

"*Help! Help!* For God's sake, *help!*"

"Slow, I hope." Antonio smiled to himself as he cut an arm's length, attached it to the explosive, laid the stick of dynamite at the edge of the pool. "Now, if this plan does not agree with you, then by all means—you should come over here and pull out the fuse, no?"

"You know I can't! Don't! *Please,* don't! McCord will know what you've done and have you arrested! You'll rot in jail!"

"I'll tell him I started a rockslide while trying to pull you out. He'll forgive me." Antonio lit the fuse and winced at the burst of sparks, then let out his breath in a sigh. "It seems to burn slowly. I thought as much." He set the lighter back in place. "So that you may watch it burn."

The German shook his head dully, back and forth, back and forth. Antonio smiled and shouldered his pack, turned to go…then paused. He swung slowly back around.

Beyond the pool, beyond the black upon black that was a gap in the rear cavern wall, something rattled, a tiny cascade of clicking sounds.

Both men sucked in their breaths. "What was that?" the German asked.

"Hush!" Antonio stood on tiptoe to peer, his mouth rounded to an O.

*Ssss-clickety-clickety-clickety Click*… A shimmering, rushing sound, like a star crumbling to sand, then sifting down from a midnight sky. Or a monstrous slithering creature, its scales rasping dusty stone…

"What is it?"

"I—I don't know, but it's *yours!*" Antonio whirled and fled.

Grunwald whimpered deep in his throat and tried to turn toward the noise. But the mud sucked at him. His feet slipped on his perch and he froze, but for his trembling. Footsteps approached. But they were coming from *within* the cliff, not without. How could that be?

Sssssssss-clickety-clickety-clickety Tik! In the corner of his blinking eye, the darkness gathered—something large looming out of it, padding round the pool, to stand above the sparkling fuse.

"Oh, God!" Grunwald whispered, then, "Yes. *Yes!*" He nodded frantically, dipping his nose nearly into the muck. "Oh, yes! Stamp it out!"

In spite of Raine's pleas that he run on ahead, McCord refused to leave her. "You said he's safe, and meantime I say we stick together." He tugged her along behind him, while Oso trotted ahead, proudly waving the flashlight. "If none of you fools had wandered off in the first place, this never would've happened."

"Are you always this grumpy when somebody wakes you?"

"Try me sometime, when it's just the two of us and it doesn't involve mud-wrestling. That damn fool Grunwald."

Crabby or not, they were making good time. "Maybe a quarter mile to go," Raine gasped as the trail sloped upward.

Oso stopped so suddenly on its crest, they almost plowed into him. McCord caught his arm, holding him on the path.

"¡Hola!" said Antonio, walking up beyond the boy.

"You left him?" Raine cried.

"I never saw him. You did not tell me, *señorita*, that the cave was haunted."

"Oh, for pity's sake! It's haunted by quicksand. That would give any place an ugly rep! So he's been waiting there all alone?"

"We can fuss later! Let's go whip him out of there before he has a conniption fit." McCord herded the Raramuri ahead of them, as he squeezed Raine's hand in warning.

He was right, first things first, but when this was over she had a few choice words for his surly pal! And her opinion of Antonio didn't improve when they reached their goal.

He sat down on the path below the cave. "It is not wise to go in there. Cannot you feel that this place is full of evil spirits?" He said something to Oso in Raramuri, making the boy swing his stricken, big-eyed gaze up to McCord's.

"Fine. You guys stay put." McCord detached Oso gently from his flashlight, then followed Raine up the slope to the tunnel, with two coils of rope slung over his shoulders, bandolier fashion. He glanced back with a frown. "First time I've ever seen him dig in his heels that way." He shrugged and handed Raine the light.

"Johann?" she called. "We're here!" Bouncing off clammy stone, her voice echoed back, its tone weirdly twisted from cheerful to jeering.

He didn't respond.

A chill oozed up her spine. "He's just around this rock," she assured McCord, moving on ahead. "Johann? Johann!"

McCord put a hand on her shoulder and kept it there. Its human warmth and weight was very welcome. They rounded the rock, to stand, staring down at the pool. It was smooth, not even a bump marring its shining surface. "This is the place?" McCord demanded as she slashed her beam of light back and forth, probing every corner of the cavern. "It's gotta be farther in."

"No…" Shaking her head, she sank to her knees. "Oh, Johann," she said softly. "Oh, God!"

McCord brushed her cheek with his knuckles. "Sit tight, sweetheart, and let me see if I can find a stick."

He returned with a driftwood branch to probe the ooze. "Gets deep again over on this side," he reported eventually. "I reckon the pit's oval-shaped, down there, with a round boulder blocking its middle. Which means..." He trailed off and moved along the perimeter to probe again.

Raine nodded her head without lifting it from her forearms that were propped on her upbent knees. What McCord meant was that there could be a gap on either side of the boulder on which Johann had balanced. Once he slipped off it, he'd sink past the rock. He might be sinking still. "Guess it doesn't much matter," she murmured. Four minutes was all the chance of survival that Grunwald would have had. McCord had been sounding the pool for what seemed like hours.

"Yeah." The Texan pulled his stick out and laid it on the bank.

She'd managed to fight back her tears till now. With this final surrender, though, she gulped around the lump in her throat, nodded and suddenly they came streaming. "Damn!" She hated to cry; it was something she'd learned to hide, growing up mainly among men. She knuckled her eyes, tried to smile for McCord, who came hurrying around the pool. "Be careful!"

He dropped down beside her and gathered her in. "I'm so sorry, Raine. If there was anything I could do—"

She burrowed against him, shuddering. "Oh, Jesus, what a way t-to..."

"Don't think about it, babe. Doesn't do any good." He kissed her temple as he stroked her shuddering back. "He probably blacked out...never felt a thing."

"Y-yeah." Not necessarily true at all, still she'd take any comfort she could get. He lifted her sideways onto his lap, kissed her eyebrow. She threw an arm around his hard hot neck and clung to him, shivering. It felt delicious to be held so, to be kissed and cosseted, enfolded in his effortless strength and warmth and comfort. He kissed the end of her nose and she laughed breathlessly. "Stop." How could she be aroused, when poor Grunwald…

"Yeah, I know, I'm sorry." He dropped his chin chastely on her hair, but his arms tightened around her, straining her against him till her ribs creaked and she huffed out a gasp against his throat. "It's just…"

"Yeah." A rotten time for the hots to hit, but maybe a natural one, too. Life asserting itself. *Carpe diem,* because how many days did you have to seize? Which brought her back to poor Johann, who hadn't had nearly enough! Her eyes flooded again; her nose was hopelessly wet. She rubbed a sleeve across it—and found herself staring over McCord's shoulder, across the pool. "Johann's pack! He threw it up on the bank when he first realized he was stuck and was trying to fight free." She scrambled off McCord's lap. "Where is it?"

"I never saw a pack. You're sure you didn't—"

"Imagine it? I opened the damned thing, took out his lighter, which I left for him, burning over…" Her breath escaped in a long shaking hiss. "Over there. Son of a bitch." She turned on McCord as he rose beside her. "Antonio! He lied. He did come in here." More than came into the cave. "That bastard! He killed Johann!" He knocked him on the head or found some way to shove him under. "I'm going to—"

"Wait a minute!" McCord caught her arm as she whirled. "Are you plumb *loco?*"

"Me? You heard him back at the fire, how he felt about damming the canyons! He got Johann alone, saw his chance, and he—" She jerked her arm. "Dammit, McCord, let me go!"

"Not till you cool down and listen!" He whipped an arm around her waist, hoisted her right off her moving feet. She snarled and kicked backwards, nailed his shin. He staggered, slipped on the greasy stone, and they both shrieked as he toppled backwards, twisting desperately as they fell.

They landed on his thigh and Raine's hip, with her boots sinking into the quicksand. "Ugh!" She bucked and shied, raising her heels out of the muck as he dragged her backwards on her butt, his arms clamped around her.

After a solid minute of shaken silence, he said, "Now wouldn't that have been pretty?"

Slumped against his chest, she shuddered, her eyes fixed on the empty slope across the pool. "I'm sorry, but—"

His arms tightened around her. "No 'buts.' At least not till we've thought this out. You're absolutely certain there was a pack over on the other side?"

She nodded against his shoulder, her temper rising again.

"Well, take a good look at that side, how steep it is. If you were moving fast, worrying about poor Grunwald, who's to say you didn't drop the pack in a way where it gradually started to slide? Kept on sliding after you left him?"

"So it ended up in the pool with him and sank out of sight? Yeah, that's likely, isn't it?"

"More likely than that a man I've known for two years— a man who's been thoroughly dependable and who has saved my neck more than once—would suddenly decide to murder somebody 'cause they didn't agree."

"Then how do you explain the missing lighter? I left it there, on that level patch. That slipped in, too? Or maybe there was an earthquake that knocked it in while I was gone?"

"No need to get testy."

"Testy? I'm ripping! And when I catch up with that Antonio—"

"Okay, here's another theory. You'll like this one better. Grunwald got out."

"What?"

"Somehow he swam himself out of there—I've heard you can swim out of quicksand if you lie on your back, spread your weight out, then do a sort of fanning stroke. It takes so much nerve to lay your head down in the sand that few people ever try it. But he got out, picked up his pack and his lighter and he took off."

"Why on earth would he do that?"

"Beats the hell out of me. He felt like a fool for all the fuss he'd made? Lord knows I'd have warted him good, once we'd hauled him out.

"Or he rushed down to the river to wash himself off, then he collapsed in relief, and we'll find him in the morning? Or…" McCord lifted one hand from her ribs to point at the back of the cavern. "Or he came to spelunk, so he's back there spelunking, the damn crazy German. I'd say the least we can do is check out the rest of this cave."

# Chapter 16

Half a mile above the canyon floor, Raine leaned against a pine tree, talking to her sister. She'd climbed up to the plateau around noon, hoping to reach Grunwald's company on her sat phone. But she'd forgotten to ask McCord the number for Mexican Information, so in desperation she'd tried Jaye in New Jersey and, miracle of miracles, they'd connected.

Poor Jaye had agreed to do her dirty work—contact the company regarding Johann's disappearance, see if she could set a recovery team in motion. "Except you're not quite sure he's actually in the quicksand?" she said doubtfully. "They're going to think I'm a crank caller."

"I think he's down there—dead—murdered by Antonio," Raine repeated, "but please do *not* go into that with his team if you reach them. I haven't got a shred of proof." A point McCord had hammered home when they'd argued this morning.

"We've searched everywhere we could think of. He wasn't

in the back of the cave." They'd followed a twisting path fifty feet deeper into the cavern, till they'd reached a dead end. "We looked for pits or cracks or some sort of exit, but nothing bigger than a packrat could have squeezed out of there." Which was McCord's latest theory of what had happened to Johann's lighter. He proposed that it had burned out—then a packie had carried it off to be the pride and joy of its cluttered nest.

"We also combed that stretch of the river, on the thought that if Johann did struggle out of the sand, then maybe he'd staggered down there to wash off—"

"And fallen in and drowned? Sounds like the poor guy had a serious case of the clumsies."

"Well, we found no tracks, so much as I'd prefer he escaped the quicksand, I'm sticking with the simplest explanation."

"Which means maybe you're keeping company with a killer? Not good, Raine."

Worse than Jaye knew. Seeing Antonio for the first time by daylight this morning, Raine had realized he looked like the runner she'd encountered with Poquita. The man who'd knocked her off the cliff.

When she'd insisted they'd met before, he'd claimed that, indeed, he had passed her on the trail days ago—traveling with a family of Raramuri that were distant cousins of his. It was a plausible explanation, one she couldn't disprove. *Yes, you've seen me, but not when and where you think.*

His story might even be true—as McCord had insisted in their private fight—but when in doubt, Raine would trust her instincts. Antonio was bad news.

"So what are you going to do about him?" Jaye prodded.

"Well, first of all, if the man held a grudge, it was Johann he hated, for his proposal to dam the canyons. He's got no reason to come after me." Except extreme dislike, which beamed from his resentful eyes on the rare occasions when he'd met her gaze. "He's been perfectly polite so far." Like frost over crusted lava. "But beyond that, since he doesn't work for me, I can't fire him. And it's his world down here. He can walk wherever he chooses."

"Then *you* walk some other direction and *pronto*."

"I can't, Jaye-Jaye. I'm on the track of something big." Per Ashaway standard procedure, they didn't discuss potential finds on an insecure phone system.

"Then be careful."

"Always am." Raine touched the hilt of her knife, concealed under her khaki pants, and smiled at her sister's distant snort. "So what's up with you?" News from home was always precious.

"Well…" Jaye hedged.

"Did you crash your BMW?" Raine prompted. Jaye loved to buzz around the Pine Barrens on an antique motorcycle that was more hazardous than anything Raine would ever face down in the canyons.

"I only wish! I…read some *People* magazines. Back issues that Eric showed me when I stayed on in New York after you'd gone. This is *not* good, but maybe this is the time to hear it?"

"Tell me," Raine said with a grimace. Her imagination was always worse than the worst of bad news. "Cade?"

"Kincade with a *K* as in skunk. The issues went back to a week after you flew to Ethiopia. Apparently Cade started dating hot and heavy the minute you left town."

"Don't tell me who." Raine did *not* want to put a face on the woman who'd knocked her out of his heart.

"Not who—a gaggle of whos. You'd think he was auditioning the staff for a new modeling agency. One slinky, empty-headed giraffe after another, with lips like the Goodyear Blimp, and eyelashes as fake as their D-cups! I cannot understand how any man who'd want you, would even look at them."

"Thanks, sweetie, but I'm fine. Really. You don't need to prop me up." Raine laced a hand up through her hair and tried to smile. "I knew it was over already."

"But I never would have thought he'd be so…so tacky! Well, you can forget about *him.*"

"Cade who?"

"Exactly! Now, the reason I laid this on you is: it's time to move on. You know what you need to do. Find yourself a Transition Man."

Raine rolled her eyes. Jaye was a firm believer in Transition Men.

"I mean it. Don't look for serious. Don't worry about long-term. Just find a nice and willing hottie and have your own personal rodeo. A week or two of that will wipe the slate clean. Put a smile back on your face."

"But I'm smiling already."

"What about this McCord? You've never had a professor before, have you?"

"He's not exactly your typical academic."

"All the better. Go get him, Tiger!"

"I'll think about it," Raine promised, to shut her up.

Back on the canyon floor, Raine followed one of Oso's pebble arrows to a pool below a waterfall. A campfire burned on its bank, and McCord sat by it, shaving in a pocket mirror. Raine dropped down beside him.

"Made some coffee if you want some," he said.

"Do I!" She filled her tin mug and lounged against her pack, watching with a mix of admiration and apprehension as he plied his lethal blade, paring away chestnut bristles to expose lean cheeks, scraped pink over their underlying tan.

"Manage to reach anybody?" he asked while he wiped soap from his steel.

"My sister." Recounting her conversation with Jaye only made her more aware of the parts she left out. *Find a man to make you smile. Go have your own private rodeo.* She could imagine palming his jaw, the damp eager heat of him... Couldn't help wondering how kissing him clean-shaven would compare with his bristly kiss back in the rattlesnake rift... What his bristles would feel like, brushing her own personal hot spots. Too late to tell him to stop shaving, she told herself, smiling behind the rim of her mug. He was halfway done, and she was totally drenched, just thinking of him. For a Transition Man, he would do.

"What're you grinning about?" McCord inquired, tipping a dark brow her way.

Besides that you're gorgeous to look upon? Shoulders to die for and buns to match, with a bonus of brains and a sense of humor? Then she remembered Grunwald, and her giddiness faltered. "Good coffee, that's all."

He grunted and made a face, tightening his upper lip to flatten the groove beneath his hawk nose.

"Where're the guys? Running ahead?"

"Nope." McCord went after the planes of his upper lip. "I sent Oso back to Lagarto, and told Antonio to see him safe home."

"How are we supposed to find the clay pit?"

"I had Antonio question him. I couldn't get a handle on how long it'll take us, but it's straight up this canyon. When we come to a fork in the river, that's the place."

"Okay, I'll buy that. But why send him back?"

His hazel eyes swerved to meet hers, then returned to his mirror. The corner of his mouth curled up.

Of course. Heat pulsed through her stomach. He'd banished the children—and now he was shaving. Half of her

wanted to laugh at his confidence; her devilish half wasn't so
sure she should make it easy. "That's a rotten idea," she said
perversely. Conviction grew as she said it. "You sent Oso off
with a killer?"

His razor paused mid-stroke and McCord turned to glare.
"I told you, Antonio's no killer. But the last thing an expedition needs is a vendetta going on. You were giving him the
Evil Eye and he knew it. What's more, if you didn't do the
math on our rations, I did. The kid ate enough for three and
we're running low. After Lagarto, Antonio's going to press on
to my base camp on the San Ignacio, pick up a couple more
weeks' supplies, then catch us up. He should make it back in
three or four days."

"Great, but I still don't think he should be trusted with a
child. Besides which, Oso adores you. You're just going to
drop him, now that he's served his purpose?"

"No, dammit, I'm— Hey, forget it. I should have kept the
kid, and sent *you* back."

"Yeah, like you could!"

"Think I couldn't?" Deliberately he folded his razor. "Are
you by any chance ticklish, Ms. Ashaway? I've noticed in my
travels that skinny women tend to be—"

"Skinny?" she said haughtily, snatching up her pack and
backing out of reach. "I'll have you know I'm *slender,*
McCord."

"Don't I know it," he muttered to himself as he stamped
out his fire, shouldered his pack and set off in pursuit of the
minx. "But not half as well as I mean to."

They'd climbed a path up to the highlands where no *gringo*
could have followed. This would cut half a day off the journey
to Lagarto, though in truth, Antonio was not anxious to rejoin
McCord. That rattling sound that he'd heard in the haunted

cave, it kept echoing in his mind, stiffening the hairs on the back of his neck. Perhaps he should ask the doctor what that might have been.

"See what I killed," Oso crowed, slipping out from among the pines. "And with only one stone!" He offered his elder a plump, bleeding rabbit.

Antonio grunted his approval. "Then we'll eat. Make a fire over there, boy, while I skin this."

By the time the fire was blazing, he'd dressed the animal and cut it into pieces. Oso trotted over with a handful of long sticks on which to spear the meat. Antonio took one and sharpened it with his bloody knife. But as he reached for another, he glanced up at the boy—and froze.

Oso's eyes were ringed with white. They were locked on Antonio's hands.

Ah, no, on the knife he held. He sucked in his breath as he realized his mistake. It was an excellent knife; he'd found many uses for it in the few days that he'd owned it. It was much better shaped for rough work than his own switchblade.

"Where did you get that?" Oso whispered, backing away.

*Where do you think, you little mud turtle? From your brother.* But this was a child of no sophistication, a country boy. If he stayed calm, spoke smoothly... "This? Why, I bought it in Creel, in a pawn shop. Do you know what that is?"

"That's my brother's knife! He carved the handle from a limb of madrone he cut under a full moon."

*Just so, little fool. And it came in very handy, the night I questioned him.* Antonio smiled. "Really? This was Mateo's? Well, he must have pawned it on his last trip to Creel. But if it was his, then I should give it to *you,* little brother." He stepped forward casually, with the blade hidden by his thigh. Just let him get within reach...

"He cut me a whistle with that knife the last time I saw him!" Oso spun, squealing as Antonio slashed, then he vanished into the bushes like the ghost of a rabbit.

Twice McCord suggested they stop for a swim, and twice Raine voted to keep walking. She wanted just a little more space and time separating them from last night and its misfortunes. Time to live with the idea that she was moving on. Taking what she wanted and needed, seizing the day. Seizing this man.

McCord indulged her skittishness, but whenever their eyes met, his burned with intention. The path swerved back and forth across the river and it was growing more rugged by the mile. They had to clasp hands to help each other balance across mossy stones. Once he had to lift her to reach a handhold on a ledge they had to pass. He stood for a moment with her held on high, his big hands almost spanning her waist. She rubbed her calf along his ribs, savoring his heated muscles, then swung up onto the rock and turned to smile down at him. *Soon. I'll say yes very soon.*

He tossed up their packs, then came up the ledge in a tigerish rush, and she laughed and fled on before him. *Soon, but not yet!*

When they reached the spot at last, they both knew it. Another pool enclosed by boulders above and below, with a beach of tawny sand sloping up into a pocket meadow. A soft bed of silky green grass starred with red and purple wildflowers.

"Break time," McCord announced, shrugging out of his pack. He reached for hers, and lifted it off her shoulders.

"Oh, *yeah!*" she sighed, lacing her fingers to stretch on tiptoe with arms overhead. She turned to find him watching as she'd known she would. "Hey, I've been meaning to ask you... I've seen you shake hands with the Raramuri twice now. Could you tell me how it's done?"

He huffed a silent laugh as he held out his hand. "Like this."

One final moment of hesitation, of freedom and loneliness—then she gave him her own. Delicately, deliberately, he stroked her fingers from first knuckle to fingertip. Echoes of his touch rippled up her arms, danced across her breasts, raising a flurry of goose bumps. She shuddered with pleasure and knew, without looking down at her damp T-shirt, that her nipples were rising, gladness rising like a tide within her. "That's how it's done?" she said huskily.

"Between the menfolk, yeah, but this…" His fingers advanced farther along hers, stroked across the back of her hand, slid beneath it to draw circles of fire in her palm. "This is for closer friends."

"Ohhh…" She gave him her left hand, and her bones melted as he greeted that one, too.

His hands encircled her forearms, gently drawing her in. He kissed one wrist, murmuring her name against her skin, then lifted her arm slowly against his face, while his lips burned a moist line from her palm to the quivering skin inside her elbow.

Half singing her hunger, she wrapped her arms around his neck, rose on tiptoe to meet his smiling mouth. His kiss was all she'd wanted and more…what she'd been needing…spring sunrise after a desolate winter…

They stood swaying and laughing and feasting on each other, till his hand found her breast. Her knees buckled, she caught at his shirt. With a groan he followed her down into the smell of bruised grass, the sound of rushing water, the crescendo of heartbeats. The celebration of flesh against welcoming flesh.

A long while later, they lay entwined, McCord still on top. He was worried about crushing her, but she'd locked her hands behind his waist and swore she didn't want this to end. Braced up on his elbows, he cupped her head in his hands. "I've been wanting to do this since the first night I met you," he drawled, smiling down at her. She'd been even better than his anticipations: generous along with her quicksilver sexiness. As eager to give as to receive.

She purred drowsily—then arched her back as a series of aftershocks hit her, shaking them both.

He thrust into her like a porpoise riding a wave—then felt the wave slide out from underneath, rolling on toward the shore; he'd missed it. He'd have to wait for the next set, which shouldn't be long in rising. He laughed, then scooped a hand under her shoulders and eased her onto her side as he turned onto his.

She hummed a wordless protest, hooked a leg behind his knee and hitched herself closer against him. A snuggler; as fiercely independent as she was, he'd never have guessed it. With her head pillowed on his bicep, he rested his cheek on her wheat-and-moonlight hair. Should he ask? Mess with perfection? He shouldn't, but still… "You never did tell me the other night why you cried."

She sighed, then pulled back to meet his eyes. "I'm going to cry now if you don't let me snooze."

"Hey…" He traced a finger down her spine to those delicious twin hollows just above her graceful hips. "Now that I've shown you the secret handshake, there's no dodging the question, Ashaway. 'Fess up."

She played with his chest hair, twining it into curls. "Okay. I…couldn't help looking back, that night."

Of course she had a past. She must have been collecting beaus since she was nine. "But now?" It shouldn't have mattered. He didn't want it to matter, but gazing into her big brown eyes, he felt a rising urge to obliterate her past—to salt it and plow it under in the only way a man knew how.

That gust of raw instinct drew a dust devil of panic in its wake. The last thing he needed was to care about another woman. But when had wants ever lined up with needs?

"Now I'm looking forward," she said gravely. Her smile curled slow and wicked and wanton. "To the next time…and the next, and the time after— Ouch!" she yelped, as he gave her buns an admonishing squeeze.

"All right, Ms. Wisemouth, I'm sorry I asked." She was here, that should be answer enough. Though the last time, with the last woman, it hadn't been.

And as for the next time…

"Call *me* a wisemouth? I'll show you!" And Raine proceeded to do so, her hair stroking a silken track down his chest, till her tongue found his navel. He groaned, rolled slowly over onto his back and surrendered himself to the demonstration. A mind-boggling, heart-stopping demonstration that put all his worries in perspective.

There was only Now.

# Chapter 17

Cradled in the crook of McCord's arm, Raine watched the moon chase the stars down the western sky. They'd pitched their camp on a ledge above what she now thought of as 'their' meadow. Though she'd have preferred to stay among the flowers, her lover had expressed an unshakable preference for high ground be it ever so rocky, when sleeping in flash flood country.

He'd have the bruises in the morning to show he'd gotten his way. It was hard ground for lovemaking, and with the consideration that seemed to be his instinctive reflex, he'd insisted she take the top. She smiled, remembering. If this was her own private rodeo, then bull-riding was the most thrilling event.

McCord chuckled in his sleep and jolted awake. "I didn't dream you!"

"Not unless we dreamed a duet." She kissed his collarbone

and her lips grazed his seashell carving. She rolled onto her side and twined her fingers around its thong. "Tell me something."

"What?" His hand smoothed her flank.

"Anything. I don't know near enough about you."

"You know all that counts."

She snorted. "Spoken like a guy!"

"Guilty as charged." His fingers stroked hypnotically. "So what d'you want to know?"

"Tell me...what would you do if you found the Aztec caravan? Is it the gold you want, or the Serpent himself?"

His hand stilled on her hip. "You still think I'm a damned pothunter."

"I don't! I know you aren't." *But what are you?*

He sighed, shrugged, growled at last, "What I want most of all is the codices I figure they carried. If they were rescuing the best of their temple, then they brought their scrolls as well as their gold. That's the real treasure. So much of the Aztecs' history, their culture, their religion, was lost when the Spanish wasted their empire. For instance, do you realize that they wrote wonderful poetry about flowers and song and life's fleeting beauty?"

"Funny, I think of them as being so bloodthirsty."

"They were people. They could match our best and our worst today. And so far we've seen the Aztecs mainly through the eyes of their conquerors. When you write another people's history with a guilty conscience, you tend to play up all the reasons they should have been stomped and pillaged, and downplay all the good things that got smashed in the process."

*You are a professor.* "So you'd study their codices. On site or would you take them somewhere?"

He stirred restlessly. "I'm not a linguist. Specialists would have to do the deciphering. I'd just like to be the hero that discovered the codices. Aside from that, my own part would be the excavating, the description and interpretation of artifacts."

"You'd want a team for that, wouldn't you?" she probed cautiously.

"You know I would. But if I found the caravan, I'd have a bargaining chip the size of an elephant. I could walk into any university, even my old dear alma mater, and demand reinstatement. Tenure." He blew out a soundless laugh. "Listen to me."

She smoothed her palm down his chest to his hard, hairy stomach and rubbed him in soothing circles. "Reinstatement?"

"Yeah." Another soundless laugh, masking a world of hurt. "Once upon a time, before I was a black sheep, I was a white. You sure you want to hear all this?"

From where he sat, hidden in a cleft near the top of the trail, Antonio watched the Lady walk across the sky, dragging her robe of stars. Not long till dawn, and still Oso had not come. Yet this was the only way down off the plateau. The only way to reach the gorge that would lead him home to Lagarto.

He'd come, surely he'd come. Most likely the boy had tucked himself into a tree or a hole last night. There'd been no way to track him in the dark. But with daylight, he'd be hungry, lonely for his mama and his safe, familiar *ranchito,* and he'd surely creep out of cover. *And when he does…* A long, long fall would solve so many problems.

It was a pity, but now that Oso had recognized the knife, it must be done.

*So come to me, little rabbit. I promise it'll be quick and clean.*

"Hanging in there?" McCord inquired as they paused, high above the river. He brushed his knuckles lingeringly along Raine's cheek.

"Doing fine," she assured him with a smile. In truth, she was wonderfully, joyfully sore in every muscle. And suffering from a major sleep deficit. But she'd have had it no other way.

"Too bad. I was thinking maybe it's time for a *siesta*."

"Considering we broke camp two hours ago, isn't it a bit early to get horizontal?"

"Who needs horizontal? With a little creativity…"

"Yeah, right. Let's save creative for when we get there." She caught his hand and drew him grumbling along behind her, then let him go, the better to balance. They'd found that their sleeping ledge was actually part of a wet-season trail high above the flood plain, so today they'd been making better time, not scrambling over the boulders below.

Some time this afternoon, Raine was sure they'd reach Mateo's clay pit. Happy as she was with McCord's company, she still had a Feathered Serpent to find. Lulled by the heat and her sleepiness, she walked on Automatic, while her mind rambled over the events of the previous night.

They'd talked for hours, slept, loved, talked till the sun rose. She'd told him about Kincade and Borneo, and she'd learned more about what made her lover tick. She'd had to coax the story out of him. Like many a proud man who'd been played for a fool, he'd come away from the drubbing with a deep sense of shame and humiliation that was totally undeserved. Yet no less painful.

It seemed that seven years ago McCord had been a rising hotshot in the archaeology department at Rice University in Texas, speeding along the fast track to tenure, with several groundbreaking papers already published. His friend and mentor was head of the department, which meant that McCord's projects received adequate funding, a crucial consideration in the cutthroat academic world. Life was looking rosy: he'd found a way to spend most of his time outdoors—an essential part of his happiness equation—and he'd found a fascinating career, an absorbing focus for his ambition and his passion.

But a snake wriggled into McCord's little Eden. He'd been running a university-sponsored excavation south of Mexico City, training Rice students in fieldwork. Then a new grad student arrived: Zelda, the young trophy wife of a middle-aged professor, a man who just happened to hold the second-most powerful position in the archaeology department, after McCord's mentor.

Soon after Zelda hit Mexico, she confided that she was separated from her husband and getting a divorce. "Sucker that I was, I didn't ask if she'd filed the papers. I took her at her word," McCord had said with a grimace. "Back in Houston I'd have steered clear of such entanglements; it was asking for trouble, mixing my business with pleasure. But the Sierra de Coycoyan are as remote as the moon. We were living in our own romantic bubble, where it seemed nothing bad could ever touch us."

To add to McCord's bliss, he'd struck a bonanza. The mound he'd chosen for his dig site turned out to be much more than the small Aztec market town that he'd hoped for and expected. It contained a jewel of a little temple, dedicated to the Aztec god Huitzilopochtli. A virtually intact jewel—and a major find. The biggest find since a highway construction crew discovered the *Templo Mayor* in the middle of Mexico City, back in 1978. Once McCord published his research, his reputation would be made.

Meanwhile he'd chosen a lover with brains, as well as what he wryly described as her "other attributes." Giving her assignments to match her abilities, he'd put her in charge of cataloguing and shipping, while he continued with the actual excavation. Each time a new load of artifacts was shipped north to be stored till they could be cleaned and considered, Zelda accompanied the precious cargo.

"And claimed credit?" Raine had asked incredulously.

"That's about the long and the short of it." And apparently

she was shuttling between her husband's bed and her lover's, waffling over whom to finally choose. But when McCord's mentor died of a sudden heart attack, her choice became crystal clear.

"By that time I figure she'd either confessed her hijinks, or her husband had heard the gossip. But in his eyes, there was no separation, just a spousal vacation—and a hound of a poacher." When the cuckolded professor advanced to the top spot in the archaeology department, McCord's fate was sealed. There'd be no tenure—no position for him at all—at the same university. Not till they danced polkas in Hell.

And worse, perhaps for her own gain, possibly at her husband's insistence, Zelda charged that McCord had purchased artifacts on the illegal black market. That he'd seeded his site, to justify his original request for funding.

The bitter outcome was that McCord had been fired, thrown off his own fabulous find, with his license to dig there revoked. With his reputation in ruins, he'd no hope of justice or reinstatement—or of finding a job anywhere else in the academic world. The man who would have fought for him was dead; the new head of the department, Zelda's husband, controlled his references, which he'd gleefully besmirched. There was no way to salvage his career, at least not from within academia.

The ultimate blow had come a few months later, when McCord had finally steeled himself to pick up the books and mementos he'd left behind. He'd found Zelda ensconced in his own corner office. She'd completed her PhD based on his work in Mexico, and now *she* was the rising young star of her husband's department.

"Oh, I'm so sorry!" Raine had kissed his shoulder.

"Hey, I'm not sorry. Now, that's enough about this. Did you realize it's just about our twelve-hour anniversary? How are we going to celebrate?"

Remembering their rejoicing, Raine laughed softly as she rounded a bend in the trail. She stopped so short that McCord bumped into her.

A mile ahead of their overlook, the canyon branched into two. Between the two gorges, a towering wedge of red rock looked like the bow of a half-mile-high destroyer, steaming right at them. They'd reached the fork in the river. Somewhere at the base of that cliff they should find Mateo's clay pit, along with—Raine hoped and prayed—the potter's most amazing discovery.

*The Canyons of the North. Autumn, 1520* A.D.

They'd made camp at the base of a gigantic red cliff. Sharp as an obsidian ax splitting a snake, it cleaved one river into two.

Before dark fell, the priests set to cutting their usual marker for those who would follow—if there was anyone in the world left to follow! Tethered to their positions on the god's litter, the slaves sprawled hopelessly in the dust.

The *pochteca* had sent out his scouts in search of game, while he himself lay along the bank of the river, making a show of tempting fish into a basket. Iuitl, the man who'd been his Second on more trading ventures than he had fingers, crouched beside him. With his broken arm he made an awkward fisherman, but he'd found a wad of red clay. He squeezed it clumsily with his good hand, till it took on a curvy shape that was undoubtedly what they all dreamed of each night—a soft, warm woman to hold and comfort them in their endless exile.

The *pochteca* handed up a wriggling fish to be stored in the dry basket, and said quietly, "Achcauhtli asked me about you this morning. He wanted to know how many days must pass before you can carry the god again." Achcauhtli was the leader of the expedition, a nobleman and a priest of the temple. A man of righteousness and blood and ruthless determination.

But priest or soldier or trader or slave, they all took their turns bearing the god and his treasures these days. They'd lost more than thirty men on the road, lost them to starvation rations and overwork and disease, to falls and drowning. They'd lost two only yesterday, when the litter tipped mid-river, crushing two slaves against a boulder before they could right it again.

"What did you tell him?" Iuitl whispered.

"Smile, my friend, Chimali looks this way!" Chief warrior of the temple, Chimali was Achcauhtli's sword arm, as savage and humorless as he was deathlessly devoted to the priests of Quetzalcoatl. The *pochteca* baited his basket, then added with his eyes on the water, "I told him that you would be healed very soon. That I thought it was a sprain, not a break."

"But you know it's not! You set the bone yourself! If I could carry, you know that I'd gladly do my share."

"I know it, yes, but if you cannot carry, Achcauhtli sees you as nothing but one more mouth to be fed. And think, Iuitl, how long it has been since we've had a sacrifice."

Iuitl gulped and shook his head. "But Achcauhtli has not touched a free man on this journey, only slaves and captives."

"Not so far, but consider how badly things go for us. We travel slower and slower each day, but go fast or go slow, we hear not a whisper of the Place of the Herons. Aztlan, *pah!* If we march till we wear our feet down to our knee bones, we'll never find it! It's a dream for children and desperate men.

"But if Quetzalcoatl does not smile on us, then Achcauhtli will try to win back his favor. He bleeds himself every night—his earlobes are in shreds, his hair reeks of blood, but still it isn't enough."

"You think I'd be enough?"

"I think you'll be the first of many, but if we sacrifice to the last free man, I doubt that the god will smile. I know *I* would not, my friend."

"Then...what should I do?"

The *pochteca* scooped up another fish with a grunt of triumph, handed it up the bank, then said, "With your one good arm, do you think you could hunt? No one throws a stone as straight and true as you."

"If there was only me to feed... Yes, I would find meat."

"If you stole this basket as well, you see how I fish? All it takes is patience and a grasshopper or two to lure them into the trap. And you remember how I nudged you yesterday, when we passed that path that seemed to lead up to the highlands? If you could make it back to there, climb out of this godforsaken crack, you should find water and game on top. Then once you'd rested and healed..."

Iuitl let out a long, slow breath. "You release me from my vow to follow you? Because know this, *pochteca*. If I escape then I won't catch up to you again once I heal. I left a family as you did in Tenochtitlan. If the rumors are not true... Even if they are true..."

While they still marched along the coast, they'd heard dreadful, incredible stories. That Tenochtitlan had fallen, had been laid waste by the rude barbarians. "How can I blame you, when my own heart would fly south? But, Iuitl, if you win through to the city, will you do one more duty to me?" The trader sat up, pulled a loop of thong over his head. The seashell dangled between them; on it, a tiny woman knelt with her arms outstretched to a crouching coyote.

"Huh, I remember this! You gave that crippled old man a sack of cacao beans to carve it, on our last trip to the western sea."

"It was a gift for my wife. I never got the chance to give

it to her. If you can find her, then give her this. She'll know you speak for me."

"Ha. So she calls you as we do, our crafty one, our trickster—the coyote?"

The *pochteca* shrugged. "I let it slip in a...moment of foolishness." After that night, she'd used it for his love name, crying it aloud when she danced beneath him. "Give her my token, and tell her that if I live, then she will see me again. I will come for her some day—by the god, I swear it."

His eyes swerved beyond his friend's shoulder. "*Hsst!* Here comes Chimali! Tonight, then, my friend, once the moon sets. I will have a fit and try to strangle Tochtli in my sleep. While the camp's in an uproar, take this basket and run for your life!"

# Chapter 18

*The Copper Canyons. Present day.*

They'd found enough driftwood for a roaring fire, and somehow this place required one. The high canyon walls closed out most of the stars, and the wedge-shaped cliff brooded above them like an enormous ax. *We're just exhausted and discouraged,* Raine told herself, blinking at the fire, as McCord sighed in her ear. He lounged behind her, propped against a trunk of driftwood, while she sat between his upraised knees, cradled against his chest. "We'll find it in the morning," she said, though she wasn't sure she believed that.

His wry grunt echoed her doubts.

They'd reached Mateo's pit only an hour before sundown. They'd found a vein of clay along the bank of the right-hand river, with signs that it had recently been mined.

But as for the something wondrous and remarkable that might have inspired Mateo to paint a Feathered Serpent on his pots... She tipped her head back, staring up at the central crag. "Maybe up there?" It didn't look all that climbable.

"Bring your junior jetpack?" McCord dropped his head to kiss the corner of her smile. She twisted half around to give him better access to her mouth, as she rubbed a hand up his nape and into his shaggy hair.

"You think?" he asked, on a husky note of hunger.

They'd made love once in the river, when they quit hunting for Mateo's wonders. Then a second time after supper, when they laid out their bedrolls. "I think I'd fall asleep on you." She smiled against his lips. "Can I have a rain check?"

"The whole dang checkbook. Cash 'em in anytime. They'll never bounce." His kisses softened, withdrew gradually to her temple, her ear, the top of her shoulder.

She shuddered with pleasure, then melted back against him, with his chin propped on her head. "So what now?" she said after a while. "Do you think this has all been a wild-goose chase?" Maybe Mateo had seen a California condor, or an amazing shape of cloud. They'd built so much on so very little.

McCord sighed again. "Maybe. But considering the goose I chased down, who am I to complain?"

"What a silver-tongued devil you are!" She pinched his thigh till he yelped. "But truly, you think your caravan ever passed this way?"

"Gotta admit I've been worrying about that ever since we hit this big-rock stretch of the river. Can't imagine they could have carried a sixteen-man litter up and over and around all these damn boulders."

"But what about those stories of the Heart Snatcher back in Lagarto?"

"Maybe they made it that far, then turned off some other direction?"

"Or maybe the trail was easier when they passed this way, then these boulders came crashing down, a couple of hundred years later. This is earthquake country, same as California, isn't it?"

"Yeah…" He smoothed his palms down her arms, then restlessly up again.

She smiled to herself; his attention was wandering. "What do you think ever became of them? Did they ever find Aztlan?"

"Doubt it. There's a lot of folks who think Aztlan might have even been located somewhere up around the Great Salt Lake in Utah—that that's the original Place of the Herons. I doubt the poor devils ever made it that far."

"Then what do you think happened to them?"

"I reckon they made it as far as the *Barrancas del Cobre,* that they followed a river up from the coast. They spent months of stumbling around this rat maze, finding no lost city, no refuge, no place of safety and welcome. And you've got to figure they'd have heard rumors along the way of Tenochtitlan's fall and they had to be worrying about their families. At some point your men break down. You run out of food and you run out of hope. When they realized they couldn't go any further, I imagine they found a safe cave and hid the treasure. Maybe they left a few men on guard, or maybe the priests killed everybody else to protect the secret. I figure whoever survived headed back to Tenochtitlan, to find out what happened to their loved ones."

"Yes, that makes sense," she said softly. "That's what I'd do."

"And either they never lived to reach the Valley of Mexico—or they did, and then they got swallowed up in the crash of a civilization. The secret died with them."

"So your hope is that they picked a nice, dry cave? And that the whole caravan, with the god and the gold and all those lovely codices, it's just waiting there for somebody clever and persistent—"

"—and outrageously virile to find it. Yes, ma'am. That's just what I'm hoping." His teeth nipped delicately at her earlobe.

"On second thought," she purred as her hips found a rhythm, "maybe I'm not quite so sleepy." She laughed as he scooped her up with a growl of triumph—turned her sideways in his lap, to kiss her dizzy and blind.

Somewhere far out in the dark a coyote howled, a sound like ghostly laughter.

Raine woke at dawn, with her head pillowed in the hollow of McCord's shoulder and his big hand splayed on her bare stomach. She smiled, blinked drowsily up at a sky fading from teal toward robin's egg, with a glorious wash of pink to the east. Another gorgeous day, after another night to remember.

*Stop gloating,* she warned herself. Today she really did have to get back to work. *How do we find this Feathered Serpent? What could Mateo have seen?*

A flicker of movement caught her eye. An eagle…high up on the red cliff between the rivers. Its golden breast appeared as it shuffled out to the brink of its ledge—then it dropped like a falling angel, wings spreading to the soft air, every feather of its wingtips etched black against the brightening sky. Fall turned to swoop, and up it soared, spiraling to greet the sun.

Glory, glory, glory on high… She blew a kiss after it—then her eyes returned to the cliff. And it hit her. "Yes!"

"What's your theory again?" McCord grumbled, after she'd poured a second cup of coffee into him.

"Very simple," Raine said, as she stirred a handful of gorp into their bubbling oatmeal. "The first time you told me about the priest's letter—the tale told to him by the *pochteca*'s wife—you said that the plan was that the caravan would march ahead. Take the god and find Aztlan. Meanwhile the high priest would gather as many as he could convince to flee with him, and these families would follow. Right?"

"Yep." He accepted the bowl she handed him, patted the tree trunk beside him.

She swung a leg over to sit astride, facing him. "How was that second band of Aztecs supposed to follow the first?"

"I don't reckon they ever did," he said patiently. "Sounds like the smallpox hit the city like an atom bomb. When more than half your population perishes within a few months, it's gotta be impossible to organize anything."

"But the men who went on ahead didn't know this. Even if they heard rumors of the disaster, they must still have hoped and prayed their families had escaped in time. So how did they expect them to follow?"

McCord scratched his bristles. "Reckon I always figured that they meant to send back a guide to meet them, show them the way."

"Maybe, but if they hadn't reached Aztlan yet, he wouldn't know where to lead the second batch of Aztecs."

"What's your point?"

"My point is that I bet they left a trail of breadcrumbs. Some sort of sign for the guys who came after."

"Hmmm." He chewed, thought, shrugged. "I've walked the whole damn route myself. Why didn't I find the crumbs?"

"I figure time and wind and water swept most of their marks away. Or people messed with them, especially in your more populated parts along the coast. But out here in the back canyons, with so little traffic, maybe some survived, if you knew to look for them."

He padded over to their fire, refilled his mug. "So what are we looking for and where do we look?"

"Well, think about highway signs. If you've got a tight budget, you don't just post them anywhere, you—"

His head swung to stare up at the cliff. "You post them at intersections or exits! Anytime you come to two or more alternative routes."

"Right! And here we sit at the fork of two rivers. Which fork did they choose, and how did they mark their choice for those who followed?"

For the next few hours they scrutinized the canyon walls foot by foot, starting with the obvious choice, the right-hand branch of the river. This fork looked as if it flowed year-round, whereas the other tributary seemed to be drying out already. If the caravan had reached here at the height of the dry season, they'd have surely stuck to a dependable source of water.

But for all their logic, they found no mark that they could swear was man-made. All the gouges and scratches in the canyon walls could have been made by the same floods that rolled house-sized boulders along the gorges, or washed monstrous tree trunks down from the heights.

"Well, it was a sweet theory." McCord braced one hand against the wedge-shaped central cliff as they stumbled back along it. Its base was buried in slopes of treacherous red scree. "But even if they did leave marks, five hundred years of floods and erosion—"

"Except that Mateo saw *something*," Raine insisted.

"Probably scarfed down a few peyote buttons, while he was out from under his mama's thumb, then sat around his campfire and—*yowza!*—revelation struck. He glanced up at this cliff and realized it looked just like Uncle Bobo's ugly ol' hatchet face, right down to that cactus up there, like the hairy wart on the end of his nose—and he knew he'd have to show it to Oso some day. Thrills are hard to come by, out here in the boonies."

"Yeah, maybe, but I'm not ready to give up yet."

"Couldn't tempt you into a short swim?"

And a long romp in the river? "Not till I've done the other fork."

"And that's why women need men. To help 'em keep life in perspective."

She laughed, but she didn't relent when they reached the end of the wedge. She turned its knife-edge corner and started up the left-hand gorge, peering up at the stone. McCord groaned and stumbled on behind.

"You know, with all this scree, maybe we've been looking too low," she said, peering upward. "If the base of the cliff has been crumbling over the years, then maybe when they made their—"

He caught her belt and yanked her back a step. "Mind the snake."

"Thanks." They detoured around a very large and sluggish specimen, too chilled to rattle, then looked up again and—

"Ho-oly…" McCord stopped short, his jaw dropping.

Twenty feet overhead, a blue-green pattern blazed against red rock.

"You gotta be kidding me!" McCord lunged at the cliff, stepped up on a toe-hold, found another. Raine scrambled up at his elbow till, clinging by their fingertips, they hung from a ledge a few feet below it. Turquoise had been inlaid into the native sandstone in a precise, familiar mosaic about the size of a saucer: a hornless *Triceratops,* covered in chips of blue.

The same design that Mateo had adapted for his mugs. The same unknown animal whose carving adorned the temple at Teotihuacan.

"Oh, you honey!" McCord crooned. "Seven long years without a single, solitary, blessed sign and now—" He turned a radiant smile her way, his eyes sparkled with tears. "I'd just about figured I'd wasted my…" He choked, overcome.

She would have hugged him, but she wasn't risking a twenty-foot drop for the pleasure. "What are his eyes made of?" Something shiny and greeny-black.

"Obsidian—volcanic glass—and that's proof enough, right there. Green-tinted obsidian was mined at the northeast end of the Valley of Mexico, at Pachuca, no place else. So this is Aztec work. The caravan passed this way."

Their fingers gave out and they scrabbled backwards to solid ground. With a whoop, McCord caught Raine up and whirled her around and around. They collapsed in yelps and laughter, to lean back, panting, against the cliff. "We found it! We actually found it!"

At least, they'd found a signpost along the way. Raine hoped it wasn't an Aztec warning for bumps ahead.


"Another damn pool!" McCord groaned, as they turned another bend in the canyon.

"No way around?" Raine studied the rock rising to either side. Their route had turned into a classic slot canyon—sheer towering walls without banks or river plain, not even one of those high-water trails that edged so many of the gorges.

"Dream on," McCord grumbled, sitting to take his boots off. For the last ten winding miles, a narrow river had hugged the left side of the canyon floor. Every so often it pooled and spread to block their road. With no way to climb up and around these pools, they had to swim across, floating their waterproof backpacks before them. The routine was getting old.

And though he tried to hide it, McCord was clearly jumpy. He insisted that she walk along the right-hand wall of the slot, while he scanned the left side beyond the little river, with each of them announcing when they spotted even a crack leading upward. Whenever they found a possible escape route, the Texan marked the canyon floor with a big arrow made by a chalky rock he'd picked up.

He was being an optimist, for sure. Given the speed with which a flash flood would roar through this canyon, no way could they hope to race it back to one of his exits. *Blender City.* Raine shivered and set the thought aside. She kicked out of her boots, and tied them to her pack frame.

This pool was colder than the last. They moaned and swore as the water climbed to their knees, then their waists, then their chests. Towing his pack with one hand, McCord caught her around the waist, lifted her off her toes. "Want a ride, shorty?" Shivering gratefully against his soggy warmth, she rode his hip for a dozen strides, then he stopped. "Uh-oh."

"What? Does it drop off?"

He swung her around. "I feel this sudden, overwhelming kiss-deficiency coming on."

"Oh, well, if that's your problem!" She hooked an arm around his neck and wrapped her legs around his waist. Soaked as two otters, they plundered each other.

"Damn, woman, we're going to set this pool to boiling, if we're not careful. You better cool down." McCord bent his knees and ducked them both. She came up yelping and laughing, wiping a forearm across her eyes, and he kissed her breast, where it tented her wet T-shirt.

Her laughter snagged in her throat, then turned to a needy whimper as his teeth tugged at her nipple. She twined her legs tighter around him, almost tripping him as he charged blindly across the pool. He stumbled up into the shallows then they sprawled on the shore, tearing at each other's clothes.

## Chapter 19

They walked on in the last rays of the setting sun, each with a smugly reminiscent smile. *You are some Transition Man,* Raine told him privately—and felt a twinge of guilt. *But am I being fair to you?* How would *she* feel if she learned that McCord was using her to get over some other woman? *If I confessed that that's what I'm doing, what would he say?*

Most men she'd met would fall over backwards and be only too glad to be of service.

But McCord? He'd been used—and used badly—already. Maybe he'd just as soon be left alone as to be taken lightly. *Is that what I'm doing?* This last time, even with all their laughter and teasing, she'd felt as if they'd plumbed a new depth.

*What the hell am I doing?* McCord asked himself, as he paused to mark another half-possible climb above flood level.

Well, he knew what *he* was doing—playing with fire—but what was Raine up to?

Enjoying herself, yes, undoubtedly. She'd scratched him like a wildcat in heat, this last time, but still, women were so damned complicated. Unlike men with their clear and simple vision, all of them were multi-taskers—able to think about two things, do three others, and hold four contradictory opinions, all at the same time. Was it possible that besides enjoying herself, Raine was also using him to get back at her last man, the dude she'd met in Borneo?

That wasn't a pretty thought. But such thoughts kept right on rolling. Like: what if she was going for a triple play? Figuring, like Zelda, that the best way to get a piece of the archaeological action was to snuggle up to the head honcho of the expedition—who could also scratch her where she itched, to bring it full circle. Ah, hell, this was surely nothing but post-coital, late-afternoon, coffee-lag blues!

That, coupled with a sneaking suspicion that anything that seemed too good to be true generally was. *But, oh, honey in the meantime...*

"This is not good," said McCord a while later. "In a couple of hours we won't see our noses in front of our faces. It's time to turn back and—"

"The last truly climbable exit was that crack five miles ago. I hate backtracking," Raine called over her shoulder as she walked on. "And if the Feathered Serpent is anywhere, he's up ahead, not behind."

"Raine, get your butt back here! I say it's time to turn around."

"Excuse me? Who appointed *you* Starfleet Commander? I thought we were partners here."

"Shit. Kiss a woman and next thing you know, you've got a partner. When did I commit?"

She could feel a blush rising as she stalked back to face him. "You didn't, Tex. But neither did I. So why don't *you* go back, if that makes you feel better—and I'll go my way." She could wait for him to catch up in the morning. A rest and a meal, and they'd both be cheerier.

"Sweet jeez in the morning, what do I have to do? Throw you over my shoulder like a sack of potatoes?" He reached out, caught her wrist.

She hissed, wrenched free and backed away, hands uplifted like blades. "Don't you ever go caveman on me, McCord! This is no place to throw you, but touch me again and so help me I will!"

He crossed his arms, rocked back on his heels. "Nice bluff, sugar, but I outweigh you by sixty pounds. You couldn't do it." When she didn't lower her hands, he cocked his head. "Could you?"

"Try me."

"Not some place where you wouldn't land softly." He blew out a breath. "Hell, have it your way. Let's go drown." He stalked off into the twilight, leaving her to follow.

Half an hour later, Raine was almost ready to admit he'd been right. If she could get past her growling stomach and her aching feet, maybe she'd concede. Not that it would do them much good. By now that hellacious crack must be nearly eight miles behind, and she was this much more spent. The lieback technique for climbing a vertical crack required oodles of upper-body strength, and hers seemed to be seeping away through her trudging boots.

"Oh, that's just perfect!" McCord spoke for the first time since they'd quarreled. "End of river. Now we get a choice: drown or die of thirst."

"Well, you can't have it both ways," she snapped, joining

him where he stood, glaring at a wide pool that hugged the left wall. The river appeared to start here, flowing back the way they'd come. "So where's the water coming from? A spring? Mighty big one."

"Dunno. Underground cave? There's enough sandstone around here to support an aquifer, as well as surface rivers. Like the San Marcos River up in the Texas Hill Country that springs up out of nowhere, runs for thirty miles, then dives again. Let's have a look."

While he rummaged for his flashlight, Raine moved around the head of the pool to the wall itself, peering up through the dusk. Could the river be flowing out of a cave in the canyon wall, which might mean there was a path beside it, leading upward and in? McCord's light leaped out behind her, to play low over the water; clearly he was hoping the same.

No such luck. The surface of the pool met the sheer rock, with no gap or arch of any sort above its inky black. In the daylight she might have suggested they swim along the wall, see if there was some sort of underwater passage, but the temperature was rapidly falling, as it did every night in the thin, dry air. Besides, after Grunwald's fate, she was sort of off after-dark caving.

"*Nada*," McCord growled. "How about an elevator to the top floor?" His beam rose to dance along the wall, which, except for some hairline cracks, was utterly sheer, offering nothing to climb.

"Wait! There, go back! To the right and up a little. Do you see it?"

"Not a friggin' thing. What are you—"

"Maybe it's my lateral angle." She squinted, tilted her head. "Walk ten feet to your left and shine it on the same spot."

"Still don't see pididdle."

"Leave your light there and switch places with me."

When he did so and Raine shone the light, she heard him suck in his breath. "Good—no, *great*—spotting, Ashaway!"

She smiled to herself. Truce? As well as a further mystery. She'd found a repeat of the Quetzalcoatl design. But this time only a thumbnail-size scrap of turquoise remained. The rest of the inlay had fallen out over the centuries, leaving the original carved indentations in the native rock. Lit from the side, they cupped enough shadow to be barely visible; by daylight, they might well have missed it.

"You know what this means?" McCord muttered, staring upward.

"That something's wrong with my theory?" Because this time the sign didn't mark a divergence of routes. Maybe it had been posted simply as encouragement. But who would go to such an effort, climbing forty feet up from the canyon floor to post such a platitude?

"Well, that too. But aside from that, I'd say the original turquoise didn't fall out of the design—it washed out in a flash flood."

Her stomach twisted suddenly and it didn't feel like hunger. A forty-foot wave of water scouring these canyon walls? These gorges were the sluice gates for thousands of square miles of upland, concentrating all that run-off into a narrow slot. Might as well be an ant in a Jacuzzi when they turned on the taps.

McCord shrugged into his pack. "Let's get up *pronto*. In the morning we can come back here, figure what the heck they were thinking, sticking a design in the middle of nowhere."

A good plan, but easier said than done. They covered the next hundred yards slowly, each using his flashlight. "This might do for apes and mountain goats," McCord called. His light zigzagged up the right-hand wall.

Raine crossed over to join him, peering upward. "I can buy it for the first twenty feet, but after that? Where's your route?"

"Let me climb up and see." The Texan shrugged out of his pack, stepped to the wall, made his first move easily, then the second. Five feet off the floor, he paused, turned to look up the gorge in the direction they'd been headed. "What the—?"

Raine heard it, too, a far-off wavering snarl, like a dog worrying its prey. And it was growing louder. The racket rose to a yammering roar as something shot around a distant bend in the canyon, racing right at them. Ruby eyes glowed in the beam of her flashlight as it bounded.

"Holy shit!" McCord jumped down beside her. "Up. Quick!"

"Is that Jorge?"

He shoved her to the wall. "Climb. If that's Jorge, it's Jorge on steroids!"

"You come, too!" she cried, pulling herself up to her first hold, then the second.

"Jeez! Are you nuts, boy? Down! Git! *Raine!*"

From the corner of her eye, she glimpsed the leaping form just as its teeth clamped in her pants cuff. Eighty pounds of living weight swung past her heels, wrenching her foot off the rock. She toppled sideways with a cry. A ten-foot fall onto rocks would be a bone-breaker! Instead, she sprawled in McCord's waiting arms. He staggered and tripped, dipped to his knees and set her down on the ground.

The coyote spun around—roaring, yelping, darting, charging—all snapping teeth and flaming eyes. "Hell!" McCord snatched up his backpack and held him off as they retreated, herded like a couple of terrorized cats. "What's the matter with you, George, you *loco?*"

They bumped into the left-hand canyon wall to stand at bay, McCord fending off each lunge while Raine drew her parasol from its pack scabbard. She'd need a minute to set up her blowgun. "Hold him and I'll—"

"Hold him? Are you kidding?"

Suddenly the coyote shut its ravening mouth, pricked its ears.

McCord didn't drop his defense. "What the blue hell got into you, you toothy luna—"

"Shhh!" Raine whispered. "Do you hear something?"

McCord paused, rotated slowly in the direction the coyote had come from, and listened.

A sound, no louder than the ocean in a conch shell, a tiny murmuring roar at the end of the world, headed their way. "*Flood!* Get back to the other side, we gotta climb for our lives!" The coyote leaped, snapping his teeth an inch from McCord's nose. He staggered against Raine, knocking her around. She caught herself against the cliff, and there, before her face, was a foothold. "McCord, here! A notch. I think maybe we can—" She stepped up against the vertical face, hand fanning the stone overhead.

"We're dead if we can't." The sound was growing louder, gaining resonance, a high thin singing laid over a cannibal growl. "Climb!"

Her fingers found a niche, just where it should be. She dragged herself higher, found the next, spaced as regular as stairsteps, cut by a thinking mind.

"Faster!"

She flew up the rock, glancing back once toward the floor. By the light of her fallen flashlight, she caught one last glimpse of the coyote, racing off down the canyon. But he hadn't a prayer. A cool humid breeze was blowing down the gorge, bringing with it a sound like a leafy forest bending to a gale.

"Faster! Faster!"

Her world narrowed to the next toehold, the next handhold, another blessed niche just where it had to be.

Not ten feet below her flying heels, the wave rumbled past, silvery and sucking, bearing tumbling trees, a dark whirling shape that might have been a drowned horse. Crying in terror, deafened, praying, Raine mounted the shuddering stone. *Is McCord alive?*

She couldn't look down. As long as she didn't, there was the barest chance that he had made it above the flood's crest. Life won or forfeited by inches; time measured in laboring heartbeats and sobbing breaths. At last her terror ran dry and Raine stopped, her forehead resting against cool stone. *Is he alive?*

McCord's fingers closed around her ankle, squeezed mute comfort. She laughed through her tears and kissed the rock. *Thank you!*

He tapped her boot heel impatiently and she hauled herself upward.

"No, it's not a crack," Raine reported as her head rose above a ledge. "It's a—a sort of landing?" She rolled over, scrambled into the closet-sized nook, bumped what felt like a small tree trunk with her head. "Hope to God it's not a dead end." There wasn't room enough to lie down, though at least the floor of this crack was flat. She scrunched in against one wall, giving McCord space to clamber over the edge.

"Who's complaining?" He collapsed against the opposite wall, with their upraised, shaking knees almost touching.

"You wore your pack!" She'd dumped hers at the base of the cliff, along with her parasol. Never could have moved fast enough, if she'd held onto it. "Are you insane?"

"Call me crazy when I'm taking you out to dinner?" He unzipped a pocket, pulled out a bag of gorp. She could see the gleam of his teeth in the shadows as she reached for it greedily. "And if I'm really nice, I might even share my bedroll tonight."

"If we find a place to spread one." She glanced up the dark rift.

"No, don't tell me this is a dead end. Somebody was surely cutting steps to somewhere, bless his busy little soul."

"Bless your pal, Jorge," Raine said soberly. "Do you think there's even a chance that he made it?"

McCord sighed aloud. "Not unless he had wings."

"He saved us, you realize. We'd never have found a way up in time where we were climbing first. But how did he know that this route was here?"

"Now don't go all mystic on me. He was running from the flood and I suppose he panicked, which is why he attacked us. As for the rest, it had to be pure, dumb, wonderful luck, which, if it continues…" McCord paused to knock stone.

"Anybody who believes in knocking on wood to confuse the evil fairies, ought to be able to swallow an intelligent coyote. There's some sort of stick over there in the corner, if you need to make that official."

He switched the light on and swung the beam to the back of the space, to where a crude wooden post rose from the floor.

"I figured that for a tr-tree," Raine gulped, as his light climbed to the white knob on its top.

A skull grinned down at them, mouth agape and emptily laughing.

"Oh, mama," McCord said reverently. "And it's still weeks to Halloween!"

# Chapter 20

"Somebody really doesn't want company," Raine said, when McCord joined her on the second landing. It was identical to the first notch in the cliff, some two hundred feet below, except for one improvement.

"*Two* scarecrows!" McCord muttered, when he switched on his flashlight. That had been his explanation for the first skull on a stick: an emphatic Do Not Disturb. "A double underline, in case we were dim enough to miss the earlier message?"

"I'd say so." Raine examined the skulls by his light. "Are these as old as the other one?" McCord had tentatively dated the head below, figuring it to be a hundred years old, possibly much older.

"Looks to be," he said, rubbing a fingertip across a dusty dome.

"That's a comfort. Anybody who treasures his solitude this much, well, I could pass on meeting him."

"Could have been worse." McCord passed her his canteen. "These niches feel like guard posts. What d'you bet at one point in history, a visitor would stick his inquisitive head up over this edge, and there'd be somebody waiting up here with a big knife to lop it off?"

"Charming. Do you think this was your Aztec buddies? The Quetzalcoatl mark was only a little ways back down the canyon."

"True, but there's no way my caravan carried a sixteen-man litter straight up this wall. To say nothing of packloads of gold, and whatever else they were lugging. No, this type of hand-and-toe trail has been found at plenty of other sites around the southwest. Might be Anasazi work, or it might be a universal response to vertical challenges."

"The decor sure smacks of Aztecs."

"But not every skull is a sacrifice. These two could be Grandma and Grandpa Raramuri, gone to their just reward, then recycled for the good of the family." McCord pulled a notepad out of his pack, switched on his light, and started printing.

"I give up. You're just determined not to be excited."

"Don't get your hopes too high, hotshot. Let your artifacts speak for themselves." He finished his note, then wedged it into the eye socket of a skull. He'd left a similar note for Antonio below.

"He'll probably guess that we kept on climbing," Raine said dryly. She had her doubts that Antonio would follow—or find that note. McCord had left him an arrow made of pebbles back at the fork in the rivers, along with a second arrow indicating the turquoise mark of the Feathered Serpent. He seemed to be confident that his assistant would catch up with them within a day or so. Probably just his stomach talking; they had only two day's worth of rations left, since her pack had been swept away.

"He will, but Raramuri tend to be superstitious. He's not

going to be happy, meeting these sweethearts. Anything I do to encourage him is effort well spent."

Raine would rather scrounge for packrats and prickly pear than share camp with the troublesome Raramuri. She hoped the flash flood had risen high enough to wash McCord's arrows away, in which case Antonio would probably follow the wrong fork of the river.

McCord rubbed the nape of her neck. "Can you make it the rest of the way?"

"Someplace we could stretch out without roommates would suit me just fine."

When Raine finally crawled over the edge of the rim, her legs were spasming. She turned around to see McCord heave into view.

He struggled out of the pack and they collapsed on their backs, gazing up at a night ablaze with stars. Raine hitched herself closer; McCord encircled her with an arm. She snuggled her face into his warmth, wrapped an arm around his ribs and floated off into oblivion.

They woke shivering maybe half an hour later, judging by the stars. The Texan sat up with a groan. "So, after all that, where are we?"

On an island in the sky, Raine realized as she stood. The top of a craggy mesa—fairly flat, without a single tree in sight. The cliff they'd climbed meandered off to her right in a razor-edged darkness. Step off that rim and you'd find yourself down in the slot canyon again, much the worse for wear.

Ahead, the rocky terrain stretched to a low ridge, which obscured whatever lay beyond. Off to her left, a long slice of velvety blackness suggested another abyss. "Pretty bleak." Why would anyone have ever bothered climbing up here?

"And no water, it looks like," McCord said grimly. "Which

means tomorrow morning we climb down again, if there's none to be found."

They made camp at the base of the ridge; it blocked the chill wind that was blowing. With no wood for a fire, they settled for string cheese, jerky and a swallow of water apiece. "I still think we're on to something," Raine insisted, struggling against the blue funk into which they were sinking. "In the morning, when we can see what we've got here."

"Yeah, there'll be heaps of temple gold, and a whole library of Aztec codices just begging to be dug up."

Raine crawled into his circle of warmth. He pulled his blanket over them both. "Been meaning to ask you," she mumbled drowsily, with her forehead against the slow beat of his heart, "when we find the caravan—and we will, McCord; I've got this feeling—how do we split the booty? If you take the gold and the codices and the dig site and the academic glory, can I have the Feathered Serpent, and equal credit for the discovery?"

She felt him jolt. His arms hardened. "What?"

Tired as she was, she'd spoken without thinking or finesse, although even if she'd approached the issue tactfully, this was how she saw the deal. "That is, if the Quetzalcoatl turns out to be based on a dinosaur. If there's no dino connection, then I've got no claim at all." He could have her help for free.

McCord caught her arms and shifted her out where he could see her face. "This is Mexico, Raine. They got tired of pothunters making off with their national treasures a long time ago. They're strict as can be when it comes to their archaeological heritage. No way will they let an unlicensed *gringa* scoop up the Quetzalcoatl and skip over the border."

"You don't exactly have a license yourself, do you?"

"Nope, but the minute I find something significant, I've got leverage. I'll know where it is and they won't—but they'll really, really want it. First thing I'd do is cut a deal with a top-flight American university; let them obtain the permits and negotiate the final agreement. But any deal will end with the best artifacts going to the *Museo Nacional* in Mexico City. I get the fame and control of the dig site and the books that'll be written—but they get the goodies. That's a rock-solid given."

She squirmed free and sat up. "Fine, I can work around that. We've got an expediter back at headquarters—Trey— he's a wonder at cutting deals. I don't have to end up with the Feathered Serpent himself, but I do want the right to have him CAT scanned. There's technology nowadays that will map the bones under the turquoise point for point—that is, if there are bones—then cut a three-dimensional, life-size perfect copy. Ashaway All sells museum-grade casts of fossils, sometimes, in situations like this." Given the glamour of the original creature, the profit could still be enormous.

"So it's been business all along. You'd think I'd have learned by now." The Texan scrambled to his feet.

He was equating her with his conniving Zelda? Yet she'd never tried to disguise her motives, or seduce him into anything. "Look, McCord, I'm a dinosaur hunter. A *professional* hunter, not somebody's subsidized academic. I can't go prancing around the canyons for fun; I've got to turn a profit. You've known that from the start."

"What a jerk I've been, spilling all my dreams while you lapped them up, wide-eyed."

"It wasn't like that! I never tried to—"

"Reckon I thought business had been set aside, when we— Shit." He stooped, found his boots, stomped into them.

"You mean you thought I'd give up my claim—my very deserving claim—to a share of the prize once we fell into the sack? Well, grow up, McCord. I'm not some blond bimbo to boost your ego and cheer you on, while *you* find the treasure! I'm a *partner*—or if you're too stingy for that, I'm a competitor."

"Hoo, boy. There you go. Glad we finally got *that* clear. A competitor. Another ball-busting Zelda in search of her own corner office, and watch out, any guy who gets in her way!" Off he stalked along the ridge.

"McCord, dammit, come back here! It's too cold to— Aw, hell. See if I care. Freeze your selfish butt off." Raine wiped her cheeks—when had she started crying? Damn, she hated tears.

And now what was she supposed to do, stay snug in his bedroll while he iced his stubborn Lone Star backside? "Oh, do men ever give me a pain!" All tender pride and towering ego, and somehow they always turned every disagreement into an issue of balls.

As if any sane woman would even want her own set, when there were plenty of loaners for the asking. She wriggled into her clothes, snatched at her boots, stood and yelled, "The bedroll's all yours, McCord!" She wouldn't have taken it as a gift.

Since the egomaniac had stomped east, Raine ended up at the western rim of their island. Huddled on a boulder, arms wrapped around her goose-pimpled knees, she stared grimly down into the bottomless black.

"Ashaway?" McCord called behind her.

She shrugged her shoulders, didn't bother to turn.

"Has the concept of rimrock entered your empty little skull?"

*Oh, yeah, like that's gonna get my attention.*

"Not all cliffs erode straight up and down, sugar. If this side of the mesa's been undercut by a river, then that rim you're sitting on could be thin as a potato chip."

Her stomach did a loop-de-loop as she pictured it. On the

other hand, here she was, perched on a several-ton boulder. Probably her seat was good for the next thousand years or so. Plenty of time.

"I would just as soon not walk out there and grab you, but so help me, if you don't—"

Somewhere far below, a light flared. Raine blinked. Had she really seen it? No, *there*—a shower of sparks! "McCord, come look at this!"

"You haven't listened to a word I've—"

"A light! Some sort of fireworks? What the heck *is* it?"

He joined her in three strides. Stood, with one hand on her shoulder.

It reminded her of the sparklers she'd loved as a child. Every Fourth of July, her father would give in to his off-springs' begging and buy boxes of the treats. She and her siblings would chase each other through the Colorado darkness, shrieking with glee, whirling fiery pinwheels. "Looks like somebody's celebrating something down there." Whoever it was was ducking and dodging and whirling his sparkling wand. "Gotta be a kid, which means a *ranchito?*"

"I've never heard of a settlement out in this part of the world."

Abruptly the light fizzed out. They strained their ears for some sort of human sound, but heard only the wind sighing among the rocks. Who could be out here celebrating in the stony heart of darkness?

"Show's over," McCord decided finally. He stooped—hoisted her high in his arms. "So come to bed, you grabby bitch."

"Such gallantry, how could a woman resist?" Still, she found herself smiling as he strode back toward the only bedroll in a hundred cold and lonely miles. No doubt he'd confuse the forthcoming stupendous sex with an apology, but still…it would be a start.

* * *

Hard as the ground was, they slept late. Raine rose finally, muttered something and vanished beyond the ridge. McCord's arms felt empty without her, so he hugged himself, shivering. Images blossomed in his waking mind—the flood, the fight, the fabulous aftermath with anger like a match to their passion. He wriggled his toes, somewhat warmer with the memory.

*What the hell am I doing?* They'd gotten even closer this last time, body and soul, but he was starting to feel like Brer Rabbit after he'd kicked the Tar Baby. Every time he made love to her, it became that much harder to pull back into himself afterwards; his borders were fraying. He'd been so long on his own, and perfectly content that way. A change like this was scary. All the scarier for being so damn irresistible at the onset, then so blissful in the doing, and so heart-glowingly satisfying at the end that right now, if she'd come back to bed... His pulse quickened with the possibility. *Oh, this is bad. Really bad!* Raine was turning into a major distraction, just when he ought to be locked on tight to his quest.

Though they'd reached a climax last night, they sure hadn't hammered out an agreement. The thought of his trusting her professionally—of sharing an epic find with another ambitious woman, of giving up control... *Am I out of my friggin' mind?*

"Hey, lazybones!" Raine stooped, pulled the covers off his head, kissed him till his brains melted. "Rise and shine. Shall I wait for you to go look at the gorge?"

"You *better* wait," he growled as he rolled to his feet.

Her dark brows rose at his change of mood, then she shrugged, turned away with a sunny smile. She found his comb in the unzipped top compartment of his pack and held it up. "May I?"

"Uh, sure. You can use my toothbrush, too." He was lost. He'd never once shared a toothbrush with Zelda. Now, though, the thought didn't repulse him. The fact that it didn't froze his blood.

"Thanks, but I used my finger and a lot of your paste."

And what did *that* mean—that *she* was drawing some kind of line? Scared as he was, why should it bother him if she was cooling her jets? "Whatever." He stomped off over the ridge for some blessed alone time.

They walked stiffly and silently to the boulder from which they'd looked down into the gorge last night, and stood beside it, staring. "That can't be what it—" McCord dropped his pack on the rock, snatched out a pair of binoculars.

"It's a…cliff house?" The far wall of the gorge, the only wall Raine could see from this angle, had yet to catch the morning sun. But in the depth of the shadows about halfway down the face of the cliff…she could barely make out squared shapes giving structure and volume to the shadows. "It *is!*" Like the ruins at Mesa Verde in Colorado! This was not just a *ranchito,* but a village complex, built within a gigantic water-carved alcove.

Bracing the binoculars against his face, McCord murmured, "Holy Mother of God, I must still be dreaming! Pinch me, Ashaway, quick. Ouch!"

"Stop pigging those glasses!" She snatched for them.

"Wait your turn, shorty." He fended her off with an elbow. "If you'd held onto your own pack…"

Swearing with impatience, she jittered beside him till he finally took pity and passed her his binoculars. "Jeez, McCord, it's as big as the Cliff Palace site!" She panned slowly along the alcove. The canyon below them wasn't straight like a city block; it curved gradually away in a big lazy clockwise bend, till an outcrop of the cliff they were standing upon blocked the rest of it from view. "Is there anything like this anyplace else in the Copper Canyons?"

Silence. She brought the glasses down, to find him collapsed on the boulder, with his head between his knees. "McCord?" She knelt before him, caught his bristly face in her palms, kissed his grimace that struggled to hold back the tears. "Oh, love, you did it! *We* did it!"

His voice was a rusty whisper. "No, honey, there's nothing like this in all of northern Mexico. I'm not sure what it is, but it's big."

"Which means you're back in the game," she said softly.

"Big-time." He wiped his nose and reached for the glasses. "My turn."

*My turn, partner,* she almost corrected him. But he'd waited and worked for this moment for so many years. So she left that for later.

# Chapter 21

"Do Aztecs build cliff houses?" Raine wondered. They'd settled on the boulder, trading the glasses back and forth, while they chewed handfuls of gorp.

"Not that I've ever heard, but try this for a scenario," McCord said, from behind his lens. "You see that creek down there at the base of the wall? If we trace its course to our left—" Which they couldn't; another outcrop of the cliff they sat upon blocked that view. "It has got to hit a dead end within a quarter mile or so, a sort of headwall.

"Well, what do you bet that in 1520, when our caravan came trudging along the canyon we were walking yesterday, they came to a little fork in the river? Right about where you spotted the second Quetzalcoatl design last evening. So they made their signpost, then they turned *left* at that point—where we kept walking straight—and that brought them through a narrow passage into this side canyon."

"You mean this river here is the same spring that pops up on the other side, seemingly out of a solid wall? But how—"

"The Aztecs didn't build cliff houses down in the Valley of Mexico, but their temple-pyramids were big as any cathedral the Conquistadores had ever seen. These guys knew their stonework."

"They walled off this side canyon?"

"Yep. You remember those hairline cracks you noticed along the face of the cliff, above the pool? You were looking at a man-made wall. They left some sort of underwater arch to let the river run out, but they slammed the door on any visitors."

"But that would have taken *years!*"

"Maybe a century or more," he agreed, passing her the binoculars. "And they likely didn't start right away. But at some point they must have realized what was coming—the Spaniards, the slavery, the plague, the priests. Realizing that no tribe could resist the invaders with their gunpowder and their germs, they just disappeared. Shangri-la. Brigadoon. *Adiós.*"

"Okay, if they didn't build the cliff houses, then who did?"

"This looks like proto Anasazi construction, something that predates the Raramuris' coming by five hundred years or more."

"And what happened to these people when the Aztecs came to town?"

McCord made a face. "Well, quite possibly this was a ghost town when the Aztecs arrived. Nobody has yet figured out why the Anasazi vanished up in the American Southwest, but vanish they did. Maybe plague, maybe drought."

"And if they were still here?" Raine asked slowly, picturing the caravan as it marched into view.

"The Anasazi were shy, peaceful people, into agriculture and hunting and gathering as a way of life. But the Aztecs were empire builders, warriors through and through. I can picture 'em coming, seeing, wanting. If they hadn't found their Aztlan, still they were tired and hungry and footsore, and here was a settlement ready-made. Ripe for the taking. And this pueblo would have had one thing the caravan lacked. Something it would need, sooner or later, if they meant to survive and thrive: women."

Raine winced. "Sacrifice the men, keep their wives? Nice guys you study. Think I'll stick to dinosaurs." They munched trail mix in silence till she added, "And now?"

"Ghost town again. I haven't seen a hint of movement. Bet nobody's been home for a hundred years or more."

"But what about the light we saw last night?"

He scratched his bristles and shrugged. "It was hardly a normal sort of light—not a campfire or torch. So maybe fire-flies? Some weird sort of lichens giving off swamp gas? Ghosts of Aztecs past? Guess we'll figure it out when we find a way down there."

But as morning crept into noon, "when" shaded gradually toward "if." Hoping for a path down, they followed the cliff edge to their left, until McCord put a foot through the rimrock up to his knee. After that they retreated ten feet back from the rim and roped themselves together. Raine led the way, under the theory that McCord could hold her weight if she broke through the eroded crust.

They made it without further accidents to a point above the man-made curtain wall, which closed off this side canyon from the slot canyon where they'd almost drowned. "The top of it is about two hundred feet straight down," Raine reported, hanging her head and shoulders over the edge, while McCord sat well back, taking up her slack. "But I don't see any foot and handholds down this cliff. I don't think they wanted drop-ins taking this approach."

"There's gotta be an entrance from somewhere up on this mesa. Why else would there be that hand-and-toe trail leading up here in the first place?"

"Maybe in the other direction," Raine suggested, crawling back from the edge. "Or maybe, once upon a time, there was a hanging bridge of some sort over to the cliff house?" She'd seen some hair-raising samples of such in the Andes. "Ropes and twigs wouldn't last over the centuries, without regular maintenance."

Backtracking to their original boulder, they continued the other way along the rim. Raine crept out to the outcrop that had earlier blocked their view up the canyon. "Oh, man!"

"What? Dammit, you're having all the fun!"

"It's a natural bridge!" Arcing across the gorge below, the tawny water-smoothed ribbon of sandstone would have been carved aeons ago by the river that now ran two hundred feet below it. "It's bigger than Rainbow Bridge in Utah!"

McCord settled down on his stomach beside her. "It's freakin' magnificent! That's where they'll take our photograph, Ashaway, for the covers of *Time, Nature, Newsweek, National Geographic*. Standing right out there."

Raine grabbed his belt. "You know, if you take a nose dive, I'm not going to appreciate it, seeing as we're roped together." He nodded absently. "Is that our way down?" From here, she couldn't see where the arch joined with this side of the gorge; it started maybe four hundred feet below their present level. On its far side, the arch ended, like a rainbow leading to treasure, some fifty feet below the cliff house alcove. "You know, it looks like they've filled in more stonework over on that side. Made a causeway so they can walk straight out onto it from their village."

"Yeah," McCord said grimly. "That's just what they've done."

She snatched a glance at his face. No more jubilant smile.

"So it's a natural bridge from some point below us on this side over to the cliff house."

"Maybe. But more than that, you see that round platform right at the center of the span? That's an altar to Quetzalcoatl."

Which meant the reddish-brown streaks that banded the stone below the simple platform, like the rings on a gigantic snake... "Th-those streaks, then, you mean those are..."

The Texan nodded, one tight nod. "They're blood."

"Well, what can you expect from a pack of Aztecs?" Raine said finally. If it was nasty, still, they'd come centuries late to lodge a complaint. She turned her attention back to the cliff house, which went on and on in a series of arching alcoves. "This place is..." She shook her head. "I'm running out of amazement."

"I know just what you mean." McCord uncapped his canteen. "One swallow only, kid."

She passed it back, caught him trying to skip his swallow, poked him in the ribs. "Drink." Their eyes met, then skimmed away. Neither wanted to confront the looming problem that by the end of the day they'd be in rough shape without water. If they couldn't find a way down to that lovely little river below, then their only alternative was backtracking—and that climb down to the slot canyon would be brutal. Dehydration on top of skimpy rations would bring increasing weakness. In all sanity, they should head back this minute. "Try for another mile or two?"

"I'm game if you are." McCord's gaze drifted back to the cliff house. His dark brows drew together. "What the—!" He snatched up the glasses that lay between them.

Something stirred in the shadows at the back of a small plaza. Raine shaded her eyes and squinted.

"Son of a bitch! Is that—? No, it can't be. Tell me I'm dreaming."

"Who is it?" Raine tugged at his sleeve. Whoever it was was blond, she saw now as the figure limped out to the low stone guard wall that edged the alcove.

Swearing bitterly, McCord just shook his head.

"Give me those!" She grabbed the binoculars from his unresisting fingers, focused on the swaying figure below—and nearly dropped them over the rim. "Grunwald!"

"The crazy bastard. How did he ever beat us here?"

"He's alive!" she said with an incredulous smile.

"Yeah, till I kill him, he is. He's stolen our discovery right out from under us."

"Hell-oo, Grunwald!" McCord bellowed. They'd been trying to attract the engineer's attention for the past five minutes. Clearly he heard at least the echoes of their hails. He kept turning in mystified circles, looking high and low, then shambling back into the shadows and returning to hang halfway over the retaining wall, peering down into the gorge.

"I never took him for brilliant, but this beats all," McCord muttered. "Look over *here,* you crazy German!"

"Something's not right," Raine said. "He's dazed, or not seeing straight."

"He does seem a bit woozy." McCord yanked off his T-shirt, stood and waved it overhead as he yelled.

Raine chimed in with a series of high-pitched ululating whoops. "He sees you!"

The German had straightened to stare, transfixed. Through the binoculars, Raine could see his joyous grin spreading. He pointed up at them, burst into laughter. "He's really glad to see us, I'd say."

"Glad somebody's happy," McCord growled. "How do we reach you?" he hollered. "Where's the way down? Is he getting what I'm saying?"

"I don't think so. He's just laughing." Though tears streamed down his face. "Something's not right, Anse." She held her arms out, palms up in a wide, expansive shrug, miming, Well? What now? Tell us!

Grunwald was pointing at her merrily. She could almost hear him chortling. He caught the garment that framed his bare shoulders and spread it wide, going her gesture one better.

"What's he— He's wearing a cape?" Well, some sort of waist-length cloth of brilliant colors, over a pair of filthy khaki shorts. He looked like a child in a Halloween costume, playing Batman—whirling and pouncing and skipping, showing off for a bemused adult audience. He leaped up onto the retaining wall, wobbled along it, cape flapping, arms out-stretched. "Oh, no!" Raine covered her eyes. "What's he doing?"

"Damned if I know, but we're making it worse. C'mon, let's go." McCord caught Raine's arm and hustled her back from the cliff. "Sit down where he can't see us." He pulled out the canteen, offered her a swallow. "Whew. I 'bout yelled myself dry."

"Me, too." Raine took a tiny sip, letting it trickle down her raw throat. "He's sick or he's crazy or—"

"I'm thinking he might be out of water," McCord said grimly. "Hallucinating. I don't know how the hell he got over there, but if there's no way down to the valley floor from his side…"

A person could live almost a month without food, but only a few days without water. Especially in this arid climate. "We've got to get to him, and fast!"

"'Fraid so." McCord stood, caught her hand and pulled her to her feet. "The guy's a total pain in the butt. But I reckon he's our pain."

* * *

The hours passed swiftly, but their pace was slow as they worked their way north along the gorge. Each time they picked their way out to the treacherous rim, a stunning new vista opened, but so far none offered a solution to their problem. "Sunflowers," McCord noted, gazing down on the crumbling terraces of the narrow valley. "Gone wild now, but the seeds would have been one of their crops."

Raine's stomach growled. "Good protein, if we could get to them."

"And look at that. I do believe that's cotton down there, in that top field along the cliffs! The heirloom seed—folks are going to go hog-wild. This'll be a botanical treasure, as well as a historical blockbuster."

"If we ever get down there. Still nothing?" Raine had assumed that there'd be some sort of stairs leading from this mesa top to the near end of the natural bridge, but there hadn't been. From directly above, they'd looked down upon the arch, some four hundred feet below. McCord carried two fifty-foot nylon ropes in his pack, but the sheer walls of the gorge offered no perches that they could rappel to, then anchor their ropes for the next downward pitch.

"Nothing but a— Hey, wait, look over there!" He pointed at the cliff house ruins across the way. "See those two stone pillars set into the retaining wall? With the V-shapes notched into their heads? What d'you bet there was a polished log that ran between them, once upon a time. Run a hemp rope over that log, use it for a pulley, and with enough manpower tailing on the rope from down below, you could raise or lower a basket for passengers and cargo."

If so, the primitive elevator was long gone. "Seems a fairly inefficient way for your townspeople to commute to work. If they were so good with building in stone, why not cut flights of steps and landings?" She'd rather climb a twenty-story staircase any day, than trust her life to a wicker basket.

"I think what we've got here is a siege mentality. Even if they were never found, they led their lives expecting that day. With this system, if the enemy ever came calling, they could hoist everybody to safety, then pull in their basket. But for everyday life, my guess would be that the plain folk lived in huts in the valley, while the nobles and priests got the rooms with a view."

"Not much has changed, has it?" Raine shaded her eyes against the dipping sun and scanned the ruins. "Still no sign of Johann. I wonder if we should give this up and make a dash for his company's base camp? Come back in their helicopter."

"Not if his problem is water. I reckon four days minimum to reach his camp, more likely five or six. Grunwald wouldn't live that long."

"If only I hadn't lost my phone in the flash flood..."

McCord dropped an arm around her shoulders and eased her back from the rim. "Don't give up yet. We'll find a way down—or we'll damn well make one."

A few hours before sunset, they came at last to the northern end of the secret gorge. As they'd expected, it ended in another man-made curtain wall. "I think this might even be the same slot canyon we started in," Raine said, hanging over the outer face of the cliff, with McCord holding tight to her line. So the mesa was basically an almond-shaped island, carved when a river split to run along both its sides. The Aztecs had built their ramparts from each tapered end of the almond, to the western highlands beyond, walling their city into its hidden gorge.

"This cliff's not quite as sheer as the face we climbed up. There's a crack that angles down. Can't see from here, but it might reach the ground. Looks like we could chimney down it."

"Yeah, but where would that get us? Back in the slot canyon—on the outside, needing to get in."

"Well, the river down there flows under the Aztecs' wall. If we—"

"Oh, no. I don't mind diving with a scuba tank, but I won't dive blind—no map, no lights."

"Given the width of the wall, the tunnel beneath it can't be much longer than forty feet."

"Yeah, but what happens if they built a grate in their waterway, to keep out trespassers? You'd have a current pushing you hard up against it, with no way to turn around and swim back. Forget it."

Raine growled in frustration as she retreated from the edge. "Then we've got to find some way to get down onto this dam from up here! Take up my slack." She'd inspected the inner side of the man-made wall from a notch in the rim, some fifty feet to the south. But the rimrock along this end of the gorge was savagely eroded. Perhaps from some closer point she'd see something else?

"Watch it," McCord called. Still seated, he swung his legs around and braced his boots along the vector of her rope. "It looks rotten as Swiss cheese."

As the ground dropped out from beneath her, Raine screamed. Her out-flung arms slammed into the earth. Her feet dangled below the crust, kicking desperately.

"Are you stuck?" McCord called.

"I th-think." Her foot found a purchase along the side of the hole. She shoved upward, pressed down with her palms and broke free, a human cork escaping its bottle. She rolled onto firm ground, with her heart slamming like a pile driver. She'd have some good scrapes and bruises tomorrow.

"Come over here and I'll kiss it and make it better."

She grinned at him. "You don't have enough spit left for a kiss." She turned to peer down the hole, like Alice looking after the rabbit. Now that she'd broken through its top, the hole was perhaps a foot wider than she was. "You know, it's possible that if I chimneyed down this thing, it would take me below the rimrock." If she could get past the overhanging crust of the mesa, perhaps she could find a route.

"Not a good idea. The edge of that limestone looks sharp as a knife. If it frays one of our ropes, we're screwed."

"I can chimney down easily. The rope will only be for backup."

"Famous last words."

She smiled and slid her boots into the hole, eased herself over to sit on its rim. "My favorite line is 'Trust Me.'"

"And I do, darlin', to turn my hair white. You sure you want to try this?"

She didn't, but granted a second chance to save Grunwald, she was darned if she'd blow it. "Quite sure." She braced her boots, one before, the other behind, and lowered herself into the hole.

The stone was jagged, which was painful but good. She eased on down, her breath sounding loud in the tube. The hole curved gradually toward the face of the cliff. At some point in the next ten yards it should pierce the wall. In heavy rains this would be a stone drainpipe, gushing water down into the canyon below.

"Okay down there?" McCord called.

"Piece of cake." It continued to be an easy climb, till her free boot reached for a purchase and treaded air. "I think I'm at the end of the hole. You might want to brace yourself." Her second boot kicked thin air and she dangled from the hips down, suspended by her braced arms and torso. She sucked in her breath, wincing as she came to her last possible grip. "Okay," she muttered aloud—then yelped as her toe touched ground. "What the—!" She kicked with her other boot and struck ground again. She slipped out of the tube—to kneel on a ragged ledge, overlooking a six-hundred-foot plunge to the canyon floor.

"Talk to me," McCord called. "Whatya got?"

"A ledge of some sort, just below the rimrock, couple of feet wide. Give me a little slack."

He gave it grudgingly, unwilling to give her enough rope to fall. Raine crawled along the ledge, peering downward. She could see the man-made Aztec wall from here, with the river gushing beneath it. She swallowed reflexively.

"Well?" McCord called.

"Nothing so far," she had to admit. Though this route would let them bypass the nasty overhang, the cliff below it was brutal. They didn't have the gear to attack this, and she didn't have the nerve or the skills to tackle it free-style. Except for the underground river, they were out of options. "Nope, this is a dead end. I'm coming up."

As usual, the return trip seemed shorter. About ten feet below the mesa's level, she paused with boots nicely wedged and knees locked, to rest.

"Wish you'd get your butt up here," McCord called. "I'm really missing you."

"Ah, you're just a big, soppy romantic," she murmured, smiling to herself.

"I think maybe we should—"

Should what? She opened her mouth to inquire—and something landed on her head, slithered down her shoulders. *Snake!* Her body convulsed; a shriek jammed in her throat. But there was no place to flee, a dead-freeze the only course that might save her. The reptile slithered across her squinched-shut eyes, down her cheek, twined her bare arm, rippled over a goose-pimpled thigh, then its texture hit home.

Not snake scales, but nylon rope! McCord had dropped the rope—its own weight had dragged it down the hole, coiling down on top of her. "McCord!" she whispered. He'd never drop the rope. *Never,* not while he was alive.

A soft grunt came from above. Then the dry rasp and bump of something heavy being dragged across rough ground.

A sound that could only be a body.

# *Chapter 22*

Time blurred with the rush of adrenaline. Raine fought the rope, squirming past its coils, then a loop around her neck snagged on something below. She let out her scream in a strangled hiss, untwisted the impediment and wriggled upward. Blood dripped from one hand. A prayer sang in her brain, *Don't let him be dead, don't let him, don't let him!*

With the rope dangling from her waist, Raine set her boots and rose a foot. She paused to listen, but heard nothing except her own thundering heart. *What the hell happened?*

Something scraped a rock, then a faint vibration. Footsteps softly padding? She raised her head out of the hole by inches—paused with her eyes at ground level. Ten feet away, where McCord had stationed himself, a man now stood, his back to her, looking down at the bare ground. Black hair, dark skin, lean build—an *indio* in western clothes.

The stranger straightened, walked with hesitant, edgy steps

over to a nearby outcrop of boulders. He stared intently, then vanished around the man-high stones.

Raine flattened her hands on the ground and lifted herself out of the hole. She hauled the rope to the surface, coiling it as it came. She pulled her knife from its ankle sheath, then padded over to the last point where she'd seen McCord.

Blood stained the ground, a big, bright splash of it. She shuddered, whispering, "Oh, you *bastard!*" The ground was too rough to read drag marks, but there was no place in this barren world to hide a body, except...

She followed the intruder in a rush. Rounding the rocks, she found Antonio. And no McCord. That could only mean one thing.

As Antonio glanced up at her, she lashed out with a boot, slamming his shoulder. He grunted, rolled away with the blow and bounced to his feet.

She followed him with her blade uplifted, slicing air in tiny circles. "You bastard!" Tears blurred her eyes. She bit down savagely on her lip. "Why'd you kill him?"

"I didn't do it!" He backed away, hugging the outcrop, sped up and vanished beyond it.

"Liar. There's nobody else here!" When she circled back into view, he held two knives, a switchblade in his right, a big hunting blade in his left.

He laughed breathlessly and beckoned her closer with both shining blades. "I didn't do it, *rubia,* but come to me anyway!"

"If you didn't do it, who *did?*" She lunged on the word, sliced the back of his wrist and retreated.

*"Haaaa!"* He wiped his blood onto his thigh. "A man, an *indio,* but he was a ghost, I think. I watched from a distance. He hit McCord on the head, dragged him behind these rocks."

"Yeah, *right,* the Tooth Fairy got him, and so where *is* this guy? Where's *McCord?*"

"I don' know. I hurried to help, but by the time I reached this place…"

"Liar! *Snake!* You walked right up to him—so easy to do, when he thought you were his friend! You knocked him out and then you threw him over."

She twisted away as he rushed her, scything his blades left and right. He had more courage than skill; she had the speed, plus all the moves Trey had taught her in years of combat coaching. But blade-on-blade she'd never match Antonio's strength, and he had the reach on her by half a foot.

They paused, panting, as they took each other's measure, then circled again. Her eyes flicked toward the hole. If she could lure him in that direction, distract him… Even better, enrage him; rage would make him careless. "What did he ever do to you that you'd want to kill him, you ungrateful worm?"

"What did he do? He showed me a world I could never have. Any time he wanted, he could go back to his Houston— drive a shiny car, get a good job, a fine woman. But me? I'm only an *indio,* unwelcome in my own land! No passport, no money, no schooling. Here I rot in my canyon, which soon will be a lake for other men's profit. *Pah!*" He lunged.

Backpedaling, she stumbled on the edge of the hole and fell to one knee. She groped the ground frantically with her free hand.

"And so, *putita!*" His knife slashed down at her face.

She swung the coil of rope. It whacked his nose, tangled his leading blade. She kicked his kneecap, then rolled desperately, bounced up and backed away.

"For that you die ugly!" Antonio massaged his leg. Blood spilled from his nose, dripped over bared teeth. His ebony eyes were ringed with crazy white.

*What are you doing?* Trey's voice sounded cold and clear in the depths of her mind. *You gain precisely what if you take him? And, Raine, I'm not sure you can. Vengeance is for chumps and comic-book heroes. Cut your losses, girl.*

"I didn't kill the *Tejano*, but I promise you this—I would have," Antonio snarled as he wiped the blood from his chin. He limped past the hole, stalking her. "I had no more need of McCord. After all my waiting, he brought me to what I seek." He hooked a knife toward the gorge at his back. "To the Aztec treasure, which is surely below."

McCord's pack lay on the ground where he'd left it. Raine grabbed it and kept backing, making for the cliff that over-looked the slot canyon. "So that's why you worked for him."

"But of course, why else? Now I have only to kill you, and the secret is mine." Antonio stooped, snatched up a chunk of ragged limestone the size of a baseball. "And that will be a pleasure!" he grunted as he drew back his arm and threw.

She swung the pack up just in time. The stone smashed into it, rocking her on her heels. Steel against steel, she might have held her own. But he'd just changed the game.

Antonio stooped again. She glanced desperately behind her as she backed up. Five yards to the cliff. He rose, showed her his missile with a smirk, wound up like a major-league pitcher.

In cultures without guns, men often hunted with rocks. A well-aimed stone could be lethal as a bullet; at ten paces, it surely trumped her knife. Raine held the pack chest-level, edged another few feet toward the cliff.

"You can jump, or I can break your bones like I'd crush a rabbit. The choice is yours."

One more stone, if she could survive one more… *Distract him.* "What will you do with the treasure if you find it, Antonio? Will you use it for lawyers? Find some way to fight the dam, save the Copper Canyons?"

"That's what my uncle, the doctor, thinks to do with it. But me, I don't know. A man can buy so many things with gold.

I will have to consider long and—" Quick as a lizard, his arm looped out and around.

She jerked the pack up to guard her face.

Pain exploded in her thigh. "Bastard!" She wobbled on the edge of the abyss. But instead of stooping for more ammunition he charged.

She whipped her blade, dropped to her knees, rolled over the edge and jammed her boots into the diagonal crack she'd spotted earlier. Then she dragged the pack after her.

"*Aiiii,* you—!" Antonio teetered overhead, clutching at the hilt of her knife, which bloomed from his shoulder.

She'd missed his throat. What a pity. Raine tucked farther into the crack, set her boots—and started the long descent.

Above her, he whimpered once, then grunted with effort, sobbing like a lost child. Droplets fell through the bright air—red rain in a dry land.

Her boot hit horizontal ground, jarring her to her back teeth. Her spasming legs stayed bent for a while—then collapsed, leaving her slumped at the bottom of the rift.

Though her heart had dried up and blown away, her instincts persisted. She crawled toward the burble of moving water, fell on her face and lapped like a dog. When she'd drunk all she could hold, she rolled over onto her back in the sand.

She blinked up at the stars. Last night, she'd watched them with her head pillowed on McCord's shoulder. Her tear ducts were working again; the stars smeared, then drizzled down the sky. She moaned, rolled over, drank some more. Then she folded her arms and rested her aching head on top of them. Should she sleep right here?

*You're not done yet,* a cold little voice objected. She could drink her fill—but Grunwald could not.

And McCord: No archaeologist would want his bones scattered to the four winds. He'd want some sort of grave, his body arranged neatly for future colleagues to dig up, then describe in learned papers. No doubt he'd like the favorite tools of his trade to be left at his side, maybe a note tucked into his shoes for posterity.

*And if your name is Ashaway, then there's one thing more,* that same cold little voice insisted. *There's a serpent in turquoise, still waiting to be found.*

McCord had feared that the upstream end of the underground river might be blocked by a grate. But Raine had no strength or patience to seek another route. She was too numb for fear.

She found the smashed pack that she'd dropped during the climb. After she'd wolfed down the last of their rations—not from hunger, but for fuel—she used McCord's razor to cut the pack away from its crumpled frame. She poked holes in its waterproof compartments, so they wouldn't fill with air when she needed to dive. She girdled it around her body with loops of his nylon rope, then she limped into the river, wading out to where it seemed to vanish along the canyon wall.

When she reached what must have been the center of the curtain wall, she could feel the current sucking at her legs. She treaded water, breathing deeply, and found she hadn't lost her fear, after all.

But would McCord leave her to lie where she'd fallen? *Don't stop to think, just do it.* She gulped one last precious breath and dove, letting the current take her.

The cold cut through her numbness. Horror followed. *What the hell am I doing? If there's a grate...* McCord would *not* have wanted this!

And no dinosaur, no matter how rare and fabulous, could be worth what the next sixty seconds might bring.

Too late now. The current sucked her faster and faster toward some narrowing gap. Something rasped along her arm, then her leg. She flailed away from the tunnel's side, spinning in the blackness. Her head slammed stone. She shoved frantically against slimy rock. *Oh, God, is this the grate?* Then the current tumbled her past. *How long, how long can I stay under?* Her lungs shuddered, convulsed. Lights pinwheeled behind her closed eyes. Frantic, she kicked faster, crying inwardly, *Oh, you stupid fool!*

Air burst against her face! With a sob, she rolled onto her back—*this* way was up? She'd have bet her last chance at life on just the reverse, but the stars didn't lie. Coughing and gagging, she grounded on a sandbar. She lay there, hugging herself while her teeth chattered. She was in.

When she drifted back to consciousness, the stars had wheeled across the night. She dragged herself a few feet up the beach.

*Don't sleep down low, honey,* drawled a smiling voice at the back of her mind. *You're still in flash flood country.*

"And you're still bossy," she mumbled, nestling her cheek into the sand. You'd think dying would teach him to mind his own… The thought fell apart and she slept.

Dawn danced on the heights when Raine sat up with a groan, crawled over to the water and drank.

A fish jumped midriver and her stomach growled, but finding food would come later. She stood, closed her eyes and reached for her center. *I've got to be strong.* She squared her shoulders and trudged east to the sheer wall of the gorge. McCord would have landed somewhere at the foot of this cliff.

Half an hour later, Raine turned to look back at the curtain wall. Starting from there, she'd walked the base of the cliff, zigzagging in and out till she reached her present point, maybe a quarter mile south. Given the time Antonio would have had—possibly five minutes from McCord's last words till she popped out of her hole—there was no way he could have dragged him for a hundred yards along the rimrock, before pitching him over. He'd have chosen the shortest path to the brink.

The sheerest thread of fragile emotion plucked at her numbness. She ripped it away. She'd come to some sort of terms with her sorrow. It would only hurt more when she found him, if she let herself hope.

She returned to the beach, pulled McCord's binoculars from his pack. One lens had shattered in the fall, but the other eyepiece had survived. She sat and leaned back on one hand to scan the heights. If he hadn't hit the ground, then he'd snagged on some ledge.

But an hour's scrutiny of the cliffs overhead found no ledge wide enough to catch a falling body. Rubbing her neck, she lay back in the sand. Had Antonio told the truth?

But by his own admission, Antonio was a murderous hypocrite, hating McCord while he faked friendship. No, she'd be crazy to pin her hopes there. Besides, she'd seen for herself that there was nobody else—and no body—on the mesa.

She sat up and turned toward the curtain wall. "Then he landed up there!" The man-made dam was a good forty feet wide, she'd estimated from above.

But this inner face was as smooth and sheer as the outer side, and it rose almost two hundred feet above the beach where she lay. She hadn't the strength to climb to its top, nor any way to lower McCord's body if she found it. If his body was up there, there it would have to stay until she brought a team in, with the proper equipment to recover his remains.

Another fish jumped and she turned gratefully towards its splash. She'd eat because she'd need strength for her next goal: Find Grunwald and bring him water.

She'd lost her hat in the flash flood, but she found several gallon-size plastic bags in McCord's pack. She baited one of those with grasshoppers, and soon had perch for breakfast. Sunfish sashimi.

Viewed from above, the terraced fields of the secret canyon had appeared relatively smooth. The situation on the ground was something else again. McCord had predicted that the dark hedges that divided the slopes would prove to be maguey. The juice of that spiky cactus had been used by the Aztecs—was still harvested in modern Mexico—to make *pulque,* a potent fermented whisky.

But this was also tactical cacti, Raine suspected, planted to confound and impede invaders. Should an army succeed in breaching the curtain wall, it would then be faced with impenetrable, head-high hedges of the fearsome plant, cordoning the valley from east to west. Each row ended precisely at the river, which now flowed swiftly in a man-made canal at the bottom of ten-foot, seamless stone walls.

Dodging brambles and rattlesnakes, she prowled the hedgerows. Each wall had a person-wide gap hidden somewhere within its vicious spikes, she soon discovered. But these passes were placed at random—again, the better to confuse an invader.

Sweaty and sore and thoroughly exasperated, she battled her way through yet another hedge, then paused. A smile stole over her face. Sunflowers run riot! This field blazed with the glorious giants, a crop in every shade of butterscotch and flame and umber. Larks and redwing blackbirds and finches swooped away in all directions, to settle anew, on the drooping, black-eyed blossoms. "Break time," she muttered, and joined the birds in their harvest. She took off her shirt and turned that into a bag of plunder.

With enough protein gathered to last a few days, she pressed on, craning her neck to peer up at the towering cliffs. How had Grunwald ever climbed *up* there? And where was he now? If she couldn't reach him before sundown today, would he still be alive tomorrow?

And darkness would come early to this valley, she reminded herself—earlier still to the cliff houses above. McCord's flashlight had been smashed in the fall, but she'd found waterproof matches in a film canister in his pack. "I'll need torches," she muttered, and began to pick dried plant stalks as she walked.

Also, she'd need water. McCord's neoprene canteen had survived the fall intact. She'd filled it when she started out this morning, but at this point it was two-thirds empty. "Fill that again," she muttered, "and soon."

The sun now stood directly above the natural arch, which loomed higher and higher in the sky as she advanced, a bloody gateway to the lower valley. A fantastical bridge uniting the two walls of this enchanted kingdom. Raine squirmed through another hedge. From here she could see for the first time that the side of the bow that joined the eastern mesa ended at the mouth of a dark archway. Even from this distance the entrance looked enormous—two or more stories tall, and bordered with elaborate carvings. So both walls of the canyon contained living space. "McCord, you should have seen this!" she whispered.

That thought started the tears again. She brushed them angrily aside, and turned to look up at the western cliff. Still no sign of Grunwald, but there were the stone pillars McCord had pointed out, sticking up from the guard wall of the alcove. Forget her earlier qualms about a basket elevator. If she'd found one waiting for her now, equipped with a dozen Aztec hearties to hoist it two hundred feet in the air, she'd have gladly stepped into it.

Her breath caught as her eyes registered what she was looking at. Along the vertical route of the one-time passenger basket, she could see regular dark squares cut into the rock, leading from the foot of the cliff all the way to the guard wall.

"A hand-and-toe trail!" Maybe the elevator had been a later improvement on a more primitive route? Or possibly the hand and footholds served the same purpose as the ladder that ran up the shaft of most modern elevators. "For basket repairmen?" Her way up at last.

# Chapter 23

First, she'd need water, but the river still ran at the bottom of its channel, unreachable from ground level. Raine sank wearily on the flagstone embankment. She tied one of her ropes to the neck of her canteen and tossed it down.

It took her almost an hour to fill her zippered plastic bags. With those stowed in her pack, she drank all she could hold, filled the canteen a final time, then attached it to her belt. It was going to be a brutal climb, with forty pounds of water on her back.

She tied her torches and her shirt full of sunflower heads to the top of the pack, started toward the cliff—then stopped. She hadn't realized; she had one more hedgerow to cross to reach the foot of the ladder. "Is *nothing* easy around here?"

Wriggling through the spikes with her bulky load, she emerged scratched and swearing, to stop short with a startled *"Whoa!"* Below the stone rainbow, the canal widened to a perfect circle, then narrowed at its southern end and flowed on.

The pool lay precisely beneath the altar—beneath the ominous drip-marks on the arch. If McCord were here, he would have explained the ritualistic implications. "*Damn you, McCord. If you'd watched your own back, instead of flirting with me…*" She swiped her forearm across her eyes, swung toward the cliff, then blinked—turned slowly back.

A curving structure, surely man-made, flanked the margin of the pool at its far end, where it narrowed again to a canal. Some sort of…rack? Built of sticks and grayish-white, regularly spaced rocks, it was the first artifact she'd seen in the valley that wasn't made entirely of stone.

Her breath blew out with a *whoosh*. The white stones…weren't stones. The dark, regular spots on the sun-bleached objects took meaningful form. Hundreds of eye sockets stared mournfully through her into eternity. This was a skull rack like the one Antonio had described that night by the campfire. This collection wasn't nearly so ambitious as the one the Conquistadores described. A rough multiplication of the racks by the rows gave her three thousand.

And the pathetically small skull on the top row, nearest her end, looked awfully fresh, Raine reflected, while she bent over the lake and returned her fish breakfast from whence it had come.

At least, the crow perched on top of it seemed to find it fresh enough.

A third of the way up the hand-and-toe trail, it hit her where that child's skull might have been obtained—the rifleman's missing kid brother!

How many days back had she and McCord met those trigger-happy drug packers with their mule train? Five? And the kid had gone missing a day or two before that.

How long did it take to clean a skull? She shuddered and

climbed on, rising two more handholds before the obvious question filtered through her weary brain: Who around here was collecting skulls? This time when she shuddered, it nearly rattled her off the cliff.

A ghost. Antonio said he'd seen a ghost. And the doctor had told her the canyons were haunted by werewolves and ghosts. "Like I believe that!" she whispered. And yet, when you considered the alternatives....

*So consider this,* her mind babbled on as she heaved herself skyward. The kid brother went missing somewhere near the quicksand cave—but ended up here? As did Grunwald.

She wished she had a map. *Let's see: after the quicksand cave, we went up the big-rock canyon, turned left at the fork in the river, found the hand-and-toe trail in the left-hand wall of the slot canyon and climbed it. Then I climbed down the north face of the mesa and hung a left, swam south through the tunnel...* Why, they'd been circling counterclockwise for days!

By now, she was possibly no more than twenty miles northeast of the quicksand cave—which lay southwest of her in a straight line, directly through this highland. "*That's* how Grunwald beat us here!" That's how he ended up at the top of a nearly impregnable alcove. He hadn't climbed down to it from above—or climbed up this harrowing ladder. He'd traveled straight *through* the rock! Through a twenty-mile cave system. When they'd searched beyond the quicksand pool, somehow she and McCord had missed its entrance.

A cramp lanced through her calf. Oh, God, no. Make it stop. Eyes streaming, she flexed her toes frantically—and abruptly the spasm retreated.

Now she was scared to move. But if she froze here till another cramp struck, or till her strength gave out...a hundred-and-twenty-foot drop onto hard ground? "You can do it," she said, though she was starting to doubt it. She reached up, hooked her aching fingers into the next hole, heaved herself up—up another, then another…past too many to count.

The chant wended gradually through her consciousness, maybe something she'd heard once upon a time. Or her befuddled brain's synapses firing in a rhythm to match these stones, this baking heat, the wind whispering through the haunted alcoves above. A clicking atonal song…a hoarse croaking…ravens nesting in the back of her mind.

The sound grew louder as she climbed. Maybe it wasn't her imagination. Raine braced herself and peered south over her shoulder.

Something moved above her line of sight. She glanced up, squeaking as that gesture unbalanced her. No… *Yes!* There… A billow of dark cloth. Something—no—*someone!* He was half truncated from this angle by the bulge of the stone, but that was definitely someone moving out onto the arch from the alcove above.

Against a blue sky the bony black silhouette wore a high headdress and stretched a wiry arm back toward the shadows, beckoning impatiently—then grasping a paler extended hand.

Grunwald staggered into view, bare-chested, foolishly grinning. His free hand clutched his colorful cape. Like a toddler led out on the Easter Parade, he was flaunting and flirting it, lifting it to the rising wind.

His companion bobbed, bent from the waist in a rhythmic move—a shuffling dance? The chant rang louder as the wind whipped it her way, then faded in the eddies. Grunwald laughed, tried a clumsy imitation of the same hunch-backed step, then cha-chad on behind his leader.

*They were headed for the altar!*

"Oh, *no!*" Raine sucked in a breath and screamed it over

her shoulder. "Nooo! Johann, you come back here! Don't you dare—"

The chanting rang louder as the wind gusted. Could he hear her? Grunwald seemed mesmerized by his companion's moves as he was drawn gradually out on the bridge. "Johann! No! Listen to me! *Don't!*"

For a second, she thought the chant wavered. The tall, black-skinned apparition seemed to straighten and turn. But with the sun shining directly into her eyes, perhaps she was mistaken. The harsh croaking resumed, even louder.

*Get to Grunwald, get there quick!* She didn't want to think what the plan was, up there. *Go, go, go!* Raine glided up the ladder, aching muscles forgotten as the adrenaline roared through her veins. Another handhold, another step, till at last her groping fingers touched the top of the guard wall. She lunged up, fell over it, leaned against it, panting. The chant sounded distantly.

Raine staggered to her feet, tearing at the ropes that bound the pack to her waist. She dumped the pack, raced along a promenade that skirted the cliff edge. The cliff houses were built back from this walkway, under the grand sweep of the overhanging rock. "Johann, wait!"

He and his companion had reached the circular altar. The black-skinned leader patted the top of the stone and Grunwald stepped up to stroke it, too.

"Johann, you idiot, don't— Ooof!" Looking over her shoulder, she slammed shoulder-first into stone, scrabbled down it and fell. She crouched, holding her arm, panting and stupefied as she stared up at the barrier. A natural wall—extending from the back of the alcove all the way out to the guard wall! Her promenade ended in a dead end? Incredulous, she scrambled to her feet. The causeway leading out to the altar started at some point *on the other side* of this wall?

"You moron!" she whispered, as she realized. From up on the mesa, she and McCord had noted that the cliff houses were built within three separate alcoves, three teardrop-shaped caves, linked together like baroque pearls on a string, but divided by thin interstices of natural stone. She turned a frustrated circle. "There's *got* to be a way through." She wheeled toward the arch.

Grunwald now sat in the center of the altar. His ghost, his host, his evil twin swayed above him, shaking some sort of device on a stick. As Raine craned out over the wall, the creature pressed on Grunwald's shoulder and he lay back on the stone! "No! Johann, look at me! Listen to me!"

This time the creature—was he human?—turned her way. And went still.

Even at a hundred yards, his gaze staggered her. She flinched back a pace, swallowed, then found enough spit to yell, "Leave him alone, you lunatic! This is the twenty-first century!"

With the slightest of shrugs, he turned away, looked back down at Grunwald—who'd finally heard her. He turned his head, smiled and flipped her a coy wave.

The priest, if that's what he was, tapped the German on his chest, sternly reclaiming his attention. He stepped over his body to kneel at his side, blocking Raine's view.

"Jeez, oh, God, oh no, don't listen to him, Johann!" Raine spun toward the wall. "Gotta be a way through!" They wouldn't have built a city in isolated compartments; people needed to schmooze, to visit. These guys had been masters in stone; they'd have cut a door through.

And being utter paranoiacs, they'd have hidden it in case of invasion. "Right! Yes! That's it!"

With a last panicked glance at the proceedings—all she could see was the priest's back as he bent over his prey—she spun toward the rear of the cave. In twenty feet she hit the first cliff house. Blundering and backtracking, she raced up stairways, across flat rooftops, through blind alleys. The light dwindled as she Brailled her way deeper and deeper into the maze. Tears of rage blinded her.

Some time later—ten minutes, an hour, she hadn't a clue— she stumbled out onto a flat-topped roof. "You creeps!" Of course they'd cut a way through the natural wall—up here, two stories above the floor of the cave! A squared-off window opened onto the next alcove. All she needed was wings. Or a gangplank. An alley maybe eight feet in width separated *her* rooftop from the rooftop she could see beyond the cut-through.

Swearing, weeping, she leaned over the edge of the roof, looking down. "Where's the bridge?" Either the security- mad residents of this hell-hole city had hidden it, or the cen- turies had crumbled it. Didn't matter. Nothing mattered but getting over there.

She backed up to the roof's parapet—not enough room for a good running start—and ran.

Half a lifetime later, Raine hobbled up to the guard wall. She'd sprained her ankle in the jump, and that plus the crazy- mazy jumble of the cliff houses had cost her precious time. "Johann?" she whispered, half blinded by the daylight.

For a second the scene looked much the same. The dark, spider-like shape crouched over Johann, then his back straightened and his joined hands wrenched toward the sky.

His chanting changed to a howl and the wind rose to meet it. He stood—turned in a slow, triumphant circle with his offering raised on high. The last rays of the setting sun made it glow like a ruby.

All that haste and effort wasted. Raine's knees gradually buckled. Her neck drooped, her forehead grounded on cold stone. She sighed into the dust—and blacked out.

* * *

Consciousness returned with a jolt. Now in the twilight Raine struggled to her knees and peered over the guard wall. A fire crackled on the altar, and Johann's body had vanished. Had it been thrown into the pool below?

Something moved between her and the flames. Angular and nimble as a praying mantis, it took form as it advanced along the arch. The priest, coming at last.

She stumbled to her feet and fled.


Something rattled, a tiny cascade of clicking sounds. Raine froze with one hand splayed on a wall. Rattlesnake? She held her breath, craning her head through the darkness, but the sound didn't repeat itself. She shrugged and limped on.

Before night closed down entirely, she'd found the wall that divided the middle alcove from the one to which she'd first climbed. On the far side of this barrier lay her pack, with its makeshift torches, rations and climbing rope. And truth to tell, she wanted the escape route down to the valley as much as she wanted her gear. She'd had about all the good times she could handle, at least for this day.

*Sss-clickety-clickety-clickety Click...* A shimmering, rushing sound that raised the hairs on the nape of her neck. She couldn't guess its direction, the way sounds echoed in this maze of adobe and stone. She shivered and groped on in utter darkness. She hadn't tried to find the rooftop to which she'd leaped from the first alcove. With her weakened ankle, that route was now closed. But with blind luck and persistence perhaps she'd find another cut-through, something at ground level, before—

*Sss-clickety-clickety-clickety Tik!*

Not a snake. More like the clicking of tiny bones. She stooped, reached for her knife—and touched the empty ankle sheath. Right, she'd left her knife embedded in Antonio. She straightened and pressed on, fingers skimming rough stone. She could find her way through this maze if she kept one hand forever on the same wall and followed it to the bitter end. But the problem with that method was it could lead her back the way she'd come, back to meet whatever it was that was stalking her.

*Sss-clickety-clickety-clickety Clack!* She glanced behind, swung forward again and let out a muffled cry. A long, wavering figure stood with hands upraised, mocking her own startled stance.

*Me!* That was her own shadow confronting her, cast on the creamy wall of a house. Which meant—she whirled to see a form crystallizing behind her, a glowing archway that she'd just passed through without knowing it. Torchlight edged it with gold...crept toward her along the walls in a flickering stain. *Somebody's coming and he's got a torch!*

She spun, choked back a cry as her ankle twisted, and hurried on, her way now lit by her pursuer. Through doorways, down alleys, up a staircase, then down, and always the light followed. She should find a place of ambush, stop and make her stand. But weaponless, not knowing what she'd face...

*If I could just find a way through!* She ducked into another doorway, this one led her out of a building and— Dead end. She'd reached the back of the alcove. A wall of unworked sandstone slanted overhead, into the dark.

A narrow alley led right and left along this barrier, behind the cliff house city. Which way? Left would take her south, farther into the unknown. Right would lead her back toward the dividing wall between this alcove and the one she wanted.

Her shadow formed on the wall before her as torchlight spilled from the house she'd just exited. Raine spun right and broke into a lopsided jog. *Let him guess the wrong way, let him go left...*

The alley twisted along the irregularities of the natural cave, carrying her beyond the light. But her eyes were dark-accustomed; she saw the wall before her at the last instant, threw up her hands and fell against it.

*Sss-clickety-clickety-clickety Tok!* He was coming *this* way, tracking her by the smell of her fear?

She slammed her fist against the barrier. Natural stone again—she'd hit the dividing wall, and there wasn't a cut-through as she'd dared to hope. She glanced behind, and yes, veins of reflected light came scurrying toward her along the stone. For an instant, beyond a twist in the trail, she caught a glimpse of actual flame. *Oh, he's coming all right!*

Time to make her stand. He'd expect her to turn right along the dividing wall and bolt for the front of the alcove. She turned left, limping into the angle between this wall and the rear wall. Not much time, she could see her hands before her now. Also, a few feet to the left of the corner, the light revealed a black lightning-bolt streak, staining the rear wall.

She hobbled closer, reached to touch this streak—and her hand moved *through* it. A jagged shadow, not a stain. A fracture in the rock, taller than she was, but only half as wide. Could this be the passage she'd prayed for? Turning sideways, she edged into the rift, leading with her left shoulder.

The inside of the crack was black as pitch. She inched in farther, groping before her. *Please, let it widen, just enough for me.*

Holding her breath, she sidestepped ahead. The gap narrowed; rough walls brushed her breasts and her shoulder-blades. Her fingers explored the contours ahead, still narrowing. But did it widen beyond this choke point?

Maybe this was a fatal idea, but it was too late now. The canteen at the back of her waist scraped the stone. If she took that off, she'd be narrower by inches. She whipped off her belt, lowered the canteen stealthily to the ground—sighed with relief as she squirmed another foot inward...then stuck.

This was the end of the road.

*Sss-clickety-clickety-clickety Click!*

Her nose brushed rock as she looked behind. The threshold of the crack warmed to gold, then flames blossomed like a rising sun. A long, bony arm thrust the torch into her hidey-hole.

She gulped and tried to squint past the smoky flames. *"Buenas noches. Habla Español?"*

No response, except that the torch moved closer. "Do you speak English?" She flinched as the flames scorched her cheeks.

God, if he set her clothes ablaze, lit her hair... "If you want a look, how 'bout you let me out? I'm perfectly harmless."

At least, wedged in here, she was. Given elbow room, she still had a fighting chance.

As the torch stroked closer, skimming her figure from her feet to her face, a dry cackling chuckle needed no interpretation. In any language on Earth it meant, "I got you where I want you!"

"You do, don't you, you heart-ripping pervert?" Raine kept smiling, telegraphing surrender on all conceivable wavelengths. "And it's a wonderful joke, but if you *really* want some fun—"

But this guy had his own agenda. The torch was raised higher—he was tall, she calculated; he had half a foot on her at least. Then his other arm insinuated itself into the gap. From its bony fingers dangled a rope, with a hangman's noose sized neatly for her head. He swung it invitingly.

"Yeah, in your dreams!" She couldn't even cringe when he tipped the torch toward her hair and clicked something in his beetle-like speech. "Okay, okay! You're the boss."

He flipped her the noose and she caught it, meekly fitted it over her wrist.

Another clickety-clack command, and it didn't sound like pleasure. He jabbed the torch at her face.

"All right!" She dropped the noose over her head and he tightened it with a downward jerk. "But just keep this in mind: You're going to be sorry."

When he tugged on her leash, she obeyed.

# *Chapter 24*

Sexism was not a modern invention, Raine reflected dourly, while she lifted a gourd and poured cold water over her head. Here she'd stumbled into sixteenth-century Mexico, or as good as, and the Aztecs had their own version. Her captor smelled like a pile of roadkill, but he wanted *her* to take a shower.

He'd marched her along the alley at the back of the cavern, heading south, pricking her backside with what seemed to be a sword whenever she faltered or swerved from his determined path.

When they'd reached a man-sized boulder that bulged out from the back wall, he'd stopped, swung it out from the wall on invisible hinges—and chivvied her into a grotto. Moisture dripped down one glistening wall to gather in a slanting channel cut near the floor. This trough emptied its trickle drop by drop into a waiting gourd. More gourds were lined up along the wall, both empty and full.

While he'd given her a tour of the facilities—gourds, a bowl of fine sand with which to scrub her skin—then pantomimed what he expected her to do, she'd watched for a chance to jump him. But he'd kept his distance and he'd stayed wary, giving her no slack in her leash.

Never mind, her chance would come. Probably soon, she thought grimly, as she scrubbed her hair. He'd made a couple of clickety-clack remarks when she'd stripped—his idea, not hers—and fixed his eyes upon her.

It was hard to see much else by smoldering torchlight. His ankle-length toga was dark, fastened at one shoulder with glinting gold, and his skin was black, as if stained with ashes. His hair hung in clotted dreadlocks past his bony shoulders. And the smell! Fresh blood overlaid something ranker and infinitely rotten.

Quivering with disgust, she sluiced the last of the sand off her legs, then brought the stem of the gourd to her mouth. It had been hours since she'd stopped to drink.

He sputtered in outrage and tugged on her leash. She paused, water dribbling down her chin. "If you don't want me to drink the bathwater, why don't you come over here and stop me?"

He glowered, yanked again. She shrugged, tipped the gourd and drank. Water was life out here, and who knew when she'd get another chance to— A whistling *whoosh* and her gourd split in half; its precious contents splashed down her breasts. How could a stone-age sword be that sharp?

He jerked his head toward the exit, giving her no time to get dressed. She stalked haughtily off in the direction he indicated, still south along the back of the alcove.

On through the empty city he marched her. They came to another dividing wall and he swung another seemingly fixed boulder out from the stone, to show her a passage into the third and southernmost alcove. "*This* is why we didn't find a way out of the quicksand cave—you had a secret gremlin-door, didn't you?" No doubt he'd nabbed poor Grunwald and marched him back here.

He yanked on her lead, and pointed his sword in a new direction. "Could we just stop please?" She'd never been so tired in all her life.

No such luck, he prodded her on through countless twists and turns, till at last she caught a breath of clean air, a cool wind whispering. They were approaching the front of the alcove! Outside and freedom. Her eyes filled and she brushed at them angrily. No time for weakness now; she should be reviewing every dirty street fighter's trick that Trey had ever taught her.

He pulled on the leash, then indicated a doorway leading into a house. Her skin crawled. If this was their destination, then it was show time.

The flames at her back danced over a large room with a rush mat on the stone floor, a primitive broom leaning in one corner. In the far wall, near another doorway, a niche had been cut into the adobe. It held a large black burnished pot, gleaming in the torchlight.

When she reached the center of the mat, her captor pulled her to a halt. Raine closed her eyes and breathed deeply, reaching for serenity, preparing for explosive action. She opened her eyes to find that he'd padded past her, and now hovered at the doorway to an inner room.

With a last warning glance he walked out of sight, uncoiling her leash as he went. *Quick!* She pulled frantically at the noose—but it didn't loosen. Knots in the rawhide, some trick that allowed the running part to tighten, but not slide the other way. She'd have to fight with a choke hold around her neck.

Raine gulped and gave it up, reached the pot in four strides. She hefted it and approved of its weight. No doubt McCord was leaning down from heaven, shaking his fist at her. A priceless relic and she was going to use it to brain an endangered species of Aztec? *Well, tough!*

From beyond the room, her captor tugged on her leash— or somebody did. She froze as another male voice clicked in a lower register. *Oh, God, two of them!* And her with only one pot. When the line tugged again, she gritted her teeth and obeyed. No sense telegraphing her resistance. The leash tightened further, drawing her toward the door.

"For me?" drawled a familiar voice.

*No…oh, no.* She was dreaming. Stress overload, hallucinations. Wistful fantasy.

"Aw, you're too good to me, Gramps. What is it, a pony?"

This was no time to cry, but tears streamed as she limped through the doorway. *Can't be. Cannot possibly be. Don't you dare hope, you silly fool!*

In the inner room, lit by flickering torchlight, her captor stood beyond a floor mat, tumbled with bedclothes. Upon it a genuine, blessed, Lone Star miracle sat cross-legged, reeling her in.

The pot dropped from her numb fingers, shattered at her feet.

"Raine? *Sweetheart!*" McCord opened his arms as she dove into his embrace.

Above them, her captor made a few choice remarks about clumsy, inconsiderate females. Raine was laughing and weeping too hard to care. "It *is* you, oh, it *is!*"

The priest swept up the shards of pottery and stomped out. He took his torch with him, leaving the room lit by a red glow of embers smoldering in a stone brazier. As soon as he'd gone they fell on each other, rolling and laughing in the blankets. There'd be time for questions later, but now she needed to kiss him. Needed him inside her—tangible proof that she wasn't dreaming, that she hadn't conjured him out of grief and terror. That he was here and real and safe in her arms.

But though she wanted him *now,* the harder and faster the better, McCord was in another place. A place of dreamy caresses and slow-motion friction. When she bit his shoulder and tried to speed up the action, he simply laughed and pinned her with his weight, eased inch by inch into her aching center—and settled to a rhythm slow as the rising of the moon.

She writhed in protest and he smiled—stroked into her ever slower, ever deeper; finally she gripped his flexing butt and surrendered to his tempo.

It must have been just about moonset when he rocked her right off the edge of the Earth. She came in a shuddering, boiling darkness, in an arching convulsion that lifted them both off the floor. He laughed breathlessly, covered her face in butterfly kisses—then started all over again. "I c-can't!" she whispered, twisting beneath him.

He laced his fingers with her own, drew her arms over her head and stretched her out to a taut and trembling bow as he whispered, "Stay with me, baby! Sta-ay."

This time when she came, she brought him with her in an endless, rushing wave, carrying him someplace they'd never been before. Someplace beyond consciousness, beyond ecstasy or fear. When at last they grounded, she lay like a shell on a beach in Paradise, filled with the roar of the ocean, the heat of the sun.

Raine woke when he stirred, lifted himself to his elbows. The embers had died, leaving them adrift in velvety darkness. McCord's dear rough fingertips traced her cheekbones, laced into her hair as he cradled her head. "What are you *doing* here?" She clenched her muscles to hang onto him.

He shuddered and shoved into her a gorgeous inch. "Here's where I was born to be."

*Oh, yes!* "But I mean *here*. In a five-star hotel in Aztec City."

He scooped an arm around her waist and rolled them onto their sides. "Why don't I tell you in the…" His chest expanded in a luxurious sigh. "…in the morning?"

*No, now!* The rational part of her brain protested. Then they should move—run—while their enemy slept. "Don't you think we better—"

"Yeah. Better sleep…" His voice trailed off into blissful breathing.

She was too tired, too happy, to argue. She nestled her head under his chin and, with his pulse tapping softly against her temple, she faded away.

*Sss-clickety-clickety-clickety Click!*

Raine yelped in her sleep and struggled against the arm that pinned her to a stony altar…a knife descending out of a merciless sun.

*Sss-clickety-clickety-clickety Clack!*

"Easy, honey. That's just our wake-up call." McCord's voice…McCord's hands soothing and stroking her. "I'll get rid of the geezer. Go back to sleep."

She snarled and pulled the blanket over her head. Lay rigid while bare feet shuffled rhythmically around their pallet. Voices clicked and murmured, then silence.

She woke again, only seconds later. Or had she slept longer than that? She bolted upright. "McCord?"

No answer. Had he been stolen away again? Or worse, had she dreamed him, dreamed last night? She snatched up a blanket, whipped it around her and hurried into the outer room, then let out her breath in a shaky sigh.

McCord stood, mother-naked, drinking lustily out of an

upturned, golden flask. Like a Stone Age butler, their captor stood before him, holding a tray of hammered gold. His yellowish eyes met Raine's, then returned to McCord's throat, pulsing as he swallowed. There was no smile on the old man's cadaverous, hawk-nosed face, no expression at all, yet somehow he radiated satisfaction. Smugness.

"Ah!" McCord wiped his mouth on his forearm. "That hit the spot. Nothing like *pulque* in the morning." He clicked a word or two, then added, "Thanks, Gramps."

The tray held a couple of golden bowls mounded with a greenish porridgey-like substance, plus a second flask— meant for her? Raine swallowed in reflex, then said, "Your friend there sacrificed Grunwald. Cut out his living heart."

"Oh," McCord set his empty flask on the tray. "Did he? Well, shoot."

"Shoot! That's all you've got to say?" She caught his arm, swung him around. "He *killed* him! I'm not kidding. I saw it!"

An aimless smile wavered across the Texan's face. He patted her fingers. "I'm sorry to hear that. Reckon it smarted."

"Jesus, what's wrong with you? Do you understand what I'm saying?" Raine grabbed his upper arms, rocked him on his big, bare feet.

He chuckled and leaned to kiss the top of her head. "Take it easy, honey."

The priest clucked reprovingly. Lifting the other flask, he offered it to Raine.

She didn't spare him a glance as she searched McCord's face. He looked…different. Childish, in spite of his beard shadow, all his facial muscles subtly slackened. The wry awareness of a conscious, edgy adult had smoothed to a bland contentment. His eyes were dilated, just a sliver of hazel iris surrounding a fathomless dark.

The priest clucked a command as he nudged her bare arm with his flask. "You bastard!" She spun, smacked it out of his hand. It clattered to the floor and rolled. "You drugged him!"

"Raine, come on, that's no way to behave. We're guests here," McCord protested while the priest burst into sputtering outrage.

Gramps set down his tray to chase the rolling flask. He scooped it up, gave her a murderous scowl when he found it empty.

"We're not *guests!* Do you treat guests like *this?*" She held the braided leash out from her neck. "You know what he means to do with us?"

"I reckon now that Grunwald's gone, I'm the next *ixiptla*."

She stamped her foot in frustration. "What the hell is that?"

Gramps stored his tray along one wall, then drew a long stick from his braided belt. Its head ended in a small, carved gourd. When he lifted it and rotated it in tiny circles, a slithering, rattling hiss filled the room. *Sss-clickety-clickety-clickety Click!*

Raine shuddered and turned away. "Could you tell him to *go*, McCord?"

Eyes fixed on some inner vision, the priest circled the room as he shook his gourd. "If he keeps that up I'm going to break that rattle over his bony head!"

"Oh, don't do that, honey, he'll be finished in a minute."

She gritted her teeth as the sound sifted down to her bones. Drugged, just as Grunwald had been drugged into giddy acquiescence! But how long would the effect last? And whose side would McCord take if she forced a showdown?

*Sss-clickety-clickety-clickety Clack.* Treading his slow-motion moonwalk, Gramps shuffled on into their bedroom. McCord rotated like a sunflower, following the sound.

"What's an *ixiptla?*" she insisted.

"Umm?" McCord's eyes stayed locked on the doorway. He beamed when the priest emerged, still shaking his rattle.

Gramps held something folded over one black scrawny forearm. He shook it out like a tidy housewife, then spread it reverently over McCord's naked shoulders. A waist-length cloak of iridescent green feathers.

Raine's hand flew to her hammering heart.

"An *ixiptla* is the Chosen of the god," McCord told her while the priest fastened a golden catch at his throat. "Quetzalcoatl's...well, reckon you'd call him the god's rep on Earth. His avatar, till he calls him home."

The priest turned, and this time his lizard-dry lips curved in a smirk as his gaze clashed with Raine's. He shuffle-danced to the outer doorway, then vanished beyond it. Gradually his rattle dwindled to a cold and dusty silence.

"And when will the god call him home?" Raine whispered. *How long have I got to get you out of here?*

McCord shrugged and gripped the edges of his cape— lifted it to some inner wind and cruised dreamily around the room. "Beats me."


"What makes you so sure you're the *ixiptla?*" Raine asked later, as they walked hand-in-hand. She hoped to retrace her path of last night, but was this the way? "I mean, wouldn't Gramps have you chained up or something?"

"The god's fair-haired boy?" McCord said scornfully. "No way! The *ixiptla's* s'posed to roam through the city, singing and dancing and spreading holiness and good cheer. And he gets the best of everything—the best food, the finest *pulque,* the most beautiful girl, which is why Gramps gave me you." He scooped her off her feet, broom and all, and gave her a smacking kiss.

"Big of him," she muttered, looking up into his eyes. They were still dilated to the max.

"Best present I've had since my dad gave me his ol' '57

Chevy when I turned seventeen. Lord, now there was a car! Eight cylinders, and once that baby hit cruising speed, it was a freight train."

His long-term memory seemed to be working fine, Raine reflected glumly, hooking an arm around his neck as he strode on, blithely babbling. At least for retrieval, it worked: she doubted if he could have strung the events of his life together in order. But McCord's short-term memory was dreadful and his impulse control non-existent. He'd urged her to try their breakfast of amaranth and green algae porridge, then, when she'd walked into the back room to find her clothes, he'd wolfed down both portions.

Not that she meant to sample Gramp's home cooking, even though her best guess was that he'd drugged only the *pulque.* In this arid climate, one had to drink, and if a drugged liquid was the sole choice, you drank—or died. Which is why her first goal was the grotto with its gourds of fresh water. She licked her parched lips, pointed left at a crossing passageway. "That way." She hoped. "Don't you want to put me down?"

"Nope." He waltzed her around in a giddy circle, staggered back against a wall, laughing, and kissed her again.

Maybe lugging her was a good thing. It gave her ankle a rest, and maybe exercise could sweat the drug out of him. *But how long does the dose last?* Last night its effects must have been wearing off. He'd seemed almost his old self, though she'd been so delirious with finding him alive, would she have noticed?

No, come to think of it, he had been affected—that incredible, slow-motion, mellow endurance! Her womb fluttered with the memory. *I ought to ask Gramps for his recipe.* The women of the world would come running, waving their money, to buy a drug that could turn a man into a totally agreeable, all-night love machine.

But here, agreeable was a problem. McCord would do anything she told him right now, including lie down on a nice altar to have his beating heart carved out. Just like Grunwald. "Oh! I think we cut through this house," she said, pointing her broom.

"Sure. Why'd you bring the broom?"

"Well, if Gramps pesters us again, I plan to bat him from here to Guadalajara." The priest was amazingly spry, with a big body honed down to gristle and bone, but she'd bet he was seventy if he was a day.

"What about his sword—his *maquahuitl?*"

"It's made of wood, isn't it?" Sharpened to a nasty point, but still, if she got the jump on him…

"Ironwood embedded with blades of obsidian. The Conquistadores wrote that such a sword could lop the head off a horse in one swing. And recent microscopic studies have shown that obsidian holds the sharpest tool edge known to man, much sharper than a steel scalpel."

She winced. "Reckon I'll go to plan B, then." Except she didn't have a plan B. Sneak up behind him and light his toga with McCord's lighter? She patted her pants pocket in sudden alarm, then sighed in relief. Still there. After she'd used it to burn her leash off, she'd decided it was safer in her hands than its owner's.

Once they reached the dividing wall between this alcove and the middle one, Raine found the hidden door easily. McCord moved the boulder with a grunt, then swung it back on its concealed hinge behind them. He picked her up again. "There was a trap door like that up on the mesa, wasn't there?" Antonio hadn't lied, after all.

"I don't remember."

"Tell me the first thing you do remember." He had a nasty

knot on the side of his head. Gramps must have snuck up behind, then clocked him one. The priest would have known they were trespassing on his mesa, because they'd spent that morning yelling their lungs out at Grunwald.

"I'm…looking at a flame. A torch. I'm thirsty and somebody helps me sit up, gives me something to drink."

And no doubt drugged him while he was still half-stunned, she thought bitterly.

"Next thing I remember is the temple."

"A temple? Where?"

"Inside a great big cave. Before we crossed the arch. I had to be purified—washed—before the god."

"McCord, you've *seen* the Feathered Serpent? What's he like? Tell me!"

"Big. All covered in turquoise. Scary. His teeth…and his eyes…" McCord shivered. "He told me that all those years I've been looking for him…He's been looking for me."

She shuddered in spite of herself. "That—him talking to you, love? That was just all in your head."

"Right. He put his voice inside my head. Then that night, He came to me in my dreams." McCord sighed, a soft sound of resignation.

She cupped his cheek with her palm. "And then last night?"

"You came…and He stayed away."

She brushed the back of her knuckles across his lips and felt her heart twist as he kissed them. *And I'll keep Him away from you, I swear it!*

# Chapter 25

"This is it! I'm almost sure it is!" Raine tugged at the boulder. "The grotto's behind this rock. Give me a hand, McCord." She hadn't had a drink in more than twelve hours; her body *ached* for relief. When he'd rolled it aside, she stepped into the cave, sniffing the blessed scent of water. Groping for the lighter, she clicked its flame to life.

Her smile faded to bewilderment. Last night there'd been a dozen gourds below the drip trough. Now only one gourd remained. "He's been here!" The crafty buzzard had anticipated her move. She hurried across the damp floor, swallowed in painful reflex as she lifted the remaining gourd. "Oh, thank God! It's...full." Gramps had taken the rest of the containers, but he'd left her one.

Out of the goodness of his shriveled old heart? *Yeah, right!* She sniffed its contents longingly. "Smells okay." She poured a few drops onto her palm, licked them. A taste of minerals as before—plus something herbal? Or was her fear affecting her tastebuds?

Lose this bet—and she lost all. "Can't risk it," she decided mournfully, then glanced at McCord. He was smearing his hands through the slime on the spring wall, making swirly patterns as he hummed to himself. "Don't do that!"

"Okay." He stopped, rubbed his hands together like a good child.

She had a sudden, savage urge to shake him—shake the filthy drugs right out of him! Raine smacked a hand to her aching head and turned away. It wasn't his fault. *Got to find water. Got to find it soon.* Was there any chance, if she strapped her ankle, that she could make that flying leap again, through the window into the northern alcove, where she'd left her pack with its gallons of cool, clean, river water?

She had a sudden vision of Gramps pawing through her pack and cackling as he poured her water over the guard wall. "*Damn* him! Damn him to—"

And she remembered. The canteen! She'd dropped it at the back of the crack, just before Gramps caught her. "Oh, McCord, maybe—" She turned back into the grotto—and there stood the Texan, with the uptilted gourd at his lips, his throat pulsing rhythmically. "No!" she yelled, waving her arms and charging.

He whipped the gourd aside. "No?"

"Oh, no! How much did you swallow?"

"Umm, all of it? Are you mad at me?" He looked like a scolded five-year-old, trying not to cry.

"No, I'm not mad." She hugged him, rocked him on his feet. "It's just that—" *Oh, I miss you! I need your brains and your brawn and your bravery, and instead I've got Kindergarten McCord.* And now he'd possibly sucked down a double dose of Gramps's herbal lobotomizer. If he regressed any further… Well, it couldn't be helped. "Let's go, sweetie. We're not licked yet."

McCord didn't regress to his Terrible Twos, but within twenty yards he was yawning. A hundred yards north along the alley at the back of the alcove and he could barely stagger. "Nap time," Raine declared. She led him through the door of the nearest cliff house, then helped him lie down. "I'll be back for you," she promised. "Don't go anywhere." She loosened the gold fibula that pinned his cape around his neck, fingered a cord beneath it, then realized he still wore the seashell he'd carved, of the woman and her coyote. She kissed his forehead, then limped out the door to the sound of gentle snoring.

She found the crack in the back wall only a little ways north of there—and the canteen. Full, when she shook it. *Thank you, oh, thank you!* She unscrewed the cap with shaking fingers, then the thought hit her. Gramps could have found this, too!

Either thirst had driven her to paranoia, or he was devious beyond words, but which? If he'd drugged this, then… "Then I'm done for!" she whispered. She could go back and suck on the slime in the grotto, but her body needed more than a trickle. "Screw it, then—and screw *you*, Gramps." She tipped the canteen and chugged, almost weeping with relief. Then slowly she slid down the wall to sit, waiting for results.

Five minutes later Raine felt fine—wonderful. Which didn't prove a thing, she reminded herself as she drank again. The real test would be when Gramps ordered her to do something. Would she snap him a salute or tweak his hawk nose?

Meanwhile, now that she could think straight, it was time for her next goal: Grunwald's shortcut. If a secret passage linking the quicksand cave to the hidden valley existed, she meant to find it.

Its entrance should open somewhere on the alley that ran along the back of the alcoves, since that lay farthest to the west. She'd yet to explore the southern end of the alley, so she set off at a hurried hobble.

She stopped to check on McCord, found him peacefully sleeping. Limping on past the grotto, she reached the dividing wall between this middle alcove and the southern one, shortly after that. She found her way through that barrier by another swinging boulder-door and resumed her southward search.

The light had dimmed perceptibly; the sun must have reached its zenith over the bloody altar and was now sinking to the west. *Hurry, oh, hurry!* When its rays no longer reflected into the alcoves, she'd be blundering through a deep twilight. An hour after that she'd need the lighter to navigate, and she hated to waste its precious fuel. Besides, at some point Gramps surely would be checking on them.

She rounded another bend in the alley and startled at the sight of a shadow on the back wall, then broke into a gimping trot.

She halted before a closet-sized cleft in the rock, not the opening to a tunnel she'd prayed for. Still she grabbed the lighter. Flicked it—and gasped.

A life-size coyote crouched at her feet, staring at her with bright blue eyes. She blew out her breath, then stooped to its level. "You again!" Or at least Jorge's effigy, carved in gray stone. Its knowing, clever eyes had been inlaid in turquoise, ringed with white seashell. She shifted to one side to admire the stylized curls of his shaggy coat—and the eyes seemed to follow her. The Trickster, the clever one, his long muzzle was parted in the faintest suggestion of a smile. "What are you doing here?" she wondered, swinging her lighter around the alcove. Guarding something? "This isn't the tunnel I'm looking for, is it, George?"

No mark or crack marred the walls; they seemed to be perfectly solid. She stooped to study the statue itself, but that hope was dashed, too. The base of the carving was flat. It couldn't be rocked forward or back to expose a trap door, in the way of the rolling boulders.

"Okay. It was a nice thought." Wearily she turned to go— then she swung back and sank to her knees. "Jorge, it sort of seems like you've been looking out for us."

Or maybe she'd had it all wrong. Maybe the Trickster had simply been luring them here, leading them to their doom. Or maybe, after centuries of crouching alone in the dark, he'd wanted company. "Whatever. Anyway, if you're so inclined, McCord and I could use a hint. Where's the quickest way out?"

No reply. A door didn't crack open ponderously in the back wall; his stony tail didn't stir. "Well, think about it."

She moved on, about thirty yards, till the alley twisted hard to the left. She'd reached the end of the last alcove. Turning left would take her to the front of the cave. Raine folded her arms and hugged herself, fighting back an urge to cry. Now what?

"Kill Gramps," she muttered. If she could. Broom versus an obsidian-edged horse-lopping sword? "Even if I manage it, McCord will wake up and give me three kinds of hell," she realized, turning back the way she'd come. If he'd lusted after the Aztec codices with all their unknown knowledge, how would he feel about a primary source? An Aztec priest uncorrupted by five hundred years of European influence, who could be interviewed and questioned?

He'd feel the same way she'd feel if she got a chance to bag a live dinosaur. He'd never forgive her, if she deprived him of that. "Well, tough, McCord. I'm not letting you donate your heart, no matter what you—"

Her head snapped toward the nearest cliff house. Had

something moved within that open doorway? The archway loomed black and empty, but she thought she'd seen the tip of a shaggy tail, whisking out of sight. "You've got coyotes on the brain," she muttered.

Turning aside from her path, she flicked her lighter and stepped into the ruin.

And found a stairway, leading down into the dark.

By the time she reached the house where she'd parked McCord, Raine could barely see her hands before her face. "McCord? I think I've found it! Our way out." But the room was empty.

She flicked the lighter, held it near the floor—and groaned aloud.

The dust of centuries had been churned by two sets of boots, one large and one small. But another set of prints was laid on top of these at the doorway, then they diverged to circle the room in a shuffling pattern. Made by naked feet in about a size twelve.

Halfway across the southern alcove, Raine caught up with them. When she could see the flames of Gramps's torch, she stopped to stash her half-empty canteen within a doorway. Tucking her lighter in her pocket, she limped after the procession. The blood was thumping so loudly in her ears, she could barely hear the snaky slithering of the priest's rattle, or the measured stamp of his feet. McCord was stamping happily in his wake, making it a two-man conga line.

Jogging up behind them, she tapped McCord.

"Raine-baby!" He hooked an arm around her waist, waltzed her in a joyful circle. "Hey, Gramps, look what I found!" He hustled her on after the priest, who'd spun around, still shaking his rattle.

If looks could kill, she'd be one more skull on his rack.

Raine gave him a cheery wave, and turned back to McCord. "I've found our way out!"

"That's nice." He caught her hand and tugged her along till they were treading on the priest's callused heels. Gramps half turned to offer his wrinkled hand. McCord caught it, chaining them all together as he bopped on in the dance.

*Gramps is conditioning him to follow,* Raine realized, *wherever he leads.* The rattle captured McCord's drugged attention the way certain drumbeats could alter the brainwaves of a listener. "Got a question for you, McCord," *Pay attention to me!* "Have you seen anybody else 'round here, besides your pal?"

"Not a soul. I reckon he's the last surviv—" He jumped as Gramps rapped him on the shoulder with the rattle. The instrument rotated and hissed before his widening eyes, then dragged his gaze forward to the priest.

*They're all dead.* That was what she'd figured. Plague had winnowed them out, or the young ones had fled, or they'd sacrificed a few too many of the fertile ones. "Fine by me." One Aztec geezer was trouble enough.

Once they reached McCord's quarters, the routine was much like the morning's. A golden supper tray awaited them, with two bowls of porridge and two flasks. Raine gritted her teeth while McCord downed his potion. She was tempted to stop him, but Gramps put a hand on the sword at his belt and gave her the Evil Eye.

"Right. He's the *ixiptla,* and I'm expendable. Got it." There was no sense provoking a showdown. With any luck he'd leave them alone tonight, as he had the night before. Some time after midnight, they'd make their run.

She'd followed the tunnel she'd discovered at the foot of the stairway for a hundred yards, and it had bored steadily to the southwest, the direction in which the quicksand cave should lie. It was worth the gamble, she'd concluded. They could cover twenty miles before dawn. By the time Gramps discovered they'd bolted, they'd be out in the lovely sunshine. The *ranchito* of Lagarto lay a day's march beyond the quicksand cave, and she didn't plan to stop running till they'd reached it.

Once they were safe amongst Oso's people, she could relax—eat!—and wait for McCord to regain his wits. Then they'd figure out how to tackle this place with guns, cameras, sufficient supplies. "And a butterfly net for *you*," she promised Gramps as he brought her a flask. "No, thank you, I'm not drinking that."

He thrust the flask in her face.

"Well, on second thought." If she refused to drink it, then no doubt McCord would. She accepted it meekly, then— "Oops!" The flask slipped from her fingers; its contents splashed Gramps to his bony ankles.

His slap bounced her off the wall. Ears ringing, she staggered along it and fell, then looked up to find him looming above her with blade on high. "McCord, help! Tell him I belong to you!" She hitched frantically backwards on her elbows as McCord caught the priest's sword wrist. He clacked out a stern pronouncement.

Gramps looked from him, down to Raine—and bared his teeth. He added a few choice clicks.

"He says 'By tomorrow, you'll be very, very thirsty.'"

*By tomorrow I'll be very, very gone.* But she didn't dare say it aloud, for fear McCord would translate. "Could you tell him that we're tired, and we'd like to rest?"

"Sure." McCord made another speech, tipped his head at the reply, then watched as the priest picked up his tray and stalked out.

Raine sat up wearily, then accepted the Texan's hand. He

pulled her to her feet, then straight into a hug. She sighed and rested her forehead against his solid warmth. "Thanks."

It didn't take long to make their preparations. They rolled the bedcovers and rush mats into crude torches, cinched with strips of blanket. Raine went back to fetch the canteen. After that, it was a matter of nerve. How soon dare they set out? She'd known many a codger who suffered from insomnia. If Gramps took a notion to drop in for a late-night tango and found them missing, he might guess where they'd gone.

Walking out to the guard wall, which was only yards east of McCord's house, Raine took a bead on the star Mintaka in Orion's belt, rising above the mesa. "My dad taught me that it rises precisely in the east, and sets exactly in the west," she whispered, pointing the star out to McCord. "When it stands straight over the arch we'll go, love."

"Okay." McCord yawned hugely.

If she let him fall asleep, would he be rousable? Better not risk it. She sat down with her back to the guard wall and patted the ground. "Let's wait out here. What a gorgeous night." Just the smell of free air whispering down the canyon lifted her heart.

Pity to leave without seeing the Feathered Serpent. But she could be patient. He'd been waiting for centuries. *Waiting for McCord?* She shivered, reached for his arm and pulled it around her shoulders. Not to worry. She had everything well in hand.

Except for her own exhaustion.

# Chapter 26

Raine woke with a start. *Oh, no, what time is it?* McCord snorted in his sleep as she struggled out from under his arm and scrambled to her feet—and heard what must have awakened her.

Like two stones knocking, a dry and rusty chant wavered down the northern breeze. Out on the natural arch, a light flickered. It turned a slow circle, then moved on at a measured pace, heading their way. "McCord, quick, wake up!" Raine patted his cheek. "Gramps is coming! We better get back to the house. Come on, sleepyhead." He staggered to his feet. "Good, that's good." She rubbed his arms, then looked over her shoulder. "I cannot *believe* that geezer! Does he never quit?"

McCord followed her gaze toward the rotating light and chortled. "He did this my first night. Wait'll you see it."

Leaning against their cliff house, they kept vigil as the

minutes dragged by. Raine's head craned through the dark. Down the cliffside promenade to their north, a flame blossomed, a light floating above the guard wall. It turned a slow circle, then advanced. Pausing again, it rolled through a vertical plane like a tiny Ferris wheel, then moved on to the sound of a croaking chant. "He's out of his freakin' mind!" Raine whispered. Gramps was walking the foot-wide guard wall, dancing above a two-hundred-foot drop to the canyon floor.

They ought to go inside, pretend to be asleep, but Raine couldn't bring herself to budge. Besides, any minute now Gramps was going to trip and solve all her problems.

And he still wore his sword, she noted, though he'd changed to a white toga that glowed in the starlight. Like a moon-crazed moth, he swooped and twirled and slowly advanced, chanting as he came.

When he arrived abreast of them, he stopped. A pendant of sheet gold dangled from his nostrils. A gleaming butterfly with wings outspread, it masked his mouth and jaws. Swaying and croaking, he lifted his light on high.

"That's a lighter!" she whispered. "Where'd he— Oh!" Grunwald's lighter. The Aztec stepped down from his tightrope. He drew what looked like a stick from his belt. Chanting triumphantly, he wafted the flame toward the stick, and a fizzing spark erupted mid-air. The lighter snapped out, but the sizzling fire remained—twirled through the dark as the priest danced.

A sparkler in the night! The same thing they'd seen from the top of the mesa. Like a child on a hot summer evening, he reeled through the dark, drawing sputtering patterns, gorgeous as heat lightning.

With a laugh, McCord stepped forward to circle around him. The men executed a dipping do-si-do—and Raine saw at last what the priest held. *"Dynamite!"* Its fuse twinkled and swayed above the stick. "Holy shit, McCord, get away from him!"

Snagged by the rhythms, McCord lifted his arms overhead and cut a finger-snapping, foot-stomping fandango around his deadly partner. "Come on, sweetheart!"

She darted in for a look. The priest stared straight through her and spun dreamily away. There were maybe eighteen inches of fuse left, slow fuse. If she could pinch the spark out, or better, throw the whole damn stick over the wall— Dancing and whirling, Raine swooped in toward the priest, snatched for the stick—he smacked her aside.

Her teeth clicked together and she landed on her butt. She licked her lips, tasting blood. Damn, but the old guy packed a punch! "So go ahead! Blow your skinny ass to kingdom come!" But when the dynamite blew, she and McCord wouldn't be attending the party.

She flinched as the priest made a spinning pass, then scowled, watching him go.

Get the broom, Raine decided. If she waited till Gramps danced along the guard wall, a well-timed swing could knock the explosive out of his hands, out into space. *What have I got, maybe ten minutes of fuse left?* She darted into the house, came out on the run—and screeched to a halt.

Standing up on the wall again, Gramps licked his fingers and pinched out the sparkling fuse. Raine sagged in relief.

The priest tucked the stick into his belt, flicked his lighter. He turned three times around and set off to the north, chanting. Like a boy chasing the circus parade, McCord kept pace along the promenade.

"Oh, no, you don't!" Raine caught his arm and spun him around. "You stay with me, McCord." She kissed him to break the spell. He blinked. She leaned in again to trace his lips with the tip of her tongue, and his arms wrapped tightly around her.

They watched till Gramps's flame reappeared beyond the

dividing wall, moving out the causeway. It arched slowly across the bridge, then snapped out.

Raine sighed. "Guess we can go now." And yet... "The temple's over there somewhere, isn't it?" She shivered when he nodded. *So we go, and Gramps stays. And if he can't dance to honor the* ixiptla, *then I suppose he'll dance for the god.* Even an Aztec priest must get lonely.

And he had—what—twelve inches of fuse left? Depending on how he rationed his sparkly treat, he might dance one more time, he might survive two. But soon, very soon, he'd blow himself to heart-snatcher's heaven.

And if he took the Feathered Serpent with him? Possibly an entirely new species of dino, covered in turquoise and dripping with bloody history? How could an Ashaway permit that? She moaned and dropped her aching head on McCord's shoulder.

"What'sa matter, honey?" he whispered, stroking her hair.

"There's one thing more I've got to do."

Whether she succeeded or failed, they'd need to make a quick getaway. So they carried their torches and the canteen north, into the middle alcove, and hid them in the cliff house nearest the causeway. Raine patted the floor. "Lie down and take a nap." She hated to let McCord out of her sight, but if it came to a brawl, there was no telling whose side he'd take.

"You come, too." He sat and held out his arms.

"Oh, love!" She knelt, hugged him fiercely. "You go to sleep, and I'll join you in a little while." She hoped.

"I thought we were leaving."

He was arguing with her, she realized. He'd swallowed the potion some five hours ago. Give him as long again and maybe he'd be back to his own decisive self. "We are, in just a bit. Now lie down. Take your boots off and get comfy."

Raine stroked his hair till his breathing deepened. Then she stole his boots and sat in the doorway, snarling the laces together. She was terrified that he might wake, go wandering in search of her.

But these knots should fixate his attention the same way a rhythm did. He'd stick here till he untangled the mess, and by then... *Hope I'm back to help him.* She stood, listening to the sound of his breathing. Then she squared her shoulders, picked up a torch, her leash and the broom, and headed up the starlit arch of the causeway.

With no sun or moon to mark the hours, time moved differently. Sometimes Antonio thought it oozed like a gigantic worm sliding through the earth. Later he thought it moved as fast as the beats of his own heart, like a man battering the stone walls of a prison, screaming to break free.

But fast or slow, the tunnels wound on forever through the endless night. He chanted the turns he'd made so as not to forget them: "Right, then left, then right and right, then left again." Always descending. *To the treasure,* he told himself.

Later he whispered it aloud. "Treasure, Aztec gold, a serpent in turquoise." When these things were his, then nothing and no man would stop him! He would be free!

He came to a place where the tunnel split into three, then stood, swaying and whining. Which way had the ghost and McCord gone? Which way should he choose?

But three was one choice too many. He sank to his knees, then onto his side, hugging his flashlight to his stomach. "Turn it off so that it doesn't burn out, Antonio."

"I won't!" There was something out there in the dark. Some *thing,* prowling beyond the electric circle of firelight.

"Do it. You're a tough guy. A modern man. You've walked the paths of the Internet. You've toured New York and Paris and Hong Kong, though your feet never touched the ground.

Ghosts are for old men like the doctor. For fools like McCord. Turn off the light!" He squinched his eyes tight, then his shaking finger pressed the button.

He woke, curled up in a shivering ball. He ate some jerky from his pack and stumbled on, stiff as a corpse walking down to Hell.

He slept again. He ate when his stomach growled. He stopped often to whirl and listen, but the Beast padding behind him made not a sound. It crouched beyond his light with a terrible patience.

"Time to go back, Antonio." He could find another way into the valley; this way was no good. "Time to go back!" But if he met the Thing that followed?

He felt its hot breath on his neck and as he spun with a shout, the flashlight smashed into the wall. It fell from his hand and its light burst, a tiny star exploding.

Darkness pressed in from all sides. Black sand poured into his ears, his eyes. Black dust sifted down his nostrils to clog the scream in his throat. Coughing and gagging, he batted at the darkness, and Mother of God, he remembered—the lighter in his pack! McCord had given it to him, brought it back from Creel that first week after he'd hired him, tossed it to him with an easy, "Reckon this might come in handy."

"I hope you're dead!" he raged as he ripped off his pack and dug it out with shaking hands. "This is *your* fault, you and your dreams! And look where it got us!" He lit it, and the flame leaped.

The Beast sat back down in the shadows.

Antonio turned and headed back the way he'd come.

The Beast rose and shambled on before him.

So he walked and he cursed, when he didn't whimper, and finally, in the way of all fires, his flame burned out. Too numb for fear, Antonio stood.

The Beast padded up to him—walked *through* him! Then walked on. Antonio giggled and wiped his tears away. He put a hand to the wall and staggered after the monster, down, ever down, and came at last to the cavern where He dwelled.

The Beast crouched on his altar at the top of the steps. Flames leaped in the brazier before him, touching His scales to glistening blue. Gold glittered all around him. Antonio sank to his knees. Treasure! Even in Hell there was treasure.

Raine had hoped to find Gramps's cell, or whatever one called a priest's bedroom. With any luck he'd be sleeping off his trance. She'd snitch his deadly sparkler, then toss it off the arch, down into the lake, on her way back to McCord.

But the alcove beyond the bridge was enormous, with black mouths of caves leading off from its craggy walls on all sides. The entire mesa must be one vast honeycomb of eroded limestone. No way could she hope to search this hive. Instead she stuck to the road, tiled in flagstones and pebbled in swirling mosaics, that led straight east into the cavern.

It ended at a carved and gilded archway tall and wide enough for an elephant—for a Feathered Serpent—illuminated from within by a ruddy glow. Raine stamped out her smoldering torch and walked through. Her breath snagged in her throat.

Coral eyes rimmed in white, each as large as the light on an oncoming locomotive, stared at her. Teeth grinned a lethal welcome. The Feathered Serpent crouched on his dais at the far end of the temple, but he seemed to lunge. A trick of the flickering flames that burned at the foot of his stairs?

His blue scales glittered and shifted with a beast's heavy panting. *So, you've come at last.*

Raine shuddered as she was drawn helplessly inward, to stand, looking up.

*I've been waiting for you.*

She shivered and fisted her hands. "And the world's been searching for the Quetzalcoatl ever since You fled. I've come to show You the way back." Under his armor of turquoise, he *was* a dinosaur; like a gigantic *Styracosaurus*, with that spiked neck-frill. "The whole world wishes to see You and admire."

*Ha! You think to seduce me?*

"What is a god without worship? A pile of turquoise and petrified bone, gathering cobwebs in the dark? Soon there will be no one left to tend this fire."

Her words were met with a blast of pure rage.

Raine rocked on her heels. *Hold it together. Whatever else that thing is, he's a dino and I'm a dinosaur hunter.* And after skipping two days of meals, of course she was hallucinating in Technicolor and Surround Sound and chatting with fossils. She turned her back on the creature and walked toward the exit.

Came the faintest, plaintive whisper behind her: *But I must have blood. Hearts!*

"I'm *not* having this conversation." Bad enough she had to deal with his priest.

She stopped, looked around the temple, taking it in for the first time. Now where to set up an ambush? Her eyes lit on an untidy pile near the archway and she blinked. Gold. Heaps of it—chalices and chains and sconces and statues. "What the hell?" Had Gramps been doing spring-cleaning? Or was it polishing day?

Or… Yes, that made sense. The priest had been gathering the temple treasure. At some point he must have realized that he was the last. He must be planning to bury it.

Antonio watched from hiding while the bitch talked to the Beast. So, she, too, could hear him speak, or were they both going mad? No matter. When she walked over to his gold, he growled under his breath and reached for his knives.

But she didn't stoop to caress it or kiss it, as he had. She shrugged and returned to the entrance, where she tied a rope to a carving on one side of the arch, then stretched it along the floor to the other side. Then she took a broom and planted it handle-side down in Antonio's pile of treasure.

She lit its straw, then walked back to the archway and yelled, "Gramps, you heartless, heart-snatching ol' geezer! Come out, come out, wherever you are! We've gotta talk!"

Truly the darkness had stolen her mind. Or no, now she crouched by the doorway, holding the end of the rope in her hands. She'd set a trap! Smothering his giggles, Antonio crept toward her along the margins of the cave.

A patter of approaching bare feet sounded beyond the archway. Raine tightened her grip on the rope, braced her boots.

Gramps came in a rush, then drew his sword and charged her decoy. She yanked up the rope and he crashed in a flying belly flop, with his face in the gold. His sword clattered away.

She sprang onto his back, whipped the noose she'd made over his head, yanking it tight. She twisted his right arm up behind his back—grasped his big thumb and bent it back toward his wrist; a control grip that never failed. If he struggled, she'd pop it halfway out of its socket.

With her other hand, she reached under his clotted hair, feeling for the pulse point under his jaw. Press there and he'd faint, then she could tie him up, swipe his dynamite. But squalling with rage, he bucked like a bronco. "Be still or I'll hurt you!" She gave him just a taste.

A normal man would have been reduced to cringing obedience. But this was a guy who stuck thorns through his earlobes, when he couldn't find a better sacrifice. He yelled, rolled and trapped her left leg as he spun.

She popped his thumb and kneed him in the kidney, scrambling to break free. But she was weaker than she'd realized, and he was stronger—and the pain drove him wild. He crushed her down, and his horny old hands clamped around her throat as he climbed on top of her.

*Go for his eyes!* But she couldn't see them. Lights swarmed behind her lids and somewhere the Beast was bellowing his laughter. She writhed and twisted, then slid one hand down along her thigh. If she could reach his crotch—

*"Uck!"* He jolted on top of her, then went utterly still. His choke hold loosened.

Raine gulped in a burning breath as his fingers fell away. Gramps's eyes stared through her—then rolled up in his head. A hand grasped his shoulder and threw him aside.

"McCord…" She sucked in another breath, but it was too rich, too wonderful. She was sinking away, floating down into delicious darkness. "How'd you untie those shoelaces so fast?"

# Chapter 27

Raine woke when McCord pulled her roughly to a sit. Metal rattled, as something cold and heavy was draped around her neck. Chains, a necklace coiling round and round her. "Too heavy." What the hell was he doing?

"Yes, they are," said a voice that wasn't McCord. Now he was wrapping more coils around her elbows, pinning her arms to her sides. "That was my problem, which you have now solved."

"Antonio?" Her brain wasn't working too well. What was *he* doing here? Baring his teeth in a feverish grin.

"Up!" He hauled her to her feet.

She swayed, tried to throw out her arms for balance but only managed to flap her hands and forearms like a penguin. Up on his dais, the Beast was laughing uproariously. *Oh, shut up!* she told him, looking around.

No McCord, that had been mere wistful imagination. Gramps sprawled facedown, with the hilt of a knife sticking out of his back. Antonio was shoveling golden artifacts into a pack. He grunted as he hoisted it, then slung it onto his shoulders. "And now, *rubia,* you will show me the way out of this pit."

"Is he still alive?" she said, then wished she hadn't. But the stain on the priest's back seemed to be spreading.

Antonio knelt heavily beside him, gave the knife hilt a vicious jerk. "No." He started, then touched something on the priest's belt. "My dynamite! How could that—" He laughed, shrugged, pulled the stick free. "It may yet come in useful." He gave her a playful glance.

Swell. But she had enough problems already.

A surge of adrenaline cleared Raine's head as they trudged up and across the arch. The wind was blowing harder and if she stumbled, she'd roll till she dropped—two hundred feet to the lake.

"What happened to McCord?" Antonio asked behind her.

"The priest sacrificed him on this altar yesterday," she said as they passed it. Whatever befell her, McCord still had a good chance of survival. *He'll wake tomorrow, wonder what happened to me—if he remembers I was here, at all.*

Antonio cackled. "Life is a joke, is it not?"

*Yeah, then why are there tear marks in the dust on your face?* But she shouldn't provoke him. Let him think she was docile, beaten. Somewhere in the long trek ahead, she'd get her chance. First thing was to sneak past the house where she stashed McCord.

No chance. He sat there in the doorway, bent over his shoelaces.

"You lied!" Antonio grabbed a handful of her hair. His blade pressed against her throat and he nudged her forward. "McCord!"

"The priest drugged him," she said quickly. "He's harmless. Like a child."

"Ah, as if I'd believe you! McCord, my old friend, look what I've got!"

The Texan looked up from his task and frowned. "Antonio, that's not nice."

"See what I mean? Don't get up, McCord. We were just going."

Antonio yanked her hair. "Shut your mouth, *puta!* I give the orders."

"Then order him to do something. You'll see. He's drugged. He'll do anything you ask."

"If this is a lie, then I cut you. McCord...slap yourself."

The Texan gave him a wondering look, then did so.

Antonio giggled. "Truly, this is a night to remember! McCord, stand on one foot! Now hop! Hop!"

"You see? So you can just leave him here," Raine pleaded. "He doesn't know the way out. He's no use to you."

"Do you never stop talking, woman? If he's stupid as a burro, then let him be a burro." Antonio shrugged out of his pack.

The first ten miles were a nightmare of exhaustion and thirst. Raine stumbled in the lead, down the narrow passage toward the quicksand cave, while McCord followed, lugging the pack full of gold. She'd prayed that Antonio would leave him free. At some point in the night, the Texan might come to his senses and save them both.

But though the Raramuri was crazed, he was taking no chances. He'd tied McCord's elbows behind his back, and he held the tether.

As she trudged along, Raine wriggled her arms, hoping to work the chains free. In an open space, without a load of gold on her back, in the peak of condition, she *might* have been able to take Antonio with no hands, kickboxing, but given this situation, she'd need all the edge she could get.

He meant to kill them, that was clear, but while he needed them to carry his miserable treasure, they were safe. She figured Antonio would unload them when they reached the quicksand pool. He could hide the gold there, come back for it later. The quicksand would be their grave. *So how long do I have to take him, another ten miles?*

The scent of water set her parched throat to working before she recognized its fragrance. Raine stumbled into the shallow stream and fell. She choked and rolled frantically to one shoulder.

"Clumsy bitch!"

Sticks and stones. She leaned down and lapped. Delicious! McCord dropped to his knees beside her.

"Get up! Get up or I'll cut you both!"

"If we drop of thirst, Antonio, then who will carry your gold?" Raine sucked down more gritty liquid while he thought about that. McCord had also rolled awkwardly to his side, so he could drink.

Antonio grunted, then crouched to scoop water with his free hand. When he'd drunk his fill, he kicked them to their feet and on they trudged.

But that drink had made all the difference. The passage narrowed even more; McCord's body blocked most of Antonio's torchlight and therefore his view of her. Raine flexed her arms and wriggled, and somewhere she felt a coil slip. *Yes!* She flexed again, and the loosened chain jingled. That wasn't good.

"Shhh! What's that?" Antonio jerked McCord to a standstill.

Raine paused and looked back. "I didn't hear anything."

"There're things in the dark," Antonio whispered.

"Yes." *Like your own guilty conscience.*

"Faster, go faster!"

She moved on, stomping her boots to hide the clink of her chains as she wriggled and writhed.

"There *is* something! Don't you hear it?"

"I hear it," McCord spoke up cheerfully. "Sounds like a big dog. My dad used to have this ol' coon hound. When he was running down a hot trail, he'd—"

"Shut your stupid mouth, *Tejano!* Move."

The echo of a sound whispered down the tunnel. A huff…a puff…the faintest, irregular padding?

Antonio shouted. "Run or I'll cut your man's throat!"

Damned if there *wasn't* something back there. Raine turned and broke into a stumbling trot. McCord lumbered along at her heels.

Another torch was coming up behind, to the sound of labored panting. Something whistled through the air.

"The ghost!" Antonio shrieked. "*Dios mío,* a ghost! Move, McCord. Let me by! Help! *Keep away from me!*"

Guttural snarls and an animalistic panting could be heard over Antonio's gibbering and the tramp of their boots.

As Raine ran, a hand reached out and snatched at her chains, She stumbled, yelped as she fell. McCord landed on top of her.

"*Keep away from me!*" Antonio vaulted over their bodies, ran on.

Something growled and stumbled over them—then past—with a wild sweep of torchlight, a wolfish eager whining. Raine peeped up through her tangle of hair. She glimpsed the back of a bloody toga, a sword wielded left-handed, scything hungrily back and forth through the air.

The sound of the chase diminished in the distance, along with its light.

"Can you stand, sweetheart?"

She burst into laughter. "McCord?"

"On your feet, babe! Back the way we came. Quick!"

Leaning against each other, they struggled blindly to their feet. "How long have you been...you?"

He dropped a kiss on her mouth. "Come on, Ashaway. Run now, chat later."

They'd made it maybe two hundred yards, when—

B-B-B-B-B-B-B-BOOOOOM! The explosion blew them off their feet.

After the echoes rumbled and died, they lay in the dark, stunned and half-deafened, choking on rock dust. Finally, they rolled to face each other, squirmed close enough to touch noses.

"Antonio had the dynamite," Raine said in a too-loud voice.

"Sweet jeez on a biscuit! If that greedy ingrate took out the last priest of Quetzalcoatl in the whole friggin' world—"

"Yeah. And just when your research into Aztec rituals was getting *really* interesting."

Curled in a screaming ball, Antonio rolled down the tunnel on the scorching winds of dynamite. When he came to rest, he lay like a flood-battered turtle, limbs waving feebly, too weak to move. Any second now the ghost would stagger out of the smoke to take his revenge.

Blood trickled down his back and buttocks where the phantom's sword had scourged him. But those cuts had given wings to his feet, while the ghost that pursued him was an old ghost, a wounded ghost. As he'd drawn ahead, Antonio re-membered the stick of dynamite. He'd lit the fuse only inches from the stick, held it till the last possible moment, then tossed it over his shoulder. *Eat that, you demon, then go back to Hell!*

But could dynamite kill a ghost who was already dead?

If he waited here, he'd get an answer to that question! With a groan, Antonio staggered to his feet and hobbled on. His torch had blown out, but the way was narrow, with no choices to confuse him.

A long time later, the passage ended at a boulder. He stood with his hands on it, whining in desperation, then remembered: The boulder on the mesa he'd found, which swung on an unseen hinge! He pushed and pulled and finally it moved. He stumbled out into a larger cavern, fell to his knees in the dim light, laughing and sobbing. "A miracle!" He was back in the quicksand cave!

"Perhaps I dreamed it all?" Maybe Grunwald had sunk below the surface of this shining pool only minutes ago, while he'd drifted off into wild and gold-drenched dreams.

"No." He looked back toward the secret door. Limped back to it and rolled the boulder back into place. "No, that was no dream." The hidden valley was real, the temple was real. "The gold—that was real!"

And the ghost? As he skirted the greasy slopes of the pool and found the path toward the sane light of day, Antonio began to wonder. Could an old man have lived through that stabbing? Lived for revenge? Antonio's lips stretched in a parched grin. "Why, then, this time he is truly dead!"

At the entrance to the cave he paused, as the meaning of this filtered through his weary brain. "This means it is safe to return." If McCord and the bitch had lived through that blast, they were still tied up. He hoped they'd die of thirst and starvation in the cave. But he must make sure that they did. After that, the gold was all his.

He limped out of the cave to stand, blinking owlishly.

Perhaps an hour after dawn—the light dancing along the canyon walls was pink and tender. The river ran clear at the foot of the hill. Life was rising in him, hot and bright as the coming sun. His eyes swept his beautiful world—and froze on a circle of men, crouched downstream around their campfire. Raramuri.

A boy jumped up from the group. He pointed and cried, "There he is! That is the man who killed my brother!"

Oso.

Antonio stepped back, cast a frantic glance toward the path, but the men of Lagarto had already risen. Light-footed and lean and unsmiling, they spread out to each side, picked up their rocks. And started up the hill.

A week later, when Raine and McCord climbed the rough stone steps to the *Casa de los Picaflores,* they found its owner drinking coffee on his veranda that overlooked the canyon. A hummingbird darted and hovered in the scarlet honeysuckle that twined the cedar pillars. Dr. Luna rose when he saw them, swept off his hat to Raine, then gestured at his chair. "My friends, I wondered when I would see you next! Please do sit down while I tell Maria to bring more coffee."

"Don't trouble yourself," McCord drawled as he propped his shoulder against a pillar. "We just dropped by on our way into Creel."

As soon as they got their provisions, they planned to return secretly to the hidden city. They needed to document their find with photographs, then rush north to secure sponsorship. With the backing of a major American university, they'd stake their claim, negotiate with the Mexican government for McCord's rights to head the excavation. And Raine's right to study and replicate the Feathered Serpent.

"Ah." The doctor hadn't missed the frost on that statement. His dark eyes shifted from one unsmiling face to the other, then he nodded to himself and pulled up another chair. "I see," he said heavily. "Then how may I be of assistance?"

Raine leaned forward in her seat. "You haven't seen Antonio, have you?"

"My nephew stopped by two weeks ago, on his way to find you. Did he not succeed in tracking you down?"

Raine shared a glance with McCord, then said, "If he hasn't turned up by now, then we thought you should know. It's doubtful he'll ever come back."

When they'd passed through Lagarto to make sure that Oso had made it safely home, and to tell him that some time soon McCord would be in need of an assistant, they'd asked after Antonio. Had anyone seen him?

The answer from one and all in the *ranchito* had been a blank stare, followed by the soft, flat words: "That one is gone."

"I see." Luna planted his cane between his legs, folded his hands on its knob, then rested his chin on his knuckles. "A pity."

McCord stirred restlessly. "We also thought you should know this: The Copper Canyons won't be dammed and flooded."

"You've found it?" The doctor jolted upright. "You've found Aztlan!"

"We've found something that'll stop the bulldozers, at least for your lifetime." McCord hadn't wanted to risk their find by revealing even this much, but Raine had insisted.

She stood now and crossed to the Texan, took the arm that he offered. "This means, Doctor, that you have no further need for dynamite."

He opened his mouth to protest—then slowly shut it as he met her ironic gaze. With a charming smile, he shrugged.

"We've bought you time, *señor*. Use it to find another way

to fight for the rights of your people. And if we can help you in this, we will."

The doctor rose. "You have given me much to think about, *señorita. Señor.*" He bowed diplomatically, then stood motionless as a stone idol at the top of his stairs, gazing out over their heads as they descended, his eyes fixed on the cliffs that turned to copper in the last rays of the sun.

McCord's arm moved to her waist as they came to a steeper pitch in the path. "He took that better than I expected. Antonio, I mean."

"Gotta sacrifice some pawns, if you hope to checkmate." Raine glanced fondly up at her lover. He was too good-hearted ever to understand someone as ruthless as the doctor. "You know, I was looking at him, and he reminds me of someone—that hawk nose. Those eyes. But I can't for the life of me figure out who."

"Funny. I was thinking the same thing." McCord opened the door to his dusty Land Rover and helped her up onto its seat. "Maybe somebody we met in Lagarto?"

"I'm going to miss this place," Raine murmured, as they sat on the guard wall, watching twilight creep over the hidden valley.

In a whirlwind three days, she and McCord had documented the temple of the Feathered Serpent, the cliff houses and the fields below with sketches and photographs and videos. They'd chosen a small selection of artifacts plus a codex that should reduce any knowledgeable Meso-American archaeologist to a stuttering frenzy of lust and curiosity. Tomorrow they'd take their enticements and head north to secure the backing they'd need for the next stage in the project.

McCord rubbed her shoulders. "We'll be back before you know it."

But they both knew it would never be the same. This was the last time they'd share the city's mysteries alone. They'd hike out tomorrow on their own scuffed boots. But when they returned, they'd come in helicopters, with excavation teams and film crews, with science writers and politicians, bureaucrats and curators. They were trading mystic peace and ancient silence for twenty-first century excitement. For power and knowledge and fame.

*And how will that change us?* She'd fallen for a rag-tag adventurer, who walked the canyons on his own dusty lonesome. She figured she'd stay the same—this wasn't her first world-class find—but when her drawling treasure hunter metamorphosed into Professor Anson McCord, a chaired professor at Yale or Stanford or Harvard, and a darling of the media, would he still be the same? Feel the same about her?

McCord kissed her ear. "Now don't go all end-of-the-dig blue on me, Ashaway. Just picture you and me in a five-star hotel. Hot tub for two. We'll send out for pizza and champagne and key lime pie, and when we crawl out of there, we'll crawl straight into a kingsize bed and they won't see us for a week. Then after that, I've got this perfectly sinful fantasy I want you to help me with."

"Another one?" They raised 'em wickedly inventive back in Texas, she was finding. Last night's episode had involved the feathered cape of the *ixiptla* and a giggling game of hide and seek through the moonlit city.

"Yeah. I want to see you in a dress, Ashaway. A tight, short, red strapless dress, and I want us to go out dancing. And I plan to take your silk stockings off with my teeth."

She laughed and swung around to stand up. "Would that be before we dance or after?"

"I was thinking during, but let me get back to you on that."

"Well, meantime, there's one more thing I want to show

you." By common accord they'd stayed away from the alley to the west of the alcoves, but she ought to pay her respects before they left.

"Jorge!" McCord exclaimed when the beams of their flashlights fell on the statue of the crouching coyote. "It's George right down to the grin!"

"Exactly what I said. I hoped at first that he was guarding our escape, that this niche would be the gateway to the quicksand tunnel. But I couldn't find a way to roll him aside like the boulders."

"No, that rectangular base wouldn't roll, but…" McCord lowered his torch, as he peered along the edges of the statue. He knelt, blew along the base, sneezed and sat up. "But there's a crack where it meets the floor. Maybe this statue is a stopper?"

"Hiding what?" she asked as he moved to the rear of the statue and took a grip.

"Give me a hand here, Raine. Shouldn't be too heavy. I'm thinking maybe it's a grave marker."

"Lie down with archaeologists, wake up with mummies," she said resignedly, as she grasped the shoulders of the coyote. "I think this is a pretty poor return, for all the favors Jorge did us."

"Maybe he wants us to find— Easy! There we go!" The statue rose with a grating sound. They shifted it carefully to one side, then McCord lay on his stomach to flash his light into the hole revealed. "Yowsa!"

"What? Is it a mummy?"

"No such luck. It's a couple of— I'd say they're cremation urns. But still, that's a spectacular find. Aztec grave sites are rarer than rare."

She wriggled into place beside him, peering down. Two simple pottery urns sat on the floor of the pit, amid a litter of jade and obsidian and golden artifacts. "A pair," she said. "Husband and wife?"

"Most likely. And the objects arranged around them are goods for their afterlife. I imagine that golden plate there held food, the day the grave was sealed. And—" McCord grunted, then reached. His fingers closed over a cord that had been looped around the shoulders of the smaller urn. Leather worn fine and dry as chain, and dangling from it, a white and purple pendant. "Will you look at this!"

A seashell carved like a cameo. On it a tiny figure knelt with her arms outstretched to a crouching coyote. It was the same scene that McCord had envisioned, then carved, except that here the coyote didn't stand; he crouched before the woman—in obeisance? In adoration? Waiting for a word?

Raine touched the edge of the fragile token. "I don't understand. You told me that the *pochteca*'s wife wore a carved seashell, a gift from her husband. But that was in the Valley of Mexico—Mexico City—*after* she'd become a slave. The priest noticed it, wrote about it to his brother in Spain in— When did you say?"

"In a letter dated 1538. Eighteen years after her husband's expedition headed north."

"But then…" Raine peered down at the urns. Side by side they nestled, with their unglazed shoulders touching. "I don't get it. How did that necklace come to be buried *here?*"

"Reckon the explanation is easy, sweetheart." McCord gently rearranged the cord around the pot's shoulders. "Some guys get in a rut. They find that flowers work for them with one babe. So they give that gift again, the next time they go courting."

"You mean this urn might be the *pochteca*—and that would be a woman he found later on? With a duplicate necklace."

"That'd be my guess. Now wouldn't that be something, if here is the guy who started it all?"

"Yes." And McCord's explanation made sense, yet... *If he felt about her the way I feel about you he'd never want another lover.*

They lifted the statue of the trickster, the clever one, back into place. "Good night, Jorge!" Raine whispered, as McCord's arm settled around her shoulders. Then, side by side, they walked off toward the dawn.

# *Epilogue*

*Tenochtitlan, Valley of Mexico. 1539*

What was one more beggar in a city the size of Tenochtitlan? The one-eyed cripple found a corner in the marketplace and there he sat, day after day, lifting a shaking hand to the passers-by.

Patrolling soldiers glanced at him, then curled their lips and tramped on. Gray of hair and scabrous of limb, he was too old and diseased to make a slave for their mines or their fields. Let the friars feed him or the dogs take him, it was all one to them.

On the third day, the priest's woman came to do her master's shopping. She bargained for melons and cacao beans, then her errands led her down the walk past the beggar.

"Have pity, sweet lady, oh, pity for an old trader!"

"A trader? You were once of that guild?" Her eyes darted around the square, then she whisked a melon from her basket and pressed it into his hands. "My husband was a *pochteca*, in the Time Before. Now quickly, hide this! Should anyone see me—" She hurried on to the stall of the maize grinder, made her purchase, then turned and gasped.

With a forked stick for a crutch, the beggar swayed before her, his hand outstretched. "Wife of a *pochteca*, I—"

"Oh, please! Hush! That was long ago and now I am nothing. If my master heard that I gave his food away— I can give you no more, Old One."

"But I can give *you* a message. From a man who sent you a seashell a lifetime ago."

Her hand flew to her throat, to touch a cord that vanished below the folds of her shawl. "A seashell?"

"From the one you called the Coyote."

Tears brimmed and spilled. She pulled the shawl over her face and spun away, walking much faster than an old man could hope to follow.

When she reached the passage that led toward the cathedral, she stopped and stared blindly off the way she should go. She winced as she heard the old trader limp up behind, but she didn't look around.

"He promised that some day he'd come for you, lady."

"And if I could have waited, I would have. I *would!* But it wasn't for me to choose."

"He knows that."

"It's too late now! Years too late! I am not who I was!"

"None of us is. How could we be?"

"You d-don't understand. I was given—*taken*. I belong to the priest now."

A hand gripped her elbow and it wasn't the grip of an old man. He steered her into a doorway, where no one could see. "But first you gave your heart to me! And I never gave it back."

"Oh, is it really…" She choked, turned her head aside. "Is it y-you?"

A knuckle stroked away the tear rolling down her cheek.

She shivered, but still she wouldn't turn. "I always thought that I would know you. But the years have used you—"

"Yes, but not as ill as I'd have the Spaniards think. A syrup of *maguey* juice to glue this eyelid shut, more syrup mixed with colored earth makes my scabs. A sharp rock in my sandal causes my limp, lemon juice whitens my hair… It's a poor suit in which to come courting, my lady, but a wise one."

She laughed through her tears and peeped shyly over her shoulder, and he touched her smile. "And so…here I am. Have I come too late? I cannot promise you an easy life, but I can promise you we would be free. Will you come?"

She trembled, then a smile broke like a bird spreading its wings to the breeze. She touched his face and he kissed her fingers, then drew them to his heart. "Then I'll meet you tonight in the alley behind that place where you dwell. We will be long and long on the road, so wear your strongest sandals. And, wife?"

She laughed wordlessly at the title and looked her question.

"When I saw you last, you were with child. It would be too much to hope for, but do we—"

"Oh, yes! We have a fine son. The Fathers took him into their school and he trained for a scribe."

"Ah. Would he… Would he wish to…"

She sighed and slowly shook her head. "He knows no life but this one."

"Yes." The *pochteca* found a smile for her. "So be it, Wife. Then we'll have a foot in two worlds. Perhaps some day he'll tell our story." He glanced sharply around the corner. "Have a care, here come more soldiers! Quick, scold me for a lazy fool, then be on your way. I'll meet you at moonrise."

\* \* \* \* \*

*New York Times bestselling author Linda Lael Miller is back with a new romance featuring the heartwarming McKettrick family from Silhouette Special Edition.*

*SIERRA'S HOMECOMING*
*by Linda Lael Miller*

*On sale December 2006,
wherever Silhouette books are sold.*

*Turn the page for a sneak preview!*

Soft, smoky music poured into the room.

The next thing she knew, Sierra was in Travis's arms, close against that chest she'd admired earlier, and they were slow dancing.

Why didn't she pull away?

"Relax," he said. His breath was warm in her hair.

She giggled, more nervous than amused. What was the matter with her? She was attracted to Travis, had been from the first, and he was clearly attracted to her. They were both adults. Why not enjoy a little slow dancing in a ranch-house kitchen?

Because slow dancing led to other things. She took a step back and felt the counter flush against her lower back. Travis naturally came with her, since they were holding hands and he had one arm around her waist.

Simple physics.

Then he kissed her.

Physics again—this time, not so simple.

"Yikes," she said, when their mouths parted.

He grinned. "Nobody's ever said that after I kissed them."

She felt the heat and substance of his body pressed against hers. "It's going to happen, isn't it?" she heard herself whisper.

"Yep," Travis answered.

"But not tonight," Sierra said on a sigh.

"Probably not," Travis agreed.

"When, then?"

He chuckled, gave her a slow, nibbling kiss. "Tomorrow morning," he said. "After you drop Liam off at school."

"Isn't that...a little...soon?"

"Not soon enough," Travis answered, his voice husky. "Not nearly soon enough."

**From the Heart.**
**For the Heart.**

Get swept away into the Outback
with two of Harlequin Romance's
top authors.

Coming in December...

# Claiming the
# Cattleman's Heart
BY BARBARA HANNAY

And in January don't miss...

# Outback Man Seeks Wife
BY MARGARET WAY

# TAKE 'EM FREE!

## 2 FREE ACTION-PACKED NOVELS PLUS 2 FREE GIFTS!

Silhouette® **BOMBSHELL**™

### Strong. Sexy. Suspenseful.

SBOMB06

**Silhouette®**

# Desire

USA TODAY bestselling author

# BARBARA McCAULEY

continues her award-winning series

## S E C R E T S !

**A NEW BLACKHAWK FAMILY
HAS BEEN DISCOVERED...
AND THE SCANDALS ARE SET TO FLY!**

She touched him once and now
Alaina Blackhawk is certain horse rancher
DJ Bradshaw will be her first lover. But will
the millionaire Texan allow her to leave
once he makes her his own?

# Blackhawk's Bond

On sale December 2006 (SD #1766)

*Available at your favorite retail outlet.*

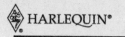

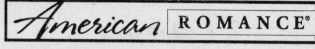

IS PROUD TO PRESENT

# COWBOY VET
## by Pamela Britton

Jessie Monroe is the last person on earth
Rand Sheppard wants to rely on, but he needs
a veterinary technician—yesterday—and she's the
only one for hire. It turns out the woman who
destroyed his cousin's life isn't who Rand thought
she was. And now she's all he can think about!

"Pamela Britton writes the kind of
wonderfully romantic, sexy, witty romance
that readers dream of discovering
when they go into a bookstore."

—*New York Times* bestselling author
Jayne Ann Krentz

**Cowboy Vet** *is available from*
*Harlequin American Romance in December 2006.*

# COMING NEXT MONTH

### #117 DAUGHTER OF THE BLOOD—Nancy Holder
*The Gifted*

For New Yorker Isabella de Marco, serving as Guardienne of the House of Flames in New Orleans was a birthright she still hadn't come to terms with. The ancestral mansion was in the midst of dangerous transition, and powerful demonic forces were aligning against her. With her partner and lover both wounded, Izzy comes to rely on a mysterious new ally for help...but does he have a hidden agenda to bring about her eternal damnation?

### #118 VEILED LEGACY—Jenna Mills
*The Madonna Key*

Adopted at birth, Nadia Bishop never knew her roots—until she came across what seemed to be her own photo on the obituary page! Was this the lost sister who'd appeared in her dreams? Tracing the murdered woman to Europe, Nadia discovered the key to her own life—her blood ties to an ancient line of powerful priestesses made her a target...and her child's father might be part of the conspiracy to destroy her.

### #119 THE PHOENIX LAW—Cate Dermody
*The Strongbox Chronicles*

The biggest threat in former CIA agent Alisha MacAleer's new life was babysitting her nephews—until an ex-colleague showed up on her doorstep, dodging bullets and needing her help. Suddenly she was thrust back into the world of double agents, rogue organizations and sentient AIs, while also helping men who'd betrayed her before. As avoiding death grew more difficult for Alisha, could the phoenix rise from the ashes once more?

### #120 STORM FORCE—Meredith Fletcher

Taken hostage by a gang of escaped prisoners during one of the worst hurricanes in Florida history, Everglades wilderness guide Kate Garrett was trapped in a living nightmare. Her captors were wanted for murder, and though one of them might be the undercover good guy he claimed to be, it was up to Kate to save her own skin. For the sake of her children, she had to come out alive, come hell or high water...or both!

SBCNM1106

*I've been waiting for you.*